Dragon Knights of the Emerald Spire

Mark Joyce

Dragon Knights of the Emerald Spire
Text © 1998 by Mark Joyce

All rights reserved. No part of this book may be used or reproduced in any manner whatsoever without written permission except in the case of brief quotations embodied in critical articles or reviews

This book is a work of fiction. Names, characters, businesses, organisations, places, events and incidents either are the product of the author's imagination or are used fictitiously. Any resemblance to actual persons, living or dead, events, or locales is entirely coincidental

For information visit :
www.spellcraftpress.com

First printed in the United Kingdom

Thank you for buying an official copy of this book and for complying with copyright laws

ISBN: 978-1-8381505-7-0

First Edition : 2022

10 9 8 7 6 5 4 3 2 1

I dream of a life far away.
A life I was always meant to live.
Now I know how to live it.

PROLOGUE

Many millennia ago, on the third planet of this system's red sun—the only planet capable of supporting life—an immense and wondrous civilisation existed. Unique and unlike any other seen today, the dominant species of this world were dragons.

In later years, these majestic beasts would be thought of as mere legends by contemporary historians and scientists, but years ago, they did indeed live.

Possessing an intense intellect and a lifespan bordering on immortality, the dragons turned their world into a paradise. Imagine, if you will, a world without conflict, poverty, or war, where all were equals. This was how the dragons lived. But some time within the dragon's fifth age, disaster was to strike, a disaster in the name of Baudrous.

Once a popular figure amongst his kind, Baudrous had fallen from the light. He developed radical views about the dragons. To him, they weren't just rulers of Earth, but also rulers of the galaxy, and the stars. He petitioned that their strength and wisdom made them transcendent and that any lesser race should kneel before them or face oblivion.

Naturally, the peace-loving dragons would never condone an act that'd lead them to war, and Baudrous's rants went unanswered by all but one of the dragon clans: the white dragons, a cold-loving species that lived in the most frigid areas of the planet. They welcomed Baudrous's plan of change and eagerly joined his side.

This was all the dark dragon required. Just one hostile clan would give him the resources he needed.

Before turning to the dark side, Baudrous was a scientist and historian. He'd dedicated his life to delving into the depths of the planet's past and had discovered dragons hadn't always been peaceful. Many years before he'd hatched, clans had warred on clans, and the planet had been plunged into chaos.

The ancient dragons had created a form of genetic technology to war against each other. These were a lesser form of lizard creatures, designed for specific and brutal purposes, known as Terramorphs.

Knowing their secret, Baudrous prepared for his new war. He and his followers set to work, designing new Terramorphs to do their bidding, each symbolising and representing the dragon's greatest attributes. Created in secret, away from the eyes of others, the dark army grew. In a few hundred years, it was ready and strong enough to tear down the dragon's civilisation and replace it with its own darker form.

Still, before he could begin, Baudrous desired a platform for his invasion. He needed a new body, a form that would inspire terror into his enemies' hearts. So, he returned to his books and the forbidden knowledge contained within to find a solution.

Finally, after poring through those dark texts, he discovered the answer. Before the ancient dragons had ceased their war campaign, they'd found a way of merging the traits of two dragon clans into one to create a far superior being. Baudrous was originally a red dragon, and with the abundance of white dragon material, his choice of genetic bonding was clear. He'd merge the strength of his body with that of a white dragon and become unstoppable.

His experiments were successful. When the army of darkness marched forth, they were led by a gigantic two-headed beast, capable of breathing both fire and ice and gifted with a strength no other dragon could hope to match. A new dragon war had begun, and unfortunately for the dragons, this would be their last age.

Baudrous and his Terramorphs were methodical in their persecution of the good dragons. Within a few years, the planet's peace-loving inhabitants had been nearly wiped out.

It was then that Maligrimance took centre stage, a powerful sorcerer and scientist and once Baudrous's mentor. He was best suited to defeat the evil dragon and his minions. He called forth the last of the dragon clans and asked them to help him save the planet.

He had an ambitious plan and a dangerous one at that, but if it worked, their planet would once again be free. Maligrimance had studied the ancient scriptures as Baudrous had, and he'd found a weakness—the Terramorphs were mindless without someone to guide them. With Baudrous removed, they'd all fall. However, Baudrous had grown beyond them in terms of strength. Even by combining their powers, they couldn't destroy him. Still, perhaps, they could contain him.

It would mean sacrificing their lives, but defeating Baudrous was worth it. So, each clan placed their last eggs within the Cave of Sanctuary, a hallowed ground where time did not pass and they'd be safe. And upon each egg was a sacred amulet artefact created for them at the dawn of their society by the age's wisest dragons.

The jewels had many powers, some lost to history, but their main function was as depositories of knowledge for the clans. One whole clan's history was kept in each amulet, preserved for all time. These they gave to their young so that when the planet had healed itself and they awoke, they'd have all the knowledge of their forefathers.

They then sealed the cave and went to their

doom. They were successful. Baudrous was fooled by their trap and was imprisoned along with the remnants of his white dragon allies within a vast block of ice. And as Maligrimance predicted, the Terramorphs lost their way, becoming mere beasts that we today call dinosaurs.

The era of dragons was over.

Time passed.

And the age of man began.

CHAPTER ONE

The sun had risen in the mountains, and the light of day sprung forth, casting a river of gold over the valley. All manner of creation set out at this time, combing the countryside to search for food and water to last them through another of this country's desolate nights.

Humans were no exception, and nestled in the valley's wintry heart, was a small log cabin. A tourist trap at the height of the season, today it played host to some very different guests.

A small group of scientists made their home on the peaceful slopes, a team from England who weren't finding the Alaskan temperatures at all to their liking.

Leading the group was Scott Thomas, a robust man of around fifty summers old. He'd been in the field for most of his life, and there was nothing else he'd rather be doing. He woke with the sun and went to his window, allowing the rays to warm his face as he stared out at the Alaskan wilderness and admired its beauty.

He and his team had been up in this range for weeks now. Originally, they'd been here studying the valley's topography for mineral deposits. Their employers, the Lazarus Corporation, had been sure that precious minerals would be buried within the outlying strata, and everything had been moving along steadily until now.

The team had been mapping the far side of the canyon wall when a group of locals came howling down the mountain. They all seemed in terrible shock and babbled to the team in their unique dialect.

Luckily, a member of Scott's team, an appointed observer from the company called Landen Collins, knew some of the language and said they spoke of a monster in the ice. Scott dismissed this as the imaginings of a superstitious crowd, but Landen seemed quite interested.

He immediately contacted Lazarus and told them about the incident. From that moment on, the team had been immersed in locating this frozen creature.

Scott wondered why the company were so insistent about the matter, especially as all they had to go on was the testimony of a group of half-frightened villagers. But Lazarus were paying the bills, so the group packed up their gear and spent the last few days hunting down the area where the locals had seen the frozen beast.

The villagers were unwilling to return to the area, and unfortunately, Landen didn't know enough of the language to be simply told its location. So, Scott and the others were left with the difficult job of searching high and low for their quarry.

The team had covered most of the mountain area the villagers had fled from but had found nothing. Hopefully, today would be different, for they had uncovered a promising cave last night that an avalanche around the monster sighting had hidden.

Scott turned from the window and dressed in his weatherproof outdoor clothing. He fastened his boots tightly and put on his insulated blue snow jacket.

Someone knocked at his door.

"Scott, you awake?" called a familiar voice.

Scott crossed the small room and flung the door wide. "Darren! Good morning," he said warmly. "What seems to be the problem?"

"No problem, Professor. Just making sure you're up. Got a long day ahead of us."

"Indeed," Scott said, leaving the room and closing the door behind him. "I've got a good feeling about this one, Darren. We're close, very close."

"I should say so. We've nearly covered the whole area. There are not many places left."

Darren was a few years younger than Scott and was second in command of the expedition. He was a smart and dependable man whom Scott held in high regard.

The pair walked down the hallway and through the sparsely decorated corridors to the stairs. They descended to meet and greet the rest of the science team, who were all wide awake and going about their business.

In addition to Scott, Darren, and the ever-present Landen Collins, the team had an additional four members—Aaron Welsh, Arthur Strangford, Jenny Edwards, and Samantha Folkirk—all experts in their respective fields.

They'd been together on expeditions like this on many occasions, and Scott knew he could count on all of them implicitly.

"Morning, Scott!" Aaron yelled. "Finally awake, old man?"

"Old? Just hope you look this good when you get to my age," said Scott.

The group laughed together. Aaron was also several years younger than Scott, tall with long dark hair. The pair were always goading each other.

"Okay, listen up," said Scott, drawing everyone's attention. "This could be it. We find this blasted thing, report it to Lazarus, and then we can get on with the job we were actually paid to do."

He pulled out a map from his bag and unfurled it onto the table. "This is our position," Scott said, indicating a spot on the map. "Today, we go back to the far side of the canyon and delve deeper into the cave Aaron and Jenny found late yesterday. Any questions?"

He didn't think there would be. The operation was straightforward and nothing everyone hadn't done on many other occasions.

"All right then, we go in, do some surveillance, and hopefully, this time, there's going to be something to find down there."

"Let's hope it's not another wild goose chase," Landen complained. The cold weather didn't agree with the fragile corporate lackey.

"Maybe we'd search harder if we knew why we were here in the first place," Arthur grumbled. He wasn't the only one sick of Landen's complaining and believed that the appointed babysitter from Lazarus knew more than he was letting on.

"I keep telling you all. I don't know why the company wants you to do this. Just be content with that. In a few more days, this'll be over, and you can all go home decidedly better financially than you were before."

Apart from Scott, the promise of ample payment for this job was the only thing keeping the team from stringing up the corporate jumpsuit.

"Now, now, everyone, let's all calm down. Sam, Jenny, can you finish packing the gear?

Darren, I'm going to help them. Make sure these two don't kill each other before we get back."

"I'll try, Scott. Just don't take too long, okay?"

Scott nodded and hurried out the door. It was turning out to be a long day.

It took a short time to sort through the group's gear, but eventually, they were on their way. The hike to the cave was a trek of some two miles in rough, snow-covered terrain. Naturally, the journey would take a bit of time, but once they reached the site, the study would go much quicker.

Scott walked in front, his trail walking stick feeling out ahead and checking for ice under the snow. Darren walked at his side, the rest of the group trailing behind. Scott had thought it best to separate Landen and Arthur, so their designated official stomped along in silence behind them.

"What do you think this is all about, Scott? I mean, it seems an awful lot of work for something that might not even exist."

"I'm not sure, Darren, but one thing is certain. That man's not telling us the whole truth."

"You can say that again. That man wouldn't know the truth if it came up and bit him on the face."

Neither trusted Landen, and this was no

longer the job they'd signed on for.

Or was it?

Scott had his doubts. Maybe Lazarus had planned this all along? But how could they've known there was something buried up here? And if they knew, why lie and send them up here to find it?

Whatever the case, they kept their suspicions to themselves. None of them could really afford to lose out on the company's money. Their profession, although enjoyable, hadn't been the most profitable of late. This money would keep Scott's team afloat, hopefully until another job cropped up. Darren had a wife and newborn son to get home to. He couldn't return empty-handed to them. The two walked on in silence, each consumed with his own thoughts and wondering what they'd find at their journey's end.

***

In a dark glacier in the Alaskan mountains, something stirred. It had existed there from as far back as it could remember, but now something brought this entity's mind back from the void.

Creatures approached.

There'd been no other contact with lifeforms in his millennia of imprisonment, and now two groups in so short a time. The last group had been fearful of him and fled like cowards, but this new group wouldn't escape. He'd make sure of it.

* * *

It took the best part of the day, but Scott's team finally arrived at the cave entrance.

Darren stepped in first. The others followed close behind with their torches switched on to light their way through the cavern. No noise broke the air. The group moved along in stunned silence, for the cave was a beauty to behold.

All the walls glistened as if alive. They'd been in many frigid caverns on this expedition but nothing as wondrous as this. The entire edifice seemed alien to them, as if brought about by some great unknown hand.

"My God," exclaimed Arthur. "Seeing this almost makes the whole trip worthwhile."

Scott was inclined to agree but soon remembered that this wasn't why they were here.

"Okay, people, let's get a bit more professional. Nothing we're not used to. We'll separate into teams, a standard search pattern. Keep in radio contact and always keep an eye on your buddy. We don't want anyone to get lost in this place."

"Hey, Landon, try not to follow that last bit too closely," Arthur said with an evil glint in his eye.

The Lazarus executive just scowled and followed Aaron into one of the joining tunnels.

"Cut it out, Arthur, and be careful, okay?" said Darren.

"You got it, boss," Arthur said with a smile before wandering off down another passage.

Scott despaired and hoped his good-natured friend would take the rest of this trip more seriously.

"Well," Darren said. "Shall we?"

The two scientists headed down the centre corridor, Darren hefting the gear to take the stress off Scott.

The cavern was immense, a frozen maze of ice sheets and crystal walls. Darren and Scott walked down ice passages and corridors that glistened and shone, filled with wondrous beauty, but as of yet, no sign of their elusive frozen monster.

Darren sighed. These locals were so cut off from the outside world that they probably thought of machines as witchcraft. He was certain they'd just imagined this so-called monster and that he was wasting his time. He walked along, musing for a while before realising that Scott was no longer with him.

Damn. How could he have lost him? Maybe he'd fallen and hurt himself. Still, why hadn't Darren heard anything? Cold fear clutched at Darren's breast. Scott was like a father to him. If something had happened, he'd never forgive himself. He ran back down the passageway, calling Scott's name, but there was no reply. He then immediately went to his radio.

"This is Darren to all team members. I've lost Scott. Head towards me and converge on our tunnel."

He didn't wait for a reply. Instead, he ran back along their route, retracing his steps. Scott had to be here. He had to be. He ran so fast that he almost fell through an ice cleft in the cavern wall.

Darren stopped and examined the break. He was sure it hadn't been here when they'd passed by earlier. Maybe Scott had seen it and taken a closer look. Perhaps he'd fallen and was lying hurt and unconscious, freezing to death.

Darren quickly squeezed through the break and was surprised to find the space quite large on the other side. He popped free of the ice and immediately lost his footing. Stumbling, he fell down the icy slope on the other side and came to rest finally with a bump, ice crystals falling all around.

He checked to ensure he was in one piece. No bones appeared to be broken. He stood, flexing his legs and thanking God for small miracles.

It was at this point that Darren saw Scott. His old mentor was on his knees, staring fixedly at the ice wall. He seemed in a trance and hadn't even acknowledged Darren's entrance. Darren edged closer.

"Scott, are you okay?" he said hesitantly.

Scott's head slowly turned to regard Darren. "I'm fine, Darren. I've found him, he who'll rule us," said Scott, his voice sounding strange and cold.

"What're you talking about? Who'll rule us? What's this madness?"

Scott turned his head, and Darren followed his gaze. There was something in the glacier, but what, he couldn't tell. Darren could make out a scaled hand and the top of what he believed to be some sort of wing.

"Is this it, Scott? Is this the beast?"

Scott chuckled. "You know nothing if you would call him a mere beast. He'll lead us. He'll rule."

Darren thought Scott had lost the plot. He was

about to voice his opinions when the light from Landen's flashlight filled the cavern.

"Hey," the observer called. "You okay down there?"

Darren shook himself, deciding to figure this out later. The fall must've hurt Scott's head. It wouldn't do for the expedition leader's abilities to be called into question now.

"We're fine," Darren said. "Mind your step. It's steep on the other side of that gap."

In a few short moments, Landen was through and standing at Darren's side, staring up at the creature in the ice.

"So, Landen, is this what you wanted to find?"

"It has to be, but we'll find out when the excavation crew gets here." Landen pulled his phone out of his pocket and began dialling.

"Excavation crew? What excavation crew?"

"The one I'm calling. You've done your job and found it. Now we'll do the rest."

Darren couldn't believe what he was hearing. Scott had perhaps lost his mind, and now Landen was about to steal away the find of the century. Things were beginning to spiral swiftly out of control.

"But what about us?" Darren stammered.

"You'll be paid as promised, but this is now

officially a matter for Lazarus." Landen ended the conversation there and typed a number into his cellular phone.

Darren could do nothing but stand there, mouth agape. "Scott, are you hearing this?" he finally managed to say. "He's going to cut us out. After all the work we did for him, we're not even getting the credit!"

If Scott heard his friend's words, he didn't show it. Instead, he simply stood transfixed and unmoving.

Eventually, the other team members turned up, arriving in time to hear Landen requesting a second team.

"What's he saying, Darren?" Arthur asked. "He's asking for a second team? Did you guys find something?"

Darren turned and indicated the wall of ice. "See for yourselves."

As one, the team huddled close to the ice, trying vainly to see the discovery beyond. Very little was visible save a dark silhouette attached to a massive clawed foot.

"What is it?" Sam asked breathlessly.

"No idea," Darren said.

"And what's this about another team?" Arthur asked, turning from the glacier.

"For that, you'll have to ask Mister Chairman of the Board over there," Darren said bitterly, indicating Landen. "As for me, I'm getting Scott out of here."

"Why? What's wrong with him?" Jenny said, taking a closer look at the still kneeling form of Scott.

"I don't know, but he's been like that since I arrived," Darren explained. "Probably hurt himself in the fall."

Aaron came forwards and took a closer look. He was the most qualified in first aid. "Well, I can't see any visible injuries," he said, tilting Scott's head. "He seems to be in some kind of trance."

"Well, whatever it is, you guys had better get him out of here," Darren said, looking worriedly at Scott. "I'll stay and see if Landen can be negotiated with."

"I'll stay too," Arthur said, shaking his fist. "I've got a few things to say to that suited snake." Arthur took an aggressive step towards Landen.

"Arthur, no," Sam said, holding onto his arm. "Darren's right. Maybe he can be negotiated with. If you go in there fists flying, we may never get a chance to study whatever this thing is. They may not even pay us."

The subject of pay always made Arthur calm

down. His mother was very unwell, and he desperately needed that money for her. "All right then," Arthur said, kneeling to take hold of one of Scott's arms. "Make sure you fight for us, Darren. Don't let him walk all over you."

"You got it," Darren said as Arthur grabbed Scott's other arm.

"I'm really worried about him," Jenny said. "He looks so strange."

By this point, Scott had closed his eyes, and his skin had gone ashen.

"We'll take him back to camp," Aaron said. "I've some supplies there that may help. He's probably just exhausted, Jenny. He's been working awfully hard."

"I knew he was getting too old for this," said Arthur, grunting with the exertion of carrying Scott. "The old fool should've stayed at home."

None among the team argued. They'd all seen Scott deteriorate as the expedition had gone on but knew how stubborn he could be.

Darren watched his friends disappear and then turned to the task at hand. If Landen thought he was getting away with this, he had another thing coming.

In the days following the team's discovery of the monster, Darren and the others had become increasingly left out of what was happening to the beast. Though he'd fought hard for the team, his efforts had gained them little. Scott had also become more distant as the days wore on, and few things now could coax him from his room.

Darren was at a loss. Landen had abandoned them, and now all they could do was wait while the company stole their prize and flew them home.

Some of the team had already left, like Arthur and Aaron, with Jenny and Sam due to leave that afternoon.

Darren had other plans, plans he'd hoped to involve Scott in, but if his old mentor didn't leave his room, Darren would go it alone. He'd planned to photograph and hopefully take a sample of the creature back to England to find out what exactly they had discovered in the ice. Still, he had to wait. He couldn't risk the others being involved in this. Thinking on it, perhaps it'd be better if Scott remained in his room. He had become unstable of late and could jeopardise the heist.

Darren rested alone in a small tent erected by Lazarus Corporation to house its employees. He was surprised after the way they'd been treated, that they still bothered to consider him and the others. Scott, of course, had remained at the cabin. Jenny and Sam were there too, stowing their gear for the trip home.

Darren checked his watch. The hour was later than expected, and he thought it'd be best to see them before they left. He stood and unzipped the tent's flap, pulled his jacket around him, and stepped into the cold air. A brisk breeze blew, and Darren was thankful for the heavier jacket the corporate staff had given him. It was also a useful disguise.

As Darren walked through the excavation site, he again ensured that his initial observations were correct. Only two guards were posted. The company weren't too worried about security, and why should they be? They were in the middle of nowhere, surrounded by ice and snow, and no one knew they were there. They could afford to be sloppy.

Darren had watched them for a while since he'd struck on the plan to take a piece of the beast with him. Apart from Scott, this was the only reason he was still hanging around. The guards changed every night at midnight. However, one group of guards would always leave before the other arrived. This left around a five-minute interval for Darren to exploit. Confident that his plan would work, Darren trudged down the valley and towards the cottage.

* * *

The beast still dwelled in its prison but could feel his power returning, memories of a time long lost resurfacing and a war long forgotten. Soon, he'd be free, and the world would once again fear his name.

* * *

The girls had taken longer to go than Darren had anticipated, but he didn't mind. He used that time to enlist Scott's help. However, his mentor continued to ignore his requests, so he'd have to go alone. He worried about how he'd get Scott to leave after his mission was over. He didn't want to leave his old friend behind if the company suspected any foul play, but he'd cross that bridge when the time came. For now, Darren had other problems.

He'd stealthily made his way up the valley sides and to the camp's outskirts. It wouldn't do to be found coming into the site at this late hour. It'd arouse too much suspicion, so he had to maintain a low profile. He jumped the small wire fencing set up to cordon off the camp and made his way to a spot he'd pre-selected.

From his vantage point by the supply tent, Darren could easily see the comings and goings of the guards. One looked to be dozing on a chair while the other tried to remain alert. Darren took another look at his watch. Not long now. Very soon, these incompetent glorified security guards would be leaving their posts.

Five ... Four ... Three ...

They never made it to two. The guard that'd been alert was obviously the designated timekeeper, for he checked his watch and then woke his companion. Both stood up together and walked rather drowsily away.

Darren smiled to himself. That was easier than he expected. He crept along towards the creature's makeshift enclosure. The door was easy to force open as the building had been hastily constructed. A short passageway opened into a cavern, and there, in the centre, half-covered by a large tent, was an enormous block of ice.

Darren had seen parts of the creature, but he never would've guessed it'd be so large. Machinery and dials flashed on and off as systems worked to keep the beast refrigerated and monitor its bio functions.

Darren pulled out a disposable camera from his utility bag and snapped pictures. Each image he knew had the potential to make him famous and solve the mystery of the beast's origins.

He was just finishing up when he heard a noise behind him. Darren stopped taking pictures and turned around, surprised to see Scott standing behind him.

"What're you doing here?" he asked.

"You finally did it, didn't you? Finally made it in, all that talk, and you finally made it. Thank you, old friend, but I can take it from here."

"Not again, Scott, this is serious. Can you at least see sense for a few minutes? We have to get out of here before we're discovered."

Scott chuckled to himself, a deep mocking chuckle as he looked at Darren with piercing eyes. "You fool. You still don't get it, do you? All this was orchestrated to allow his return. From that day, I've belonged to him."

Again, Darren thought Scott had gone off his rocker, but he didn't have time to argue. The guards would be here soon, and if they wanted to escape, it'd have to be now.

"Scott, that's all very interesting, but we really

must be going. If those guards come back, we're in for it."

He took a step towards his friend, only to be met with a gun's barrel.

"Scott, what're you doing? Where'd you get that?"

"Sorry, I can't let you go. You see, Master is still weak and needs time to recuperate. We can't have people knowing about him just yet."

Darren was losing his patience. If Scott had taken leave of his senses, it was up to Darren to save him. He rushed forwards, intending to take the gun and not harm Scott, but he didn't get two feet before Scott fired. His mentor shot him straight in the chest and then casually walked past to operate the console behind where Darren had fallen. The last sounds Darren heard before he died were the refrigeration unit powering down and Scott's maniacal laughter.

CHAPTER TWO

It was morning in the bustling town of Kingston. Deep in the suburbs, a young lad awoke to the crisp morning air and the sound of his mother calling his name.

"Mark! Leigh! Time to get up, breakfast!"

Mark shook into wakefulness first. He got out of bed and looked around his room, bleary-eyed.

He and his family lived on the small street of Aldersbrook Drive, where he currently shared a room with his younger brother, Leigh. The latter had still yet to awaken, so Mark wandered over to his bed and poked his brother in the ribs.

Leigh looked at him once, growled, and turned over. Mark let him be. After all, his brother rarely cared about being on time for college. Mark was also hardly ever on time. He had a penchant for daydreaming, which had held him back a lot during his life.

He got himself dressed into his jeans and top. The weather seemed good outside but still best to wear a jacket, he thought. After all, he was in England, and if there was one thing that all British people believed, it was that you could never trust British weather.

After a quick wash, he headed downstairs. His mother and father had already left for work. She must've called up before leaving. He briefly checked the house for his older brother, Woody. His bike was gone, and his jacket was missing, so either he woke up early or stayed out last night.

With no one around, Mark had the entire kitchen to himself. He switched on the television and poured himself some cereal.

He really couldn't be bothered with today.

Every day he went to college, came home, and went to bed—life was becoming really dull. Why didn't anything ever happen to him?

Mark glanced up from his meal to acknowledge that the news was on the television. Whenever his parents left the house, they'd watch the weather and then the news would come on.

Mark hated the news. He had his own problems without worrying about everyone else's. He reached for the remote to change the channel in favour of a cartoon when a particular report caught his eye.

There'd been an accident in Alaska. The camera hovered over a huge crater in the snow. Apparently, a British research team had been up there searching for mineral deposits. It was obvious from the debris that there'd been some kind of explosion, but the authorities were at a loss to explain it.

It was peculiar. Mark wondered how it'd happened and hoped some of the guys from his class were watching. Maybe they'd have some ideas or wild theories. It always amazed him how much some of his friends knew. He noticed the time on the bottom corner of the news—if he didn't hurry up, he'd be late.

He rushed his last morsels of food down and

cleaned his bowl. Leaving the kitchen, he put on his jacket and got on his bike.

Mark decided to take a different route to class. He had recently broken up with his girlfriend again. For whatever reason, the two of them just couldn't get along, and he missed her terribly. There was a small forest, a few roads away from his home, where Mark and his family used to go when he was younger. This place always made him feel better. The trees had a soothing quality that Mark had never felt anywhere else in the world. He could stay forever and never feel unhappy.

Mark rode over the crossroads and down the street towards the forest's gates, his bag of books resting on his back. The journey was a short one, but before too long, he was riding through the gates and under the lush forest canopy. The sun shone through the leafy covering and warmed Mark's face. He smiled and hummed to himself. No matter what his problems, this place always made him feel better.

In no time at all, he had reached the forest interior. He checked his watch and was just about to quicken his pace when something caught his eye. By the roadside, a couple of yards in, was a monumental hole, a great crack in the Earth. He had never noticed this peculiar feature before. He stopped his bike and dismounted, resting it on the ground, and advanced on the area.

Peering down into the depths, Mark examined the hole. It appeared bottomless at first. Reaching down, he tossed a stone into the inky blackness. The pebble took some time to hit, but there was definitely a bottom.

Perhaps he'd come back after classes and have another look. Shrugging, Mark turned to leave, then stopped. He became aware of a deep groaning sound, like wood being put under too much stress. Before he realised what was going on, the ground gave way beneath him, and Mark plunged into darkness.

It took a while to regain consciousness. Mark's body burned. He stood up, shaking off the stiffness. His last memories were of the forest and a great chasm in the ground. He must've fallen in. Looking up confirmed his suspicions. Above his head yawned the chasm, although it seemed bigger now than when he had viewed it from above. A cursory evaluation of his situation told Mark that he wouldn't be leaving that way. The tunnel's height was too great and the sides too steep for him to traverse without aid. He'd have to find other means to escape.

He glanced around the darkness and assessed his options. Discounting up, the only way to go was forwards. A dim light pulsed from the end of what seemed to be a long passageway leading off from his position. Hopefully, that light was daylight, and he could get out. The route he'd taken in the forest wasn't a well-used one. It could be weeks before he was found.

He inspected his surroundings, musing on who could've built this tunnel and for what purpose. He brushed his hand against the wall and stopped moving, noticing it was warm and smooth to the touch. This in itself was unusual. What could've caused such an effect?

Mark was also now acutely aware that this tunnel was sloping and that instead of going up, he was actually being led down. He considered turning back and waiting by the hole again to be rescued, but for some reason, he couldn't bring himself to turn back. Something was drawing him to the light, an unknown force. He had to find out what it was.

Mark quickened his pace, determined to reach his goal, and carefully checked his footing as he went. Soon he was on top of the light source, but it wasn't what he expected. The light wasn't daylight but was some form of glowing rock. The strange substance littered the floor and the walls of the cavern-like place in which Mark now found himself. Each small portion of the rock glowed on and off like a heartbeat, radiating a bluish-white light. The cavern was at least ten feet tall and three times as wide. The same smooth stone proliferated the walls and encased the ceiling. Although there was now ample light and abundance of the substance, Mark still couldn't explain its origin.

He walked further in and searched the walls, hoping to find an entrance. His view was obscured by a large central outcropping of rock that dominated the cavern's interior. However, he could discern a path around it and immediately headed in that direction.

The path, from what he could see, led around the outcrop and to what he hoped to be daylight. Mark squeezed his way through and out the other side. Here, as on the other side, the glowing rock was prolific, but he still didn't see an entrance into the cavern. Then he spied something quite unexpected.

Nestled deep in the rock outcrop, held in what seemed an enormous stone nest, was an egg.

However, this was no ordinary egg, for it was twice his size, and embedded in its surface, was an intensely green jewel the size of a fist.

Mark couldn't believe his eyes. This was undoubtedly the strangest thing that'd ever happened to him. He whistled in surprise and reached out to touch its surface. The egg was warm like the stone and seemed to pulse with life. He pressed his ear to it and could discern a strong heartbeat coming from within. Something in the egg was alive. Mark hoped it wasn't hungry. He briefly lost his footing and placed his other hand on the shell's exterior to steady him. That was when his palm fell on the jewel. The green gem flared a bright, potent light, and the egg began to shake.

Mark quickly jumped back. As he did, a spider web of cracks flared out from the egg's top and worked their way down the shell. Great dark lines appeared as the egg opened to reveal its occupant. Slowly, it emerged. First the horns, then the top of a black scaled wing. The rest soon followed, but even before it was all the way out, Mark knew what it was—a dragon. A big, black dragon.

The creature regarded Mark curiously, its huge plate-sized eyes never leaving him. Mark backed up to the cave wall, trying to put as much distance between him and the reptile as possible. Babies were generally hungry when born, and Mark had no wish to be this beast's first meal. The dragon emerged from what remained of its egg, flexed its wings, and shook away any lingering pieces of shell.

Despite himself and the perceived danger, Mark couldn't help but admire the regal beast. It had a huge wingspan and a massive tail that snaked out from its lofty flanks. Even as it moved, the dragon's eyes were locked on Mark. The boy thought that perhaps the scaled creature was trying a form of hypnosis on him. After much more staring, something unprecedented happened.

"Hello," the dragon spoke. It was only one word, nothing spectacular, but it was still a word, and in English no less.

Mark continued to stare, shocked.

The dragon put on a puzzled look, as if it expected an answer.

"Erm . . . hello," Mark finally managed to say after wondering what he should say to a dragon.

"Marvellous, you understood! I wasn't sure if I'd got it right, first time speaking and all," said the dragon.

Mark couldn't believe it. More words. A full

sentence in perfect English. The dragon's voice was gravely and deep but otherwise perfect.

"How did you learn English?" Mark sputtered.

"I know a great many things. For instance, your name is Mark, is it not?"

"Okay, this is far too weird. I must've bumped my head. How do you know me? We've never met!"

"And yet, you know me all the same, do you not? Search your memory for my name."

Mark thought back, but if he had met a dragon, surely he would've remembered. Then it hit him—Charlock. Years ago, he often dreamed about a black dragon, a mighty beast who would take him up in the sky and away on the wind. Still, he could never quite see the dragon's face.

"You remember me now, don't you?"

"Y-yes. Your name is Charlock, isn't it? You were the dragon in my dreams."

The dragon nodded sagely.

"Correct. For millennia I've awaited you here, in this cave. Waiting for you to help me fulfil our destiny."

"Destiny? What're you talking about? I'm a college student. My destiny is in education, not here!"

"You may not believe me, but it's true. We

have a great task ahead of us, and I cannot do it alone."

"But what do you want of me? How can I possibly help you?" Mark asked.

In response, the dragon extended a clawed hand. In its palm was the green jewel from the egg.

"This is a gift. Place it to your chest, and all will be made clear," the dragon instructed.

Mark edged forwards, still not trusting the dragon entirely. He put out his hand and gingerly lifted the jewel.

"So, I just put this on my chest, and it will explain everything you say?" he questioned.

"Yes, the ever-man jewel is one of my kind's most important treasures. They contain the knowledge of my race, and through it, I was able to gain knowledge of you and your civilisation. It was the ever-man stone that called you here."

Mark was sceptical that one rock could contain so much power, but he had just spent the last five minutes conversing with a dragon, so perhaps anything was possible. He cradled the weighty gem under his arm and undid his shirt. He then drew the rock towards him, the pulse within the stone quickening with his heart's beating. Mark could feel a presence infuse him as the cold surface touched his naked chest.

As Mark stood there, the light from the stone flared brightly. He could feel the stone pulsing in his mind as he received the entire documented knowledge of Charlock's civilisation.

Through it, he saw many things in his mind. Great dragons flew the skies. Magnificent cities stretched before him, and at the end of this all, was an immensely dark presence. He saw fire and ash and the form of a despicable two-headed tyrant, who laughed over the scene. He briefly saw the research station on the news, and then all went black as the jewel proceeded to download the remaining information.

Once it was over, Mark lay on the hard stone floor. Looking up, he saw the dragon regarding him worriedly.

"Are you okay?" asked Charlock. "I confess I wasn't sure what effect the stone would have on a human, but I hoped at this age your mind would perhaps be strong enough to handle the abundance of information."

Mark sat up groggily. "You mean you gave that thing to me without knowing what it'd do?"

Charlock looked away shamefully.

Terrific, Bertilack thought. *Wait a minute . . . Bertilack? My name is Mark, isn't it?*

He looked himself up and down and found that was no longer the case. His body had been encased in a strange form of living armour designed to resemble that of a medieval knight. He struggled to his feet, noticing for the first time the great sword at his waist. "What's happened to me?" Bertilack stammered.

"The stone couldn't lend you all its power in your old form, so it changed it to one more suited to its needs and yours."

"So, everything I know, everything I am, that's true, I really am Bertilack, the green knight?"

"For all intents and purposes, young master, this is true. But fear not, you can remove the jewel at any time and return to your normal state."

This gave Mark some small measure of comfort. While he enjoyed the newfound strength, he wasn't prepared to sacrifice his old life for it.

"So, I can go back to Mark again just by removing this little bauble on my chest?"

"That's correct. You'll return to normal whenever the gem is taken off."

Still, the gem had given him a great deal. The armour he wore was black like charcoal, but it was also equipped with a green cloth that hung over his shoulder. A gold belt sat around his waist, and a fleur-de-lis was printed on his chest. He'd gone far beyond the lines of being just Mark. Now he was Bertilack the Defender. He was the ever-man, the green knight, defender of the weak and upholder of justice. He had a mission, a goal, a destiny to fulfil, no matter the cost.

CHAPTER THREE

After Mark had removed the ever-stone from his chest, he sat with Charlock and talked. Now that he'd overcome his shock and was aware that the dragon had no desire to eat him, he relaxed somewhat and was surprised how much he had in common with the dragon.

According to Charlock, the dragon's solar cycle calendar was like human years. The two even concluded that they shared the same birthday—February 17th.

As time passed, the ever-man stone began to feed information to his dormant form. It had told him all about himself and his past. The jewel had selected Mark as the chosen one from the day of his birth, as the first human born to this age who could awaken the sleeping dragon. Mark wondered why, and Charlock confessed he did not know. Although the mystic stone had told him much, it had left out that particular nugget of information.

"I know much of your race, my young friend. You have an interesting and diverse culture. It's greatly different from my own."

"I've never felt like I fit into this world, not really. Perhaps I would've been better off in yours as a dragon?"

The dragon looked thoughtful. "Maybe that's why the amulet chose you. Perhaps there's something about you that it sensed. A fragment from my world, which has made you unable to fit in here."

"Anything is possible. After today, I know that much. This day has definitely been unusual," said

Mark. Then a thought occurred to the boy. "Charlock, the jewel told me of other eggs like yours, and it showed a huge monster, a massive beast that was destroying everything in its path." Mark shuddered just thinking about it. "What was that all about?"

"Yes, it showed me the same vision on several occasions, and I'm at a loss to explain who or what it is. That said, I know the eggs are nearby. I can feel them."

"You can feel them? How?" asked Mark.

"Well, as you can imagine, a dragon's abilities are far more advanced than your own. My mind can sense them sleeping, waiting."

"For what?"

"What else? For someone to wake them."

"So, let's go wake them up!"

The dragon shook his head. "I fear it may not be that simple. Like me, they may be waiting for specific people to awaken them."

"Well, we won't find out just sitting here. Let's go look. Where are they?"

The dragon closed its eyes and tried to focus on the mental images of the other dragons. His mind led him to the far back wall, then beyond it, to a secret entrance. There was a tunnel and beyond that, a cavern. It was here that the other dragons resided, sleeping peacefully.

"They're near," Charlock said, finally coming out of his trance. "Beyond the back wall, they wait for us."

Mark got to his feet and walked to the wall with Charlock close behind. He extended his hand and felt around the rock's surface.

"How do we get in?" Mark said, still trying to find his way through the stone.

"I'm unsure. The mental images only led me to this location. They didn't tell me how to get beyond it."

This was a puzzle. Why would the ancient dragons seal the room with magic that neither he nor Charlock could breach? Mark thought about it for a moment. Maybe it wasn't himself that it wanted? He turned around and lifted the ever-stone.

"I've an idea," said Mark. "Your ancestors would've only wanted the recipient of this jewel to be able to pass, and since only I'm supposed to be able to activate the power within the ever-stone, that must mean it's not me that must pass but rather Berilack."

Charlock couldn't fault the logic.

So, Mark brought forth the stone. He held it to his chest and was bathed in the glorious green glow. The light spilled out, encompassing his body and changing his form. When it was over, the ever-man stepped forwards. Whereas Mark was unaware of how to access the chamber, Bertilack knew all too well.

"It's all here in my head now, dear Charlock. I know what must be done," said Bertilack. The knight reached down and held his sword's hilt.

"Bertilack, I don't think hitting it will be of much help," the dragon protested.

"That's why I'm not going to. Behold," he said in a deep voice. "I am Bertilack. Recipient of the ever-man jewel and bonded partner to the dragon Charlock. For me, the door shall open."

With that, Bertilack drew his sword from its sheath. The blade emitted a strong green glow as Bertilack touched its tip to the rock face. As it connected, it flashed briefly before the glow died away, and the sword went dark again.

The companions stood then in the dark waiting, and for a moment, Charlock began to think he'd have to break it down himself. Suddenly, there was a whirring behind the wall. Dust and debris cascaded down as a large section rose upwards. Soon it was up, and before them was a tunnel large enough to accommodate both Bertilack and Charlock.

"You see, my friend, it has worked, has it not?" said Bertilack when he could finally see what he was doing.

"Strange, the jewel didn't tell me."

"Yes, this is indeed peculiar," said Berilack, rubbing his chin thoughtfully. "Perhaps the jewel only wished to impart specific information to specific individuals."

Charlock smiled. "You think like a dragon. I like it!"

"Just as long as I don't get the urge to take flight and devour a whole cow!" Bertilack exclaimed.

"Hmm," the dragon growled. "Don't mention food. I've not eaten yet. If I were born in the old days, there would've been plenty to eat."

"That's a thought. How are you going to eat? I should imagine you need quite a bit to keep you satisfied."

"Worry not," said Charlock. "I will think of a way, but first, we must reach the eggs and find out how to release them from their sleep."

"You're the boss. After you." Bertilack sheathed his sword and stood aside as the dragon proceeded through the opening.

Within, the cave was dark. However, the dragon seemed to have no trouble negotiating the cavern. Bertilack tried to keep the dragon in sight as they moved, a task made easier by the dragon's immense size.

"How far down, Charlock?"

"Not far now," the dragon said. "I can almost see the chamber ahead."

When Charlock had mentioned this tunnel, Bertilack hadn't imagined it'd be this long. He had thought it'd be through the door and round the corner. So much for that idea.

As he moved, he examined his surroundings. The walls were made of the same smooth stone as the first chamber, yet the ceiling was much higher, obviously meant for larger traffic than the one he had made his way to the dragon through.

Charlock didn't seem to notice. The dragon stomped ahead of him, oblivious to everything else apart from his destination. Soon, Bertilack could perceive a faint glow up ahead—they must've been close. The ancient dragons must've chosen a cave full of glowing rocks like Charlock's. The knight wondered about their significance. It could be as simple as they needed to see what they were doing, and the rocks were a convenient light source. It was also possible the rocks had formed after the cavern. In either case, there was no way for Bertilack to find the answer, as the ever-stone had left out such trivial information.

The two companions were soon within the cavern, and Bertilack could see all for himself. Before them stretched rows of eggs, all different shades and colours, each containing a stone in the shell.

"Well," Bertilack exclaimed. "We certainly have our work cut out for us. How many are there, do you think?"

"I don't believe there are too many. Our main problem will be finding people to awaken them."

Charlock placed a clawed foot into the chamber, and the floor lit up like a Christmas tree. Each egg supported a row of lights around it that illuminated the eggs perfectly.

"What did you do?"

The dragon was speechless. He raised his claw and examined it and the area he had trodden on. "I'm at a loss to explain. It may be some ancient lighting apparatus, triggered to dragons perhaps."

"Did the dragons make use of such things?"

"It's certainly possible." the dragon said.

"Hear me, trespasser!"

Bertilack nearly jumped out of his skin. The voice seemed to come from everywhere and had no physical form.

"You are doomed, as are all those who seek to harm the eggs within this chamber." As it spoke, the earth began to shake. Pieces of the ceiling fell around each one, deftly avoiding the eggs below.

"Bertilack, what's happening?"

"I'm not sure, but it'd appear to be another security measure put in place by your ancestors."

At this point, the shaking grew worse, with rocks now clattering on Charlock's flanks.

"Try the sword. It worked on the door!"

Bertilack had to admit the dragon had a point. If the door opened for him, then could he not stop the earthquake the same way? He reached to his side and drew forth the blade. Sure enough, the steel was glowing again, and as soon as he had it free, the earthquake seemed to lessen a bit.

"Who draws the ever-blade?" the disembodied voice demanded. "If you be a charlatan, you shall not leave this cave alive."

The ground shook slightly as Bertilack walked further into the room with the sword drawn before him.

"It is I, Bertilack, the chosen recipient of the ever-stone's power. With me is the newly hatched dragon, Charlock. We mean no harm to you or the eggs. We simply seek to free them from their eternal sleep."

The earth continued to shake but gradually stopped and then finally died. Before them, a light glowed, and a figure appeared—the figure of a dragon.

"Welcome to the dragon vault, chosen ones. My apologies for the scare. You understand I had to be sure."

Bertilack approached the figure of light. "Who are you?" the knight asked.

"I am the custodian," the dragon shape said. "I was placed here millennia ago to await your arrival."

"For us?" Charlock said, walking hesitantly into the cavern so as not to set off any more traps.

"Indeed. The ever-stone could only hold so much information. Your mission and future were left to me to explain."

"Do you know how to awaken the other dragons?" Bertilack asked.

"I do, yes. Each shell contains a crystal, and within each crystal, you'll find pictures of the ones you seek."

"That's it? Just look in and we'll see the person chosen for the eggs? But what if I don't know the person? How will we find them?"

"You will," said the floating construct. "As you were chosen, so were they. Powerful spells were set in place so that you would never lose touch with these individuals until all the eggs were free."

These dragons really had thought of everything. It made sense from a certain point of view. After all, dragons were supposed to be infinitely more intelligent than humans.

"Well, I suppose I should go take a look."

The knight again sheathed his sword and walked towards the first pair of eggs while Charlock waited at the entrance and spoke with the ethereal dragon.

"Guardian, so many things were left out of the information I gained from the ever-stone. Who were my parents, and what happened to them? How am I connected to these eggs? If you know, please tell me."

The guardian hung in the air and regarded Charlock. "Unfortunately, my young friend, I've little more knowledge of events than you, but I shall tell you what I know. Your parents helped create me. It was their input that allowed me to appear before you. Their names were Gorkon and Esper, both of the black clan. In fact, they helped lead the black clan during the time of unrest. I suppose you could say that they were as close as dragons get to a royal lineage. They backed Maligrimance's plan and rallied what was left of the dragons to his cause. The eggs behind me are your charges," the guardian gestured with an ethereal claw.

"You have been chosen as their leader. It's your task to go from this place together with your bondsman and fight for justice. It's your task to ensure that dragons don't pass into history."

Charlock mulled this over. So, he was a prince, and his mother and father had been heroes, sacrificing themselves for the entire world's sake. Could he do any less? He was to lead this group, this brood of dragons, against an unknown threat.

It was then he had a thought.

"Guardian, your information has been most valuable, but there is one thing I must know," said Charlock. "Who is it that we fight?"

The guardian paused, as if unwilling to answer.

"Why do you hesitate?" asked Charlock. "Is it perhaps even something you don't know?"

The guardian shook its translucent head. "I know, young prince, for I have seen it and its minions. Your parents left its name out of the stones for fear that mentioning it would somehow curse their endeavour. Still, I may as well tell you.

"Before my programming was completed, my

neural interface was attached to the crystal network that surrounded the last of the dragon strongholds. The network's main function was as a monitoring device, so that your kind couldn't be caught unaware, it was through this I saw them.

"At first all was calm, and then there was a terrible feral scream that split the air. And from the forest marched the reptilian Terramorphs, genetically enhanced creatures meant to embody the worst aspects of dragonkind with the singular purpose to destroy. Wave upon wave of the beasts marched forth, a never-ending tide of teeth and claws. Soon, though, the waves ended, only to be replaced by something else—Baudrous.

"Your nemesis and enemy of all dragons of light. He was hideous. From what I could see, the beast had lost all vestiges of dragonhood and had become a monster. An animal created to inspire fear. This was all that I saw before your parents placed me here, to await your awakening. I know no more than that."

After he had finished, the guardian seemed visibly shaken by his ordeal. Truly it must have been dire indeed, if it could still wound him after all this time.

Charlock believed this was why the beast was left out of the ever-stone, so that he wouldn't fear him from a memory.

Charlock turned to Bertilack. "Did you hear the guardian's tale?" the dragon asked, as if still not quite believing it.

The knight nodded in reply. "Indeed, my friend, but fear not, your parents wouldn't have left it to you if they didn't think you could do it."

Charlock said nothing for long moments, then quietly spoke. "That beast killed my parents. He took them from me." He seemed distraught now, his voice rising. "I won't rest until I have him dead under my claws. Did you find out who we need? Who are the first two?"

"I know them well. I've been with them all my life," the knight said with a smile.

Mark returned to his original state and left the cavern. Within the egg chamber, the ancient dragons had thoughtfully provided a rope for his escape. He made the climb now with ease. As he emerged, the sun was sinking behind the horizon, and the once blue sky was bathed in a pinkish red as the fiery orb sank from sight for the day.

Mark was relieved to find his bike still present. He had half expected some enterprising young thief to have walked off with it. He mounted up, and rode home, his mind full of thoughts. His brothers would join the quest! How exciting! He wondered who else would venture alongside him.

Unfortunately, after they'd finished talking, the construct had run out of power and faded from existence. Its millennia of waiting was over, but before it'd gone, it had explained that the eggs would activate in pairs from now on. Once they'd discovered one pair, another set of magic stones would come alive, indicating the next two candidates.

Just finding this group alone was going to take some time, and then they would have to fight that monster, Baudrous. From what the guardian had told him, that was a creature Mark didn't fancy fighting any time soon.

He rode faster now, eager to get home. Thankfully, his college wasn't in the habit of phoning for short-term absences, so no one would miss him at least. Besides, he doubted his mother would believe where he'd been.

Oh, don't worry, mum. I just spent the day with a fire breathing dragon. Yeah, real original.

He crossed the field at the back of his house. A more important question was how he was going to explain this to his brothers. Somehow, he had to convince them that this was all legitimate.

He pulled his bike to a stop, opened the back gate to his house, and walked through the door. He announced his presence as he entered, but only his mother answered. She was busy making dinner in the kitchen and made small talk about her day, before asking about his.

"So, how was your day, honey?"

"Oh, you know ... average. Nothing interesting ever happens at that place," he lied.

"Well, stick with it. Just one more year and you can finally do what you've always wanted."

Since he was young, Mark had always wanted to be a palaeontologist. His only reason for going to college was to achieve that dream.

"Where are Woody and Leigh?" Mark asked, eager to get the day's events off his chest. He'd just been through the most amazing experience of his life, and as of yet, he had told no one.

"They're both still at work. Your older brother just phoned, he's finishing up and should be home in time for dinner."

Woody worked for an electrical goods shop in town.

"What about Leigh?"

"Your guess is as good as mine," said his mother. "You know your brother."

He did indeed. His younger brother had a

tendency to disappear and could get himself lost easily if he didn't want to be found. It was unfortunate that they weren't both here. He'd have to wait until they returned.

"I'm going to my room, mum. Can you call me when dinner's ready?"

"Okay, mate. It's going to be a while. Like I said, your brother isn't going to be too long, so I was going to wait for him."

"Hey, no problem," said Mark. It gave him a chance to go through everything in his head and mentally prepare for when he would explain it all to his brothers. "I'm not all that hungry at the moment anyway."

He took off his jacket and rushed up the stairs to his room. As usual, his room was a mess. Socks and clothes littered the floor. His gear from the night before mixed with his brother's stuff from the previous day. He reasoned he wouldn't have to wait long, and so tidied his room, and relaxed for a while on his bed.

His older brother had been let out of work early and had used his motorcycle to get home. Mark heard the engine roar as it parked outside the house. He leapt from his bed, flew down the stairs, and into the living room. Putting on the television, he tried to pretend he had been there for a while.

Soon, he heard the key in the door, and his brother walked in. Woody was around Mark's height, with red hair, and was dressed in bike leathers, carrying a crash helmet.

"All right, bruv," he said as he crossed the threshold. "What's poppin'?"

"Nothing much, mate," Mark answered. "Mum's just doing dinner."

"Yes, and it won't be long," their mother called. She emerged from the kitchen to ask Woody how his day had gone.

"Oh, not bad. I had this really tricky installation to do just outside of town but the boss said I did such a great job that I might as well go home early from where I was working instead of coming back to the store."

"Oh, cool. Well, I'll just get dished up."

"Great, I'm starving." Woody put his jacket on the banister and set his helmet on the floor. "So, what've you been doing today, mate?" he asked, walking into the living room.

Mark said nothing until his brother had sat down. "I've been waiting for you actually, mate."

"Oh yeah, what for?" his brother asked.

"I've got something to tell you, something

important."

"What is it, mate? Are you in some kind of trouble?" asked Woody, concerned. He had always taken the protective big brother role seriously.

"No, mate, nothing like that. How do I put this? You know those dreams I had a long time ago, the ones where they were about being with a dragon and all?"

"Yeah?" his brother said, hesitantly.

"Well, the dream turned out not to be a dream."

"What?"

"It's true, mate," said Mark. "The dragon is real, and he needs our help."

His brother stared at him for a while and then laughed. "Haha, you really had me there, mate. I thought you were serious for a second."

Mark merely looked at him sternly and removed the ever-stone from his pocket. "I am."

Woody looked at the jewel in his brother's hand, huge as his fist and glowing softly. Many emotions crossed his face all at once "Huh, well, you better explain then, hadn't you?"

Mark shook his head in reply and placed the stone back in his pocket "We need to wait for Leigh. This concerns him too."

Frowning but accepting his explanation, the

two brothers waited then for their younger brother to arrive.

He turned up rather late. So late, in fact, that both their parents had already retired to bed. Luckily enough, he was sober and seemed to take in the story, if not believe. However, here again, Mark displayed the ever-stone and captured his brother's complete attention.

Mark explained to them both that come morning, he would lead them to the cave where he had met Charlock, and there the two would be joined with a dragon each.

"Our own dragons, heck yeah," his older brother said. "And then what? What do we do then? I mean, there aren't many places to hide a dragon, so what're we going to do with them?"

"The first step," Mark answered, "is to assemble and release the other dragons. We shall cover the rest of our mission afterwards."

"Well, not being funny, bruv," Leigh said. "But there's something you aren't telling us. If we're going to do this, we've got to know everything."

Mark looked away and sighed, knowing he was right, yet afraid his brothers may not be so eager to join up if they knew of the beast.

"Okay, you want to know the truth? The truth is, I'm not sure myself what's going to happen, but what I do know is this, the dragons need our help. From birth each of us has been chosen to join this fight, and from what I've seen, it's going to be one hell of a battle.

"We're going to be fighting, from what I've been able to gather, hordes of unknown adversaries, led by a beast of unimaginable power and strength. Victory is by no means assured, and like I said, I've no idea what's going to happen. I only know that they need us, and I for one, am not going to disappoint them."

They sat in silence as Mark awaited their answer. He needed them to both say yes, the success of the mission, and the future of their world, was at stake. If either one of his brothers said no, their journey could be over before it started.

Leigh was the first to speak. "If they need us, and if there's no other way, I'm in. From what you've said, the dragons are our best option. Eventually those beasts we gotta fight will get into the world and start hurting people if we chicken out now."

Mark nodded and smiled at Leigh before turning to his older brother. "Woody, what about you?"

His brother smiled and shrugged. "Do you

need to ask? Do you really need to ask? I'd never allow anything to happen to you two. If anything happened and I did nothing, how could I forgive myself?"

Mark got up and hugged both of them. He hadn't thought either would disappoint, but there was always the chance.

"Thanks, guys. I knew I could count on you. It's settled then, tomorrow our destiny awaits."

They each dispersed to bed, lost in their own thoughts, wondering what tomorrow would bring.

CHAPTER FOUR

Following a good night's sleep, Mark and his brothers set off for the cavern. They had to wait for their parents to leave so as not to arouse any suspicion, but once they were gone, the brothers were on their way.

Mark led from the front as the three bikes raced along the roads and into the forest.

"So, where exactly is this place?" Woody said, after they had been riding for some time.

"Not too far now. Remember the small grove of trees where mum used to take us as kids?"

"Only vaguely," his brother replied. "It's been a long time since I've been there."

Unlike Mark, the other two had no reason to visit the place in many years.

"Once we get there, it's just a short climb and walk, and we're there," said Mark. He could tell what his brother was thinking. Woody had always hated heights, and he was also no fan of enclosed spaces either. The mention of a climb and a subterranean walk had made him go quite pale. "Don't worry, bro. It's not that long a climb, and the walk is well lit and ventilated."

This mollified Woody some, and they rode the rest of the way without conversation. Eventually they arrived at their destination and found the hole, just as it was last night, without any hint of being disturbed.

"Well, here we are," said Mark, as the trio dismounted.

Upon looking at the entrance way, his brothers appeared sceptical.

"Come on guys, what's the matter? I guarantee you this is the place." Mark held onto the rope and began his descent.

"Well, what're we waiting for?" Leigh said, not too confident about his abilities to descend the rope.

"It don't look safe, man."

"Come on, bruv. From what Mark's said, this is the least of our problems."

Of course, he had a point. Woody knew Leigh could be irritating like that. There was also the fact that he didn't want his younger brother outdoing him. He steeled himself and approached the gap, looking down at his brothers. He took the rope in both hands and descended slowly.

Mark glanced up as dirt fell on his head. He heard some noise and enquired with Leigh about the cause.

"It's Woody being a mug, mate."

"Shut up, man!" Woody returned. "You know, I don't like enclosed spaces."

Mark despaired. He hoped that once his brother gained powers like his, it would make him less afraid of such things. Mark finished his descent and waited at the bottom for his brothers.

"All right?" he said as Leigh came to a stop.

His brother nodded, a bit flustered.

"Come along, Wood. We're waiting."

"Don't rush me, man. It's hard enough as it is."

Mark looked at Leigh, who shrugged and said, "You knew he'd be like this."

"Fair point," Mark replied.

They waited at the bottom for Woody and eventually their older brother managed to complete the descent.

He stood still and examined his surroundings. "No way," he said finally.

"What do you mean?" asked Mark.

"No way am I going."

"Come on, bruv!" Leigh argued. "You can't go back now!"

"He's right," Mark said. "I promise it'll be worth it. And nothing bad will happen to you here, I swear it. You've come this far. You may as well see it to the end."

Woody glanced back up at the hole. The prospect of climbing up that far wasn't very appealing. He sighed and said, "Okay, fine, but if I don't like it, or can't breathe, then we go back. Fair enough?"

Mark and Leigh both agreed, but neither had any intention of doing so.

They turned as one and walked down the tunnel with Mark again in the lead. This time the journey didn't seem too long, and soon they had reached the cavern.

Mark walked in as if he owned the place, but his brothers were a bit more hesitant. Both were awestruck by the majesty of the cavern. With its glowing rocks and vast ceiling, it was easy to see why. Their previous pause was, however, just a precursor to what happened next.

Mark crossed through the narrow opening that led around Charlock's nest. His brothers eventually followed and came face to face with Charlock.

The dragon had grown nearly double in size overnight and now filled virtually the entire cavern. He looked upon the boys from his lofty perch, and let out a small gout of steam.

Woody felt like running there and then, and it took all of Leigh's courage to stay rooted to the spot, for although each of them had been told there would be a dragon here, neither truly believed it until now.

"Charlock, my friend, you're looking ... bigger," Mark said, surprised. "Was there a buffet I missed?"

"I woke this morning like this," explained the dragon. "It appears my growth had been slowed for so many years that I'm only now catching up."

After he had gotten over his initial surprise, Mark introduced his brothers to Charlock.

The dragon regarded the pair thoughtfully, and then, apparently satisfied, he extended his right front claw and offered it to the boys.

"Welcome, brothers of my companion. I've heard much about you."

Leigh jumped in shock, but eventually took the offered appendage and shook it. "Erm . . . pleased to meet you," he stammered slightly.

After that greeting, Charlock offered his claw to Woody, who shook it warily.

"I'm so pleased you came," said the dragon. "I cannot undervalue the significance of this all, for my species as well as your own."

"Right," Woody said.

"Well, come along, we have much to do."

The dragon shifted his immense form in the direction of the egg depository. He moved forwards and it was then that Mark had a thought, wondering how Charlock would move through the opening given his new size. He voiced his concerns whilst they stood in front of the opening.

"Oh, don't worry about that. Observe," said Charlock. The dragon closed his eyes, and his face adopted a mask of concentration.

"What's he doing?" Woody said, coming to Mark's side and crossing his arms.

"Not a clue, mate. I've not seen him do this

before."

Suddenly the dragon began to glow. It started at the tip of his tail, and worked its way up Charlock's back and over his head. Soon the dragon's whole body was immersed in a translucent glowing barrier.

Mark and the others took a step back as the light intensified and grew beyond him. Something was going on inside the glow—the dragon's body was shrinking.

Mark was stunned, he had suspected the dragon was capable of many things, but he had never considered this. Charlock could now effortlessly fit through the doorway, and they followed the dragon into the cave.

Mark withdrew the ever-stone from his belt.

"Mark, what are you doing, mate?" Woody said, coming up behind him.

Mark stopped just before the tunnel entrance. "Hold on a second. Trust me, you won't be disappointed."

He placed the stone to his chest and wondered if he should have a catchphrase to go with his change. He lost track of his thoughts once he felt the power course through him and the energy surrounding him. His body became encased in the mystic armour, and he was once again the mighty

Bertilack.

He turned to his brothers and drew forth his sword. "This is the power that awaits you, my brothers," he said in a gruff, manly, and dramatic voice. "Upon entering that room, you'll take up a crystal each. Your bodies will be infused with power and knowledge beyond comprehension, and it'll be in these forms that we shall battle our enemies."

Both brothers stood aghast. Mark neglected to mention this little tidbit of information. It was, to say the least, a lot to take in.

"Mark, is that really you under there?" Leigh asked.

Bertilack focused his gaze upon the pair. "It is, my young brother, but in this form, I'm known as Bertilack, the ever-man. You'll find that once you join, it'll feel very natural to be called by your new name."

His brothers listened intently, the voice coming from the knight was unquestionably Mark's, but was more confident in tone than Mark had ever been.

"You mean, if we go in there, we'll become like you? All armoured and whatnot?" Woody enquired.

"Precisely, my dear brother. All the powers I

now posses shall be yours. Surely you didn't think we would go off and fight as we are now?"

Woody had to agree it made sense, but he never considered the possibility of transforming.

"We must make haste, my friends. I'm eager to meet my brethren!" Charlock's voice boomed from the end of the tunnel.

"Well, you heard the dragon, let's go," said Bertilack. He raised his sword up so the light would shine on their path, and proceeded to walk down the tunnel. His brothers followed suit. Soon all three were standing by Charlock's side within the egg chamber. It hadn't changed since Bertilack's visit yesterday, both eggs still standing where he'd left them.

"Well, brothers," said Bertilack, motioning towards the eggs. "Those two are yours. Leigh yours is the gold one. Woody yours is silver."

Both eggs shone like the metals they represented, and upon each one was a gem. On the silver lay a fist-size blue stone of aquamarine. And upon the gold was a garnet of the same size.

The two brothers walked towards them hesitantly, each one examining the eggs metallic exteriors. The two eggs seemed identical, save for the fact that they were different colours, and the silver was slightly larger than the gold. They continued to walk around them, unsure of what to do next.

"Place both hands on the shell of the egg," said Bertilack. "Wait a moment, then stand far back."

Woody and Leigh did as they were bid. They advanced towards their respective eggs and placed their hands on the shells. At first there was no change, then both eggs began to shake. Both brothers jumped back to a safe distance as cracks formed on the shells' exteriors.

The dragon in the gold egg burst forth first, showering the cave in shell debris. The dragon from the silver egg took more time to emerge, steadily removing one body part at a time.

Once free, both dragons gazed around and took stock of where they were. They looked immensely happy to be free. So much so, that the gold dragon immediately started laughing.

"By my wings, it's good to be out of that shell! I thought I'd go mad being stuck in there any longer. Oh, where are my manners? I neglected to introduce myself," the gold dragon said, before fixing its eyes on Leigh. "Greetings, I'm Argast. I assume that you are my bondsman, little one? I have something for you—a thank you for my release."

The dragon sifted through the shell fragments

before bringing the huge red gem forth.

On the other hand, the silver dragon had yet to say anything. He sat amidst the remains of his shell, observing everyone. Then his gaze met Charlock's.

"Why don't you speak, brother?" asked the black dragon. "We're all friends here."

The silver dragon continued to regard him. "It is a wise dragon that holds its tongue until all have spoken," he said in a majestic voice. "But know that I am called Sharos. And from this day forwards, I pledge myself to the one that freed me."

Sharos looked down at Woody and smiled before removing a glimmering blue stone from his shell and extended it outwards towards Woody. "For you, bondsman."

The young man took the jewel, experimentally turning it over in his hands and studying its facets.

"Place the jewel to your chest, my brothers. Allow the power to fill you. Don't fight it, revel in it. Let it become one with you."

Both brothers did again as they were bid and were instantly transformed. Light engulfed the pair, and Bertilack now had first-hand experience as to what it was like to witness the change from outside.

It happened more gradually than he remembered. The light folded outwards to encompass them both, an awing experience, to say the least. Bertilack stared with admiration as his brothers changed before his eyes into heroes.

Once it was over, the pair watched and admired each other, circling slowly to get the full view of their new forms.

"So, what do you think?" Bertilack asked.

To his left, before the silver dragon stood an ocean-coloured elf, covered in blue ornate armour trimmed with greens and reds. A heavy black scabbard lay at his hip with a long sword within.

"I like it. I like it a lot," Woody said. "And brother, it's Caldor now." The elf warrior drew his sword and tested its weight.

"And you, my little brother? How do you find your new form?"

On his other side, stood a squat powerful dwarf, covered in hefty bronze-coloured armour and wielding a heavy axe in his mighty hands.

"It's not what I would've chosen for myself," he said, trying to get a look at himself in Argast's mirrored scales. "A bit much but I could get used to it. And the name's Keldon now, brother Bertilack."

Charlock smiled a toothy grin and turned to his newly hatched dragon brethren. "What of you two? What do your senses tell you about your new charges?"

The other two dragons looked at one another, and then at Caldor and the dwarf, Keldon.

"Caldor is impressive. He has a good heart and he is stronger than he knows. Already the joining will have removed his more irrational fears and made him stronger. He shall be perfect," said Sharos, looking at his new bondsman favourably.

"And you, Argast? How do you find your new companion?"

The gold dragon smiled back at his black counterpart. "He is fine. Absolutely fine. I can detect no flaws in his spirit. A hero and no mistake."

"Well, it's as expected," Bertilack said. "They're ideally suited. Charlock, perhaps we should leave them to get acquainted?"

"Agreed, we'll be waiting beyond when you're done," said Charlock.

The pair crossed over the threshold and back down the tunnel to the main chamber.

"Penny for your thoughts?" the dragon said after Bertilack had been quiet for a while.

Bertilack fixed him with a curious look.

"A human expression I learned from the everstone. I like it, don't you?"

"It's a good saying. I just found it strange hearing it from you. To answer your question, I'm thinking about what we do next. Where do we go? Who do we fight? We know they're coming, but we don't know who or when."

They entered the cavern, and Bertilack selected a flat rock on which to be seated. The dragon came in and lay down across from him.

"Both are good questions. For the latter, we must wait for the enemy to show his hand. As for the former, we only need to examine the next two jewels and hope your friends are not too far away."

At least they had direction and a course of action. He only hoped they were ready before whatever it was came knocking on their door.

"I pray they will be finished soon. We've got no time to lose. That thing the guardian warned us of seems terrible."

"You're right, Bertilack, but these opening conversations are as important as they were for us," said Charlock.

He was right. It wasn't fair of Bertilack to cut short his brothers when he had been given ample time to acquaint himself with his own dragon.

"What's your appraisal of the two dragons?"

Charlock appeared to mull this over a bit before answering. "I'm not sure. I've never really met another dragon, but my first impressions are promising. Sharos appears intelligent, whereas Argast has an attitude to match his brilliant colour. At this point it'd be folly, though, to make such presumptions."

Bertilack's own opinions were almost identical. The two dragons seemed to complement each other's abilities, but whether this was more magic or wishful thinking, he couldn't tell.

Charlock and Bertilack waited patiently for over an hour before the other dragons and Bertilack's brothers emerged. Still wearing their armour, they stalked out, dragons in tow.

"I take it you're finished?" Bertilack enquired.

"Yes, brother we are," Caldor said. "We have learned much about each other today."

"This scale-belly is a bit rough around the edges," the dwarf said gruffly. "But he's all right."

Argast growled. "To whom do you refer, dwarf?"

"Who do you think, gecko?"

The two bantered good naturedly. Even as a

dwarf, his brother still found ways to be irritating, but rather than bristling as Mark would've done, the dragon was actually absorbing it, and retaliating.

Sharos stood quiet during the proceedings, content, it would seem, to observe his new teammates.

"My friends," Charlock said. "It's good you all are here, but we musn't dillydally. Our enemies could strike at any time, and we're woefully unprepared."

"Indeed," said Sharos. "Caldor and I have already taken the liberty of seeing who our next teammates are."

"But how did you know what to do?" Bertilack said.

"It wasn't hard," answered Caldor. "You yourself told us what we were to do, and how you had discovered we were to be the next. We just filled in the blanks."

"Makes sense," said Bertilack.

"So, who are the next two?" Charlock asked.

Caldor turned his attention towards Charlock.

"Our friend, Gareth Birch, is one," the elf said.

"And the other is a companion of mine called Tristan Harrison," Keldon finished for him. "We know of their whereabouts. It shouldn't take us long to locate them."

"Good, we shall find them quickly, and bring them here. That way we will have at least six warriors and dragons on our side," Bertilack remarked. He would've said more, but at that moment pain appeared to course through the three dragons. They roared at the ceiling and attacked the floor in vicious manners. Bertilack and the others backed up a step.

"Charlock? Charlock! What ails you, my friend?"

The mighty dragon seemed not to hear, obsessed with imaginary demons and things that weren't there. Maybe the dragons could see something. Perhaps they were under siege, and the warriors just couldn't see their attackers. The knight drew his sword, started to cast about the room hoping to get a glimpse of whatever had beset them. His brothers stood back-to-back between their dragons, and they too had drawn their weapons.

"Bertilack!" Caldor yelled "What's going on?"

"I've no idea but keep your wits about you. We may be in more danger than we know!"

Soon, however, the dragons grew quiet, no longer screaming challenges at the ceiling, but their actions were still frantic, and erratic.

Bertilack looked to Charlock, who only now was beginning to calm down. The dragon fell to one knee, his breathing laboured, and although the danger appeared to have passed, Bertilack and the others kept their weapons handy. The other two dragons calmed themselves shortly afterwards, allowing the three warriors to work out what had assailed them.

"Charlock, my friend, what evil besets you?"

The dragon took a while to answer, his breathing still heavy, but he was soon back on his feet. "I'm at a loss to explain it. It was as if lightning had struck my brain, I'd never felt such pain."

Bertilack gazed upon his friend with a deep look of concern. "But what caused it, how did it happen?"

The dragon shook his head to clear it before answering. "It was a vision, a vision that both my brethren seem to have shared," said Charlock, looking at the weakened dragons with concern.

"Something is wrong. Something evil is awake and moving," Sharos said. "In the vision I saw a sign saying words that I cannot yet pronounce. They were on a building, but we dragons have no need for such things."

Caldor sheathed his sword and placed a hand

on Sharos's flanks. "Can either of you spell for me these words? There may be some importance to them."

Sharos mulled this over before he spoke. "I'm not sure, but I shall try. I believe they spelt two words. The first had the letters L-O-N-D-O-N in sequence and this was followed by the letters M-U-S-E-U-M."

"The London Museum," Keldon said, standing next to Argast. "Why would you dragons have a vision of that old place?"

"We cannot be sure," Argast said. "But I felt a chilling sense of dread when I looked upon the sign."

"As did I," Charlock said. "Whatever darkness is coming, it will begin there."

"So, what do we do then?" Keldon said.

"We do nothing," Bertilack said. "You and Caldor find Tristan and Gareth. Charlock and I will investigate the museum."

At this point, Caldor moved forward. "It's folly to go alone, Bertilack. Take one of us with you."

Bertilack shook his head at the elf. "My dear brother, you and Keldon must find Gareth and Tristan. A knight never flees from battle, and if there is something to this vision, then we shall need all the help we can get."

Caldor was noticeably reluctant. Sending his younger brother into such a potentially dangerous situation didn't sit well with the elf. "I still think it's risky. Why don't I go to the museum with Sharos?"

"Caldor, this is not open for discussion. I shall go, and that will be final. Please, brothers, I implore you, do as I ask for I have my reasons. Sharos cannot shrink, nor has he grown into his full strength yet."

Caldor looked like he was going to offer more resistance, but instead he relented. "You better come back safe," he said finally.

Bertilack nodded, and Charlock stood aside as the dragons and warriors filed past them.

"Remove the stones from your body to return to your original forms before you leave. My brothers will conceal themselves accordingly," said Charlock.

Neither brother knew what he meant by this and just had to hope the dragons understood.

"When we find them, what should we do? Just bring them here or do you want us to wait?" Keldon asked.

"Bring them here," the knight said. "I just hope we will not need their help."

"Amen to that, brother. Later."

Bertilack watched as his brothers and the other dragons left the cave before turning to Charlock.

"Let's go."

CHAPTER FIVE

The air was cool against his face as Charlock soared through the skies. They flew high above the clouds so as not to attract attention from those walking far below. Bertilack knew full well that no one would mistake the black dragon for an airplane.

Every now and again, the surface flashed

between the clouds, and the knight got a sense of how high up they were. Buildings and structures seemed little more than toys, strange constructions of a mad, giant child.

Bertilack just hoped the dragon knew where they were going. Not being able to see landmarks made the possibility of the knight guiding them impossible. However, the dragon never faltered or paused. He flew on with unnerving accuracy, as if he knew exactly where he was going. Perhaps their quarry was unknowingly sending out a beacon for them to follow. Whatever the reason, Bertilack believed they couldn't be far away. From what he'd been able to see through the brakes in cloud cover, they'd just entered London. The museum wouldn't be far, though with the crowds on these city's streets, it would be difficult to land anywhere.

"Charlock!" Bertilack yelled into the wind. "Charlock!"

The dragon turned his head to view his young partner. "What is it, Bertilack?"

"Do you know where you're going?"

"Of course, the air is rank with evil," said Charlock. "We're close."

"But how are we going to get down?"

"Once we're over the museum, we'll break

cover. If I move fast enough, and if we're directly over the museum, we should go unnoticed."

"Well, anything's worth a try," the knight admitted. "But what're you going to do about entering the museum? You'll be noticed within the building and we don't want to cause a panic."

The dragon smiled and nodded. "Worry not, my young friend. I have a plan, leave everything to me."

Bertilack could only shrug in reply. "As you wish, Charlock. It's your show."

The dragon continued on his present course, still keeping to the cloud cover. Bertilack tried to keep track of where they were, but it was difficult at this altitude. Any buildings he could see whizzed by so fast it was impossible to gauge their location.

"We're here!" Charlock boomed all of a sudden, coming to a stop that nearly threw the knight from his back. "My apologies, my friend. This is it, the sky here is full of evil. They can no longer hide from me."

"That's great, Charlock, just a little bit of warning next time, okay?" said Bertilack, readjusting himself.

"In that case, you may have to hold on tighter for this next bit. I'm going to descend to the rooftop."

The knight placed down his visor—which had risen when they jarred to a halt—and nodded his affirmation to the dragon.

Charlock pulled his wings up, and inhaled deeply, then without pause, dived into the cloud cover.

For a time, the pair disappeared, and Bertilack had no idea where they were, but soon the city stretched beneath them. He was caught by its sheer immensity as they plummeted from the sky like a comet. Bertilack gripped onto the two scales on Charlock's back, using them as handholds, and prayed for the strength to maintain his grip.

The dragon continued to fall, folding his wings into his body as he went. Never before had Charlock experienced such exhilaration. He almost hated to slow their descent, but all too soon, the ground sprang forth to meet them. He recognised the museum from his vision. It loomed before them now, and Charlock only had moments to decide where to land on its surface. He hoped they hadn't been seen as he swooped in, pulling out of the dive just short of the museum's rooftop.

Bertilack placed a hand to his chest, feeling his heartbeat ease, and dearly hoped he wouldn't have to go through that again.

Charlock extended a clawed foot and landed fully on the roof. "Time to get off, my friend. We must make haste for I shall begin to attract attention, if I haven't already done so."

The knight was in full agreement, eager to get back on firm ground after the plummet. He'd have to build a saddle for the dragon at some point. Such manoeuvres, while necessary, were very uncomfortable. He leapt down and made a brief check of his surroundings. The museum's roof was vast, even with a beast like Charlock up here. Bertilack had a clear line of sight of the whole area. He removed the ever-stone once he was sure it was safe, returning to his smaller human form—Mark.

"Well, Charlock, we did it," he said. "So, whatever you're going to do, do it fast."

But the dragon was nowhere to be found, it was as if the great beast had just disappeared!

Mark searched here and there but could find no sign of the dragon. "Charlock?" Mark whispered. "Charlock?" Mark wandered around the rooftop. "Charlock, where are you, boy?"

It was then that Mark heard a grating sound, like a cat caught in a box. Fumbling around, he discovered the source—deep inside a now broken air vent was Charlock. Somehow the dragon had shrunk himself and managed to fall through the holes in the vent cover.

"Charlock, is that you?" Mark asked rather stupidly.

"It is, my friend. The spell I cast has made me smaller than I originally predicted."

"A spell?"

"Yes, the ever-stone taught it to me. This is how I planned to enter the museum with you. In this form, only a chosen one can see me."

"That's good to know and one thing I don't have to worry about, but how am I going to get you out?"

The dragon shrugged and Mark casted about, looking for a way to remove the vents outer covering. Across the roof he spied a loose metal framework. He didn't know its use, but he could use its parts.

"Wait there, Charlock. I'll be right back."

Mark raced across the roof and selected an iron bar from the frame that was suitable. Tugging it free, he ran back to the vent. "I've got it, Charlock. Hold on."

The dragon moved away from the vent top as Mark plunged the rod into the breach Charlock had created. Gradually, he applied pressure to the end of it. At first, nothing happened, and the vent remained intact. Then, after a while, the metal groaned, and bent, until the hole was big enough for Charlock to manoeuvre through without hurting his delicate wing membranes.

"Well, that was fun. You okay?" Mark asked.

"Of course, but we had better hurry. My apologies for the delay."

After informing the dragon that apologies were unnecessary, the two raced towards the entrance to the roof. They found the door unlocked and descended the stairs beyond. Before them, the museum stretched outwards, exhibits of all shapes and descriptions depicting items from the past.

It took Mark only a few seconds to work out where they were. It was the Museum of Natural History. In the main hall, beyond the walkway, stood the representation of a fossilized brachiosaurus. The immense beast was a main feature at this museum and attracted quite a crowd. Mark himself had been here before, so he knew from experience how popular the beast was.

Charlock sat on Mark's shoulder, invisible now to all except his young charge.

"What is this place?" Charlock said as they stepped onto the rail.

"It's a depository for all the knowledge humans have gained about the planet's past."

The dragon looked from his perch to admire his surroundings. "Why do humans catalogue such things?" he asked.

"To better ourselves, I suppose. To learn from past mistakes and experiences. See what was and consider what will be."

This concept was alien to Charlock. Dragons lived for so long that they never forgot anything, very few things ever went beyond living memory.

Mark thought they'd best stay up high to watch for suspicious movements, and so continued to walk the balcony, though he wasn't sure what to look for. "Charlock, are you sure you don't remember anything else from this vision? Something that maybe could help us?"

Charlock moved his head and started sniffing the air. "Nothing remembered, but I can smell evil," the dragon said. "Unfortunately, it seems to come from everywhere. I can't yet lock it down."

This gave Mark no comfort. He had hoped that the dragon would be able to find the source of the disturbance once they got close but evidently it would take more time.

"Well, Charlock, my friend, it looks like we wait."

***

It hadn't taken long for Woody and Leigh to find Tristan. Their jovial friend had just finished work and was relaxing at home when they arrived to offer him the chance to join them. Just as the two brothers had been, Tristan, too, was initially sceptical. The powerful man mountain took a lot of persuading before he was willing to entertain the notion that dragons existed. Eventually and reluctantly, he relented and agreed to join them.

They moved in search of Gareth Birch next. Their last companion was never in the same place for long. They asked every friend they could find, talked to his girlfriend, and even called at his home, but no one had seen their blonde-haired associate.

"Where is he, Leigh? We've been searching for ages and we still haven't found him yet," Tristan moaned.

"I know, mate. Of all people it had to be Gareth that causes us problems."

"Pain in the backside," Woody remarked, shaking his head. "Damn it, we don't have time for this anymore. Mark could be in trouble. I say we go back to the cave and activate Tristan's dragon. Then, together we can fight whatever comes."

"Don't be stupid, bruv," Leigh said. "Mark said we have to get both or there's no point."

"But what if we don't find him?" Woody said. "Mark could be in danger and we're not helping him."

"Look," Leigh said, exasperated with his older brother. "We can better help him once Gareth is with us. Until then, just shut up and look!"

Leigh reasoned Gareth wouldn't have gone out of town without telling his girlfriend, and thus had to be somewhere nearby, so they resumed their search. He only hoped Mark was doing better on his end.

***

Mark couldn't quite figure out how things had gone so badly, so quickly. One minute he and Charlock were wandering through the museum, and the next, all hell had broken loose. All of a sudden, people poured out of the dinosaur exhibits and towards the nearest exits, stampeding the pair in the process. Mark tried to collar a passerby as he fled in terror.

"Excuse me, sir, what's going on? Where is everybody going?"

The man casted about wild-eyed. "The b-bones . . . the dinosaur bones!" the man said, stuttering. "They've come alive, we're all doomed!"

Mark let the man go, and he fled off with the others.

"Looks like we've got some action, Charlock."

The dragon nodded. "And not from an expected source, my friend."

He could say that again. Living dinosaur bones were the last thing Mark had thought of. "Shall we?" Mark fingered the ever-stone as he pushed past the crowd with Charlock clinging onto his shoulders. The first place they came to was the cafeteria. At this point, there was no one around, so Mark figured it appropriate to become Bertilack once more.

Charlock flew off his shoulder and landed on the floor as Mark placed the jewel against his chest. The power coursed through him, and there stood the green knight, the ever-man. Feeling heroic, he drew his sword, kicked the door open, and strode through.

The place was a mess. Tables were overturned, food was everywhere, and blood—there was blood on the walls. Bertilack advanced, keeping his wits about him as Charlock resumed his perch on the knight's shoulder. Bending low, he touched the blood with his hand.

"Can you tell if it's human?" Bertilack said, raising his gauntleted hand to the dragon.

"I'm afraid so, the smell is unmistakable."

Just then they heard a noise, and Bertilack spun on his heels. It had come from the back of the dinning hall, and had sounded like pots and pans were falling. Bertilack advanced cautiously and Charlock was alert for movement, wishing there was space enough to fully transform. Again, the pair heard a noise. This time it came from the side and sounded like claws scraping across the floor. Bertilack spun again, but could still not see their mystery foe.

"Charlock, can you see anything?"

"No, my abilities are limited in this form."

Well, that was no good, they were sitting ducks if they couldn't see their adversary. Again, Bertilack advanced, determined to show no fear. He kicked a table over and moved into the clear space.

"Come out, coward! Show yourself!"

"Bertilack!" Charlock yelled.

The dragon's warning came just in time as their mystery attacker leapt from the shadows. Skidding across the floor, the beast came at the knight, its bony protrusions flailing back and forth.

Bertilack jumped and batted it on the snout, causing the beast to lose balance and impact against the wall. The knight pulled back to fully appraise his foe.

Getting shakily to its feet was the incomplete skeleton of a long-dead velociraptor. The creature swayed backwards and forwards, dazed by the blow before renewing its attack. The beast's speed was impressive and in moments it was already on Bertilack.

This time the knight jumped backwards. With his initial surprise over, he was better able to deal with his opponent. He parried the first few blows of the beast's clawed hands, and returned a few of his own. The raptor bore down on him, slashing wildly. Animal ferocity fuelled its movements with no intelligent thought.

Whatever magic had once given cunning to the dinosaurs during ancient times seemed absent from this specimen. Bertilack dodged under a near decapitating blow and was able to push his adversary away. The distance this opened allowed Charlock to unleash a small gout of flame. In his small form, it did little more than annoy the beast, but the distraction was enough for Bertilack to get inside its guard. The creature's bony protrusions were no match for hardened steel, so the knight easily cleaved through his foe.

After the battle, Bertilack stood trying to get his head together as he looked at the lifeless bones.

"What's going on here, Charlock? Where did that thing come from?"

"I don't know, but we'd best make sure there are no more."

Bertilack was in complete agreement. He didn't fancy being blindsided again. The pair resolved to check out the entire museum before they left. If there was another dinosaur alive, they would find it.

Woody and Leigh had eventually found Gareth. Their trusty companion had been getting a haircut and had switched his phone off. The trio had come across him quite accidentally. As they returned home, he was just leaving the barbers on the other side of the road. Tristan spotted him first and called out to him, they all rushed over to his side and related their fantastic tale.

Of course, at first Gareth was having none of it, but after Leigh displayed his own ever-stone for him to see, they were off. The journey to the cave wasn't long from where they were, and before long, the quartet stood before Argast and Sharos in the egg chambers.

"So," Sharos said. "These are our new heroes. Not much to look at," the silver dragon mused. "But I suppose they'll do."

"Hey, come on, Sharos, give them a break. We went through a lot of trouble to get them here," said Woody, now in the form of Caldor. "Besides, appearances can be deceiving."

"That they can, my friend, and if the dragon elders chose them, then they must've had their reasons, my apologies," the silver dragon said. He stood aside and motioned for both Tristan and Gareth to stand by their eggs.

"Now what?" Gareth asked.

Caldor motioned for them to do as he and his brother had done before, and in no time the eggs began to rock as cracks appeared on their surfaces.

The pair stepped back as two new dragons burst to life before their eyes. In front of Gareth was a huge red dragon, and the same was true for Tristan. However, Tristan's dragon was also green on his belly and his scales had a greenish tinge. And where Gareth's dragon displayed the heritage of a fiery breed, Tristan's dragon belonged to another, for he was a scalus dragon—one that couldn't breathe fire.

"Welcome, new friends," Sharos said. "Declare yourselves to us."

The red dragon behind Gareth reared back on its haunches, displacing shell debris and rocks as it went. "I am called Bloodstone," the beast answered.

"And I am Khrishaw," the scalus dragon said.

"Good," Sharos said. "Now present your charges with the stones."

Each dragon fumbled about and removed their ever-stones from the debris, handing them to Gareth and Tristan, respectively.

Both men took the stones from the dragons.

"Well, now what?" Gareth said, looking stupidly at the gem in his hand. "Do you know how much I could get for this?"

"Gareth, shut up," Tristan said.

"Put the stones to your chests and hold on tight," Caldor instructed.

The two did as they were bid, and power once again filled the cave as another pair of champions emerged.

Tristan had become a minotaur. His huge broad shoulders stood higher than any of them, the battle axe he carried was a mighty instrument that looked capable of cleaving stone in two.

At his side, where Gareth had once stood, now

a red knight waited, resting an enormous flame-coloured sword across his shoulders. His medieval plate, a blood red with flames etched into its surface. "This is mad, mate!" the red knight said with a grin. "I think my new name is Gawain."

"And I'm Batras," the minotaur growled. "Am I to take it you're mine, Khrishaw?"

"That's correct, minotaur. Welcome."

"So, that means you're mine, Bloodstone. Pleasure to meet you," Gawain said, bowing to the dragon.

"Likewise, knight. Likewise."

"We can get better acquainted later," Sharos said. "We have pressing matters pending, Bertilack and Charlock may need our help."

"So, Mark is this Bertilack character?" Gawain said.

"That's right, mate," Keldon said. "And we may now have to go save his life."

"Cool," was the scarlet knight's only reply.

* * *

Bertilack and Charlock walked the halls of the museum. They had not gone very far since the battle with the raptor, and had since encountered no other opposition.

About two minutes ago, all the lighting in the

building had been cut, so the dragon and the knight were initially seeing only by what little light was filtering through the windows.

Naturally, some areas of the museum relied exclusively on electrical lights making these areas hard to search, as well as placing an unsettling number of shadows on everything else. Charlock had therefore used his fire and some wood from a chair in the cafeteria to make a torch that Bertilack now carried before him to light their way.

It was Bertilack's vain hope, however, that they would come across the gift shop, so he might procure an electric torch. "It's quiet. Everyone must have evacuated," Bertilack whispered to the dragon.

"Agreed, but why have we seen no law enforcement? An evacuation of that size should have drawn them."

The dragon was, of course correct. Even if the police did not believe the stories of undead dinosaurs, if enough people called them, they'd have to act.

"Maybe there's something wrong at the entrance? Perhaps, they can't get in," Bertilack said as they descended a blacked-out stairwell.

"If this is true, we must head there

immediately," the dragon said. "We may be needed."

The pair came down the stairs and consulted a map of the museum. They set off after discerning the quickest way to the entrance. The front doors were across the museum from where they were, but at a quicker pace, they could make it in about five minutes.

Bertilack moved the torch in the direction they were to go and followed the corridor as it had been laid out on the map.

"Where are we, Bertilack?" Charlock asked as they moved into a rather spacious room.

"This is the rocks and minerals exhibit. All the history of Earth's geological rocks are displayed here for all to see."

The dragon looked around, straining his senses in the dim light to try and make out the exhibits on the wall. He noticed something that did not belong—the shadowy silhouette of a person.

"Bertilack! Against the wall, we aren't alone."

"What?" the knight said, surprised. He flashed the torch in the direction Charlock had indicated.

Hiding behind an exhibit about igneous rocks was a man. But as the light fell on him, the robed figure snarled, and ran for the door.

"Hey, wait!" Bertilack shouted. There was something wrong with this fellow, and he intended to find out what. The knight broke into a run and burst through doors moments after his quarry.

Bertilack found himself now in a dimly lit corridor, he thought he had lost him for a moment but then he heard footsteps to his right and headed in the direction.

"Our friend seems to be heading for the exit," Charlock said as they ran.

The knight had already come to the same conclusion. Their robed mystery man was indeed heading the way the map indicated the entrance would be. The knight kept on running without missing a beat, but the man he followed was quite sprightly. Bertilack had only glimpsed his face, but it was definitely a man in his fifties and one who shouldn't be able to out-pace him and Charlock.

"We're gaining on him!" Bertilack yelled.

The figure ahead wheeled a corner and burst through a set of double doors.

Bertilack came to a halt, noticing above the door a sign indicating the main lobby. He knew from the map that the lobby was the last stop before the main entrance. He'd have to hurry, or he'd lose his quarry. The knight redoubled his efforts and came through the doors at a run, but what greeted him was unexpected.

Beyond the door was a walkway with stairs leading down, the lobby stretched below, and was filled with skeletal dinosaurs. The beasts stalked this way and that, creatures of all shapes and sizes.

The man he had been chasing was descending the stairs towards the creatures. Bertilack couldn't believe his eyes—could the man not see them? The knight ran to the safety rail and called to him as he descended.

"Hey, wait! Don't you see them? They're killers! Get away from there!"

The man stopped midway down the stairs and turned. This time the man's features were obscured by his hood as he looked at them. He regarded them briefly and then raised his arm to point at Bertilack. As he did, all the dinosaurs turned towards him, then, as if following an unknown signal, they attacked.

The knight needed no encouragement. As the bony monstrosities lurched his way, he jumped through the doors and took flight. Behind him he could hear the walls collapse as the undead dinosaurs crashed through after him. He continued to run, not daring to look back in case it allowed his assailants to gain on him.

"I thought knights did not flee?" Charlock smiled, still clinging onto the knight's shoulder.

"I'm not fleeing, it's a tactical withdrawal."

The pair continued to move at an accelerated pace. Bertilack just hoped he was going the right way. It was the knight's plan to lead them up to the roof so that Charlock could grow to full-size and get in a good shot.

Bertilack could hear claws and crashing as larger dinosaurs barrelled through the walls and scenery, continuing their pursuit of the duo.

Almost there, the knight kept telling himself, charging up the flight of stairs. He broke through the door and ran onto the rooftop.

Charlock leapt off the knight's shoulder and restored himself to stature. The dinosaurs came through shortly after and were met with a wall of flames as Charlock incinerated them all.

Bertilack collapsed, exhausted from his chase. "Well, that's that," the knight said. "No more evil in this place."

"Oh, I wouldn't be so sure of that," said a booming voice.

Bertilack turned towards the direction of the voice. In the air behind him, surrounded by a host of ice dragons, was an immense twin-headed dragon.

"Greetings, little mortal," said the twin-headed dragon. "I am Baudrous, and I am your end."

CHAPTER SIX

The giant dragon hovered in the air above the pair, a malicious glint in his eye. Giant scarlet wings framed an immense body whose very scales seemed to pulse with power. The dragon's twin heads snaked backwards and forwards as he regarded the pair.

"So, you're the defence against my coming?"

said Baudrous, his voice deep and rasping. "I was expecting a little more. Oh well, the ancient dragons were never very bright. Perhaps that's why they fell to me so easily," the beast drawled.

Sirens blared beneath him, and people shouted in horror below, yet he remained calm, like he had all the time in the world. Folding in his wings, he came to rest on the rooftop.

"So, my young black dragon, surely your house has not fallen so low, that you now consort with lesser species?" Baudrous said, indicating Bertilack. "Your parents wouldn't have approved."

"Be quiet," Charlock snapped. "My parents were heroes, protecting the world from the tyranny you represent. You have no right to talk about them."

At this the dark dragon chuckled. "You have fire, young one! Hmm, your mother was very much like you. She and your father were remarkably strong, it's a shame they refused me like all the others. It saddened me to destroy them."

"Hush, monster," Charlock growled through bared teeth. "Don't act like you're capable of sadness. You're a tyrant and a villain, and I'll destroy you."

Again, the dark dragon laughed. "You think to

succeed where both your parents failed? You're welcome to try, young dragon."

Baudrous once again took flight as Charlock lunged towards him, a murderous look in his eyes. The black dragon moved to give chase, but his path was blocked by a pair of ice dragons.

"I thought you wanted to fight, sorcerer?" Charlock yelled.

"I'm sorry, my young friend, but other matters require my attention, perhaps next time."

At his command, the two dragons attacked Charlock head on, drawing the black dragon into a fight for his life.

"That's if you survive," Baudrous said ominously.

Two others followed the retreat, leaving all the rest to battle Charlock and the knight—the latter seemed to have been forgotten about in all the excitement.

Ice dragons were the smallest of dragonkind. They came at Charlock from opposite directions, determined to catch their clearly superior foe off guard.

Although still immature, as a black dragon, Charlock was more than their equal. One swooped in low and to the right, the other high and to the left. Charlock met the first one full on, knocking him down, this manoeuvre however, left him exposed to the other dragon's attack, but not if Bertilack could help it.

The knight snapped his senses back into action and drew his sword. Leaping into the air, he slashed the white dragon across the snout. Forged from magic steel, the blade cut deep into the flesh of the dragon's nose, shocking it in mid-flight and forcing it to the ground.

Charlock regarded Bertilack briefly and thanked the knight before continuing his battle with the white dragon.

Bertilack figured Charlock could handle his opponent—he was more worried about himself.

The dragon he had given a bloody nose to was just getting to its feet and seemed rather unhappy with him. Shrieking in pain and outrage, the beast breathed a cone of ice at the knight, but thankfully, Bertilack had enough time to dive behind his shield or he'd have been the world's first summer snowman.

The beast roared in frustration at his failure and charged Bertilack head on.

The knight recovered from the ice attack in time to leap into the air and land on the dragon's head. The creature was startled at this development, and grounded to a halt, flinging the knight over the side of the rooftop.

Bertilack fell three stories before he managed to grab onto a window ledge to stop his descent. Unfortunately, the knight only had one arm free. He was unwilling to let his sword drop, leaving him in quite a predicament, as he couldn't pull himself up with one hand.

The situation was made worse when his ice dragon adversary leered at him from above. Unable to reach him, the beast was content merely to knock bits of rock and debris down on him in an effort to make the knight fall.

Bertilack couldn't even bring his shield up to defend himself. Small stones pinged and bounced off him, but a few larger rocks were causing him to slip even more than he already had.

Both he and the ice dragon knew now it was only a matter of time before he met his end. Sensing victory, the ice beast laughed manically. Using his strength, the dragon removed a huge slab of concrete, and hefting it over his head, the dragon let it fly.

The boulder approached, and the knight resigned himself to his fate, believing it to be his end. In his heart, he apologised to his brothers for letting them down and wondered what they would tell his parents.

He shut his eyes with the boulder inches from him, but nothing happened. He wasn't dead. He opened his eyes again. The rock fell in shattered pieces either side of him and landed harmlessly on the floor. Both he and the ice dragon looked around in confusion. Something must have hit the boulder, but what?

The ice dragon appeared to be uninterested in finding out and began to level another boulder towards him. Suddenly, it stopped short as a feral scream split the air, and lightning burst onto the scene as Bertilack's friends and brothers finally arrived.

The four mighty dragons cleaved through the air, the riders cheering and roaring in turn with their mighty mounts. Fire blazed from their great maws as they came like demons among the ice dragons.

The beast that had the wounded Bertilack square in its sights howled a challenge at the noble dragons before flinging its deadly cargo from the rooftop.

Bloodstone and his rider charged forwards. Gripping the beast by the throat, he flung the scaly fiend clear across the rooftops. However, in his zealous charge, Gawain had forgotten about the slab of concrete. The huge boulder tumbled free, falling towards the earth.

None of Bertilack's other compatriots could reach it in time and could only stare helplessly as the rock plunged down. This one, the knight knew he couldn't deflect. He tried valiantly to raise his shield in the hope this small defence could somehow save him, but it was to no avail. The huge rock slammed into him and flung him off the roof. The impact knocked him unconscious, and all went black.

His body dropped like a rag doll impacting the pavement and smashing straight through to the ground below.

"No!" Gawain yelled. "Bertilack!"

The knight urged Bloodstone on, determined to save his fallen comrade. But as he made to break for the sky, his leg became enveloped by a pillar of ice.

The ice dragon they had thrown was back on his feet and eager to even the score.

Gawain looked once more at the hole in the concrete and then to the ice dragon, rage built inside him like a furnace as the evil beast grinned over what it perceived to be helpless prey.

"Bloodstone," the knight said in barely audible tones. "This creature is dead. I want him slaughtered. I want to rip out his still beating heart with my bare hands."

Gawain drew his sword and levelled it at the dragon.

"Fool," the ice dragon crowed. "You're too weak."

Now Bloodstone smiled, and with a flex of his mighty front leg, the dragon was free once more.

The ice dragon had assumed that this clearly young and small example of his species would be but a minor threat, having had little time to grow into his full-size as Charlock had. However, on seeing this show of strength, it turned to run, no longer sure of victory. But it didn't get far, Bloodstone and Gawain were on it to mete out their own unique brand of justice.

***

Bertilack awoke groggily, his head pounding. Managing to get himself into a crouching position, the knight attempted to clear his thoughts. He remembered the boulder and falling five stories, but little else. He surmised he must've impacted the concrete, but where was he now?

Above he could still hear the hustle and bustle of the city streets, but this gave him no clue as to his location. He listened hard but could discern no more sounds of battle. Was it over? Had they won, or lost? Perhaps he was just too far away to hear.

His sword still rested nearby, wrenched away from him in the fall. The sight of it gave the knight comfort, he reached for it and used it as a prop to get his broken body moving. Slow, and steady he moved, his body screaming in agony with each gruelling step.

In this fashion he made his way underground. He walked further on, the pain leaving him and his strength returning, but he still couldn't find a way out. He removed his helmet in a vain attempt to feel air on his face, hoping to find direction, but he felt nothing. He kept his helmet off and continued to walk.

From what he could see by the light of the sword, the tunnel had been dug fairly recently. The soil was soft, and the gauge marks from whatever instrument had been used were fresh. But what would anyone be building a tunnel down here for? He half hoped it'd be for a new subway line, but he didn't like his chances of that after he started hearing someone chanting. The words were in the magical tongue, and none of Bertilack's men could be down here, so it would most likely be an enemy.

Of course, the knight realised that in his present condition he would be no match for a magic user, but what choice had he? Stand in the dark like a coward until they were gone? Hardly! Besides, he told himself, his injuries had gotten better, the excruciating pain in his leg had been replaced with a mind-numbing agony, so all was well.

He continued to hobble towards the light, trying to make himself as steady as possible before wandering into the sorcerer's presence.

Ahead, there was a light which led Bertilack into a cavern. Upon a dais at its centre, stood the robed man he had chased throughout the museum. He didn't notice Bertilack's approach. He continued to chant and raised his hands to the ceiling, like a man lost in prayer.

"Hear me, Baudrous's spawn! I am Bertilack, the ever-man, champion of humanity. Cease your actions at once!" Bertilack demanded.

The man barely moved. He only lowered a finger and shot a bolt of lightning in Bertilack's direction.

The knight watched it approach, but had no way to avoid it. The electricity slammed into him and carried him off the floor. Falling back, Bertilack impacted against the wall of the cave and slid to the ground. Strangely, however, the magical shockwave hadn't harmed him at all. It was only the initial surprise that had allowed him to be thrown in the air.

Bertilack got to his feet and advanced again on the sorcerer. The fall had depleted his already low amount of energy, a fact he'd hoped to keep secret from the robed maniac.

The man on the dais had begun chanting again after striking Bertilack, and was no longer paying attention to the knight.

Bertilack stood as straight as he could, taking a few difficult steps towards his enemy. As he walked, the knight's steps grew easier and more confident. Once again, he was in range of the sorcerer's spells.

The man seemed close to finishing his work, and turned to the knight to gloat.

"Foolish knight, you cannot stop me!" the man crowed. Again he levelled his finger at the knight and fired. The energies coursed forth towards their target, impacting the knight's chest plate. It struck and the energy dissipated.

Now that Bertilack was ready for the blasts, the results were less spectacular. He shrugged off the hit and continued his advance.

The wizard lost much of his confidence. He hadn't anticipated such resistance. "I misjudged you, knight. A mistake I intend to rectify.

Lightning times two!"

The sorcerer levelled another blast at the knight with double the power.

Bertilack felt a slight tingle and paused momentarily before continuing his advance.

"No, this isn't possible!" the sorcerer said as Bertilack reached the stairs to the dais. Abandoning his spell, the wizard launched blast after blast, and when this failed, he threw balls of blue flame at his assailant, but nothing worked.

Bertilack climbed the stairs, sword drawn. "Your magic has failed, sorcerer. What now?" the knight said once he was halfway up the stairs.

"This can't be! I'm supposed to be stronger! No mere mortal has more power than I!" he snarled. The sorcerer redoubled his efforts, hurling fire and lightning directly at Bertilack.

"Haven't you realised your parlour tricks won't work on me?" said Berilack. The knight brought his sword up and deflected a lightning bolt straight at its owner. The energies coursed back up the stairs, hitting the robed figure straight in the chest, and he fell with a shriek of pain.

Bertilack crossed the final few steps and placed his sword at the sorcerer's throat. "Now, fiend, I have questions, and you had better pray you have the answers."

The deposed wizard laughed maniacally. "Fool, do you believe to have won?"

Before Bertilack could stop him, the wizard pulled forth a gemstone from his robes. As it was unveiled, the fist-size rock flashed an intense light that blinded Bertilack momentarily. When he could see again, the mysterious sorcerer had gone, and whatever spell he'd been casting had dissipated. Bertilack hoped that whatever it had been meant to do, had failed.

He checked the area over just to ensure the wizard wasn't hiding anywhere and noticed an opening near the side as he searched for the sorcerer. Sheathing his sword, he headed that way and found a tunnel leading up. This had to be the way the sorcerer got in, and possibly the way he got out. Following this train of thought, Bertilack entered the tunnel.

It was dark within the passage's interior, and the knight had been unable to find a discernible light source. Its confines were too narrow to allow him to redraw his sword as well as keep hold of his shield, so the knight was forced to feel his way to the top.

Each step was difficult, and the lack of light meant the knight made more noise than a brass marching band. What a predicament! If whatever was at the end of this tunnel was hostile, he'd more than lost the element of surprise. Nothing for it but to keep going. He only hoped he'd have enough time and space to draw his sword once he reached the top. Otherwise it was going to be a short fight.

Ahead he could see a light. Finally, the tunnel had an end. He raised his shield before him and crossed the last steps at a run. As he approached the opening, he heard voices talking in hushed tones. Not wasting any time, he thrust himself into the dimly illuminated room and drew his sword in a flash. He felt a weight press on him from behind and then someone pinned his arms. Breaking free, he threw his opponent to the ground, placing a knee on its chest.

"Yield," he demanded of his unknown assailant.

"Bertilack?" said a familiar voice.

"Caldor?"

Suddenly, a light went on, and Bertilack discovered that he'd indeed pinned Caldor beneath him.

"Brother!" the elf said, embracing the knight. "Damn it, man! We thought we'd lost you."

Bertilack turned to see Keldon and two unknown warriors standing by the light switch.

"You nearly did, my brother. Tell me, who are these two fine looking warriors?"

"The big gristly beast is Tristan, or Batras, as he is now known, and the other is Gareth, now called Gawain," Keldon said.

"Then your quest was a success! I saw you at the battle, tell me all that occurred."

"We fought the ice dragons to a standstill, brother," Caldor said. "Though outnumbered greatly, the treacherous ice serpents were no match for our dragons."

"Where are the dragons? What happened to them?"

"They wait outside, this area of the city has been evacuated but we still might not have much time before the proper authorities show up."

"What of Baudrous?"

"He fled like a coward as soon as his forces took a big enough beating," Keldon said. "Whatever he wanted here, hopefully he didn't get."

"I'm not so sure," said Bertilack. He went on to tell the tale of the sorcerer he'd just met.

"Hmm," Caldor said. "An unusual development. We should discuss it more at the cavern. Now, more than ever, we need to find the other dragon riders."

Bertilack agreed. It wouldn't do to be caught in here by the police. They wouldn't understand the presence of the dragons, especially after the devastation caused. No, a conflict between them and the London police force they did not need.

"Batras, could you help me? I'm afraid my body is too weak to make the journey."

"As you wish, my friend," the minotaur said, in a gravely tone.

"And Gawain, is it Gareth?"

"Right," the red knight said, drawing his crimson edged blade.

Bertilack nodded, he couldn't wait to see what dragons the pair had been gifted with.

Caldor led the way as they left what appeared to be a subterranean café.

Bertilack's suspicions were confirmed when the group left the building. A sign on the door read that the café had once been a crypt that the owners had turned into a novelty café.

Outside, the four dragons rested on their haunches, keeping watch on the surrounding streets. Not a soul had disturbed the great beasts, a fact for which they were very grateful for.

Charlock was the first to see the group emerge and groaned in despair at the state Bertilack was in.

"Bertilack, my friend, what has befallen you? If only I'd been stronger, this never would've happened."

"Not true, my friend," Bertilack said.

"You're damn right," Argast said. "When we arrived, Charlock had defeated three ice dragons and was battling a fourth. None of us could've done better."

Bertilack smiled and swelled with pride at his dragon's accomplishments. "You see? Those fiends will think twice before coming after us again!"

Charlock blushed and then hung his head. "But I failed you, Bertilack. I let you down and you were injured because of it, I'm ashamed."

"Nonsense my friend, nonsense. No one could've stood alone as you did, and I'm proud of you."

The dragon brightened up and Bertilack hugged his face warmly before asking how they had found him.

At this Caldor came up behind the knight. "When we defeated the dragons, most disappeared, but three came this way. We followed and found they'd landed here," the elf said. "A robed figure left upon their backs, and they moved too fast to catch. Curious this stranger had come from this entrance and we'd no other place to go, we went inside and found you."

"That solves that," said Bertilack. "Well, I think it's time we made our exit. As Caldor quite rightly said, we have other warriors to find!"

With a cheer the men mounted their respective dragons and took wing, leaving London's streets far behind.

Moments later, police screeched to a halt outside the café. Charging into the establishment, the Londinium lawmen found nothing to show the dragons had been there. The tunnel the sorcerer had used had mysteriously closed, and soon, all thought of dragons vanished from mortal memory.

The dragons all flew above the clouds to come, finally diving into the forest that housed the cavern in which they made their home. Each dragon shrunk down in size as the warriors removed the gemstones from their respective bodies.

Mark climbed down the rope with the others following closely behind him. They reached the cavern and the dragons returned to their normal size.

"Time to awaken the next pair," Mark said.

They all filed into the egg cavern.

"Gareth, Tristan, you two awoke last. It's your

turn to awake the next pair."

Both warriors advanced on the eggs, each one was a greenish turquoise colour flecked with white specks.

"Look into the jewels on their surfaces and tell me who you see," Mark said.

They both did as they were bid, each one taking a gem in his hands and looking into its murky depths.

Gareth looked up from his stone. "Mine's Simon Spencer," he said shocked.

Simon had gone to school with both Mark and Gareth. He was an intelligent and trustworthy man, but Mark had not seen him in many years.

"And you, Tristan?" Charlock asked.

"I don't recognise him," the big man said.

Gareth came over and peered into the stone. "Blimey, it's Ramey!"

"Ramey?" Mark said. Ramey had grown up with him and his brothers. Mark's mother would care for him after school until his parents got home.

"So, Mark, you know them, but can we find them?" Charlock asked.

"I'm unsure, my friend. I remember where they both used to live but I cannot be sure they still live there."

CHAPTER SEVEN

The next few days were spent searching for the foretold warriors. Something deep in Bertilack's subconscious told him that the two they searched for would be important to the crusade, but he couldn't figure out why. The homes they once had were now occupied by other residents, and they didn't know where the last occupants had moved to. They were at a loss on their search.

Bertilack had spent long hours locked away in his war room. The room was a part of the dragon's original cavern, but the great beasts had since sculpted it for Bertilack, and his friends, in order to aid them in their battle against Baudrous.

Inside was a table made of rock, as well as chairs. Not the most comfortable of things, but they served their purpose.

Today, like on so many other days recently, Bertilack sat brooding on past events. Baudrous and his creatures hadn't been seen since the incident at the museum, and every lead so far to find them, or the new chosen ones, had been a dud. It was on a day like this, that Gawain entered the war room.

"Evening, Bertilack," the red knight said. "Why are you still sitting in here?"

"Gawain, what is it that I can do for you?"

"Well, first, mate, you can tell me why the chief of the newly formed dragon riders, is sitting sulking in here." Gawain had never been the brightest of people, but as the only dragon rider still within the cavern, he took it upon himself to save their leader from depression.

"You know why, Gawain. Like it or not,

Baudrous and his minions are still out there," the green knight said, slamming his fist on the table. "If only I'd caught that wizard, things would be different."

"You tell Charlock not to blame himself, then do the same? Perhaps you should practice what you preach?"

"I don't need you to tell me what to do."

"Perhaps, or perhaps you need to see your dragon," Gawain said. "You've not spoken to him in a while. Do us all a favour, go see him."

Bertilack seemed unconvinced, but promised Gawain he'd try. Saying his goodbyes, the knight left, and Bertilack returned to his sullen mood.

Gawain left the war room and travelled into the dragon's cavern where Bloodstone had elected to wait.

"How is he?" the red dragon said.

"The same, there's no change. I just wish there was something we could do."

The red reptile looked on thoughtfully. "Until the next two are found, and my brethren are awakened, there will be no peace for him. He has much on his shoulders."

But Gawain did not agree with his dragon. "Bertilack's always been like that, instead of crying, he should be acting. Where's Charlock anyway?"

"He has spent much of the last few days in the egg chambers, tending our charges. Bertilack's depression seems to have affected him too."

Gawain sighed, shaking his head. Their two strongest warriors and the leaders of the group, and both were sulking. What a predicament.

The two walked towards the chamber's entrance, but all of a sudden, Bloodstone's head snapped up, and stared fixedly ahead.

Gawain drew his sword, not quite knowing the danger, but determined to be ready for it nevertheless. "What is it Bloodstone? Are we under attack?"

The dragon shook his head uncertainly. "Someone approaches but I can't be sure if it be friend or foe."

The dragon bent into a fighting crouch, and Gawain ran to the side of the opening, keeping out of sight, his sword drawn. He listened intently, the scraping noises were louder. Gawain guessed that there were around five people coming their way. The knight motioned for Bloodstone to be ready. The first set of feet crossed the threshold as Gawain leapt into the doorway. He was met with five distinct screams of alarm as the red knight scared the intruders half to death.

"Gawain, you muppet!" Tristan yelled. "What the heck are you doing?"

The red knight looked at the group and sheathed his sword. "Hey, sorry, okay? We didn't know who you were. I was left here to guard after all."

Woody came forward and clasped the knight on the shoulder. "And a fine job you're doing but quickly now go summon my brother."

"He's not in the best of moods."

"Oh, he'll want to see what we've brought him," Woody said, smiling.

***

Bertilack started to doze off in the war room. The exertion of the last few days coupled with the knight's lack of sleep, had finally taken its toll. He rested with his back against the cave wall, his eyes slowly closing. He'd almost drifted off to sleep when he heard some commotion outside the room. He was aware of two voices speaking together, Gawain and Woody.

Apparently, Woody had found something important on his travels, something Bertilack would like to see. In that instant, Bertilack's heart fluttered. Could it be? Could it really be? The knight was on his feet in seconds and ran through the door before skidding to a halt to compose himself and hide his excitement.

As he left the cave, Gawain and Bloodstone stood with their backs to him, obscuring the tunnel ahead. Bertilack couldn't quite see what was going on. He approached unnoticed as Woody explained that they'd found what they sought, something about tracking school records. Bloodstone's wing was in Bertilack's way, so he still couldn't see what they were talking about.

"I'm telling you, Wood, we should let him rest," Gawain said. "Maybe we should let them meet their dragons first. Let him get some rest."

"Gawain, I understand your concern, but this will cheer him up. Trust me."

"What will?" Bertilack had finally made his way into view of the tunnel. "What'll cheer me up?"

Gawain stood flabbergasted. "Bertilack, what're you doing here? I thought you'd get some sleep."

"Sleep?" Bertilack laughed. "With you two arguing out here? How could I?"

Gawain and Woody stood nose to nose with Tristan and Leigh behind them, each one except Gawain had his dragon on his shoulder, but behind them stood two unidentifiable figures.

"And who are these two?" the knight asked. "Surely not Ramey and Simon?"

The two figures stepped forward, revealing the faces of his old friends. They looked at him with curiosity.

"Mark, is that really you under there?" Simon enquired. The young man who now stood before him was tall and blonde, he wore glasses and held himself with a strong bearing.

"It is, my friend, and I'm very pleased to see the two of you after all this time."

He clasped Simon by the shoulder and took Ramey's hand in his.

"And we you, but it's all so fantastic!" said Ramey. Ramey was of Arabic descent and in their time together as children, Bertilack had known him to be a smart and capable friend.

"Fantastic but true. Woody, tell me how you came by our friends?"

"When you told us which school you remembered them going to, it was easy to get to the school records and trace down their last known addresses."

"An excellent idea, my brother. I'm proud of you all," said Bertilack.

Woody beamed with pride and the group's morale raised considerably.

"What has my brother told you of our quest?" the green knight asked.

"Only that we're needed desperately. That we'd receive magical powers for use against the forces of darkness," Simon said, smiling.

"Seemed good to me," Ramey put in.

"As you can see, both Gareth and I posses such powers," Bertilack said. "You too will gain these powers, including one of these." Bertilack indicated the crouched form of Bloodstone behind them.

"A dragon. We would control dragons?" Simon said, astounded.

"No one controls me, human," Bloodstone boomed.

"Bloodstone is my friend, not my slave," Gawain snapped. The relationship between these two men had been strained since they were kids. Both liked and respected each other, though neither would admit it.

"At ease," Bertilack said, sternly. "You two are not enemies, we've plenty of those."

Simon looked ready to respond, but he reined in his anger. Bloodstone's form looming over him helped.

After he'd got that out of the way, Bertilack was eager to get them suited up as fast as possible.

He motioned for all to follow him into the egg chamber.

As they walked, the dragon riders each changed into their more heroic forms, with the dragons enlarging to full-size. They walked down the tunnel and crossed the threshold into the chambers.

Bertilack entered first and called to his companion.

The massive black had been dozing amid the discarded shells. The noise of their approach had reached his keen senses, and now he sat in a crouched guarded position.

"Charlock, my friend, it's only us."

The dragon relaxed and released smoke from his nostrils.

"We've found them, Charlock. After all our searching, we've found them both. I just pray it's in time for them to do what they were destined to do."

"They're here? Both of them?"

Bertilack stood aside to reveal the two men behind him. "See for yourself. Behind me stands Ramey and Simon, the ones foretold."

Charlock wandered forward and bowed to the pair. "Welcome, we need all the help we can get."

Both Ramey and Simon smiled hesitantly, not sure how to take the dragon's praise.

"Please, take your place beside the eggs."

The great dragon moved aside to reveal two glowing green eggs.

"Those are for us?" Ramey said.

"They are indeed," Caldor said, coming up beside him. "Simply approach and touch the shell. The dragon within will sense your presence and awaken.

"That's it?" Simon said, incredulously. "It's that simple?"

"Yes, it's that simple," Caldor said.

Both Ramey and Simon advanced hesitantly upon the eggs, neither sure what to expect and not really believing that what Caldor said would work.

Ramey was first, his almost ebony skin reflecting starkly against the deeply green egg. He touched the shell and felt the warmth of its occupant.

As with the others, it didn't take long for the reaction to take place. The shell cracked, and the new dragon sought to free itself from its confines.

On the other side of the cavern, Simon stood dumbstruck as the drama unfolded and a new life was brought into this world. And what a sight it was, unlike the other beasts on their team, this creature possessed no wings. Instead, long tapered fins bordered its arms and legs as webbing presented itself between its long-clawed fingers. It was clear to all that this dragon was meant for an aquatic environment. This dragon was also more serpentine than the others, its body resembling a snake more than a lizard. The beast roared and slithered forwards from its egg on four scaled legs. Stretching out, it looked upon Ramey with curiosity.

"You have summoned me here?" the beast said, its voice sounding strange and hollow.

"Erm . . . I suppose so," Ramey stuttered.

The dragon continued to scrutinise him before turning to look at the other assembled warriors and dragons.

"So, you're those who were freed before me? Interesting," said the dragon, grinning and displaying its impressive fangs.

"And who might you be?" Bertilack said, advancing from the group.

"I am Skalus, dragon of the sea. In the ancient days, my kind ruled the oceans of Earth," the dragon replied, sounding imperious, as if it considered itself above all the others.

"Bold words, new friend," Charlock said. "All who have witnessed the ever-stone's power know your words to be true Skalus, but here and now, you're one of us, and an equal. Please give the ever-stone to Ramey."

Skalus briefly locked eyes with Charlock as if about to defy his wishes, then shrugged and found the ever-stone. Removing it from the shell, he placed the enchanted gem in his hand.

"Use it wisely, my new friend."

Skalus's sincerity surprised Ramey at first. He was imperious and bold than he was noble and sincere. It was all so confusing, but then who was to say how a dragon should act? Ramey clutched the gem to his body and was transformed. Sparks flew, and energy pulsed as the power of the stone changed the young man into a new warrior.

As the light receded, the mighty man Kazar appeared. Dressed in a red suit, his trousers striped in blue, his shirt open, revealing a bare chest, and his ever-stone attached to a chain. He moved forwards and made his hands glow brightly.

"This feels great! I feel pumped and stoked for this now," Kazar said, laughing. "Hey, Simon, hurry up, will you? You won't believe this." He turned round and bowed to his dragon. "Skalus, I can tell this is going to be a great friendship."

The dragon bobbed his head in agreement.

"I don't know if I'm ready for this," said Simon, who still hadn't transformed. "What if something goes wrong? What if I don't like who I become?"

Simon's doubts were understandable. None of them had known what would happen when they joined with the stone, but each had gone and yielded positive results. Now, it was his turn.

"Simon, my friend," Bertilack said, coming to his side. "This is your destiny, never forget that. You were chosen to bear this burden. No one else. It has to be you."

Simon still seemed unconvinced.

"Come on then," the knight continued. "Come look into the jewel on the egg, if you have any doubts this will clear them." Bertilack stepped aside to give Simon access to the egg.

Simon still hesitated, but eventually relented. Advancing on the orb, he touched the gem. As he did, the stone flared into brilliance, bathing the room in a greenish glow. The reflection in the stone formed a face he recognised. His face, as clear as day, appeared before him. Every line, every curve, and every bit of his image, and he was smiling. A cocky grin played on his lips, and he winked. Simon dropped the gem, as if it had suddenly become hot coals in his hands, and stared ahead as though seeing a dream.

Kazar went to go to his friend's side, a look of concern on his face, but Bertilack blocked his way.

"No, Kazar, now isn't the time. We must wait for Simon to make his decision."

"But why does he stare so?"

"His ever-stone has granted him a vision. When I first became Bertilack, I was told to do this in case one of the chosen ones wouldn't take up the challenge. It will show him his future."

Kazar relented and stopped his advance, waiting for Simon to make up his mind.

Moments passed, but Simon's expression remained unchanged. He just continued to look ahead of himself.

Kazar looked to Bertilack with that same worried expression on his face, and Bertilack too, thought that perhaps he'd made a mistake.

This wasn't a good idea. Bertilack had just made up his mind to interfere when Simon's head moved and looked to the ground.

"It is indeed my destiny," the young man said in a shaky voice. "If I don't do this, all will be plunged into darkness. Everything I care about will be destroyed and there will be nowhere for me to hide."

He brought his hand up and placed it upon

the egg shell. "For my family, for my friends, for all in the world, I will join with you, Balnase, guardian of the marsh."

The young man's call resonated through the rock of the cavern. It shook and rumbled like never before, as the gem of Simon's egg shone with the brilliance of a thousand stars. The egg underneath cracked at the top and flew apart to reveal its mighty occupant—Balnase.

The great green dragon roared its approval at being awakened, and stomped forward, its emerald tail swinging from side to side. The beast stopped short of Simon and looked down to regard his young charge.

"Your words reached me inside that egg, Simon, and I echo your sentiments. I will join you, and together we will banish the darkness from this world."

The dragon riders, young and old, voiced their approval, and the dragons roared in a great crescendo.

Balnase reached into his shell and retrieved the ever-stone. "It's yours," the dragon said.

Simon placed the stone to his chest, becoming now and forever, the powerful elven mage, Thorlastas, whose mighty form and lofty brow stood higher than even Bertilack himself.

"My friends, hello to you all. Know that I, Thorlastas, though you may call me Thorn, together with Kazar, will open the portal to another world and give us a home of our own."

His words brought many gasps of surprise from the other members of the dragon riders.

"Bertilack," Keldon said. "What madness is this?"

"No madness, brother. Consider it, did you really think the dragons would be able to live freely now in this world or that we would be able to fight at full strength here? The ancient dragons must have foreseen all this and planned accordingly."

Thorn gave a regal bow of acknowledgement. "Bertilack is correct. Within my ever-stone was encoded the knowledge to traverse dimensions," the elf said. "Before the last of the great marine dragons died, they created a way of traversing dimensions in a hope to flee Baudrous's persecution. Their experiments were successful, but before they could finish, a call came out from a dragon sorcerer called Maligrimance. It asked for all surviving dragons to come to him and help him preserve their world. The marine dragons almost didn't accept his offer. For the longest time they resisted, hoping to find peace in a new land.

"The wisest of them, though, soon realised however, that even if they were successful, Baudrous would find a way of following them. The devilish dragon had always shown great resourcefulness in matters of magic and technology. So, the last of the marine dragons travelled to Maligrimance, bringing with them the last eggs of their kind, and the knowledge of portals that were placed within the ever-stone," said the elf. He paused for a moment and looked meaningfully at the group.

"Kazar and I will construct the portals immediately, and then we shall be able to move everyone to this new land. From then, it will just be a case of finding the enemy."

The group had fallen silent. Sharos was the first to speak. "You two have this knowledge?"

Both the wizards nodded.

"And you're sure it's safe, there is no risk to us?"

"Quite sure," the elf answered. "It may take us a few days but we most definitely can accomplish this task."

"Then I'm all for it. If it'll mean gaining a home and being able to fly unhindered outside of this cave, I'm with you," said Sharos.

Bertilack stepped towards the dragon riders,

his palms flat. "Sharos's words are wise, but we cannot make this decision until all are decided. Keldon, what say you?"

The gruff dwarf shouldered his axe and smiled. "Though I'm now a dwarf, and thus at home beneath the ground, I hear the wisdom in this cause of action. Argast and I are in."

"As are Bloodstone and I, just as long as there's plenty of fighting to be done along the way," said the red knight, followed by a hearty laugh.

"Batras, what of you?"

"Ha! There's no place that Gawain would dare go and I not. My axe, is as ever, at your service, and Khrishaw's strength, at your disposal."

"Then it's agreed. We keep a vigil until the mages are done. Then we find Baudrous and deal him his death."

Bertilack's words reached all in the cavern, and they let forth a mighty cheer, for the first time they had a positive plan and a fiery direction.

CHAPTER EIGHT

"It's dark," said a voice.

"The light's gone again," another sighed.

"Well, relight it," the first snapped.

As they spoke, they heard a scrapping noise invade their vicinity.

"It's very dark in here," a deep voice rumbled. "Mind if I turn on a light?"

A gout of flame erupted forth and lit a torch on the far wall, illuminating the faces of two rather befuddled wizards and one very confused dragon.

"What happened?" Balnase asked.

"Kazar's spell backfired and the torches went out," said Thorn. The elf dusted himself off and fixed Kazar with a stern glance before turning to the dragon. "What is it that you need, Balnase?"

"Gawain is waiting down the hall," the dragon said. "He was sent by Bertilack to obtain a progress report."

The wizards both sighed, this was the third time in the day that the knight had asked.

"You may tell his high-exalted one that we'll be ready soon. Opening a portal is tricky business, if we get it wrong the whole structure of reality could be affected," Thorn said gruffly.

The dragon had found his companion's mood and speech to be very strained as of late. Not wishing to push the issue further, the dragon politely bowed before departing the cave.

Once he had gone, Kazar looked at Thorn despairingly. "I hate to say it but he's really tiring us out."

"I know, Kazar, I know," the elf replied. "He's so desperate to open this portal that all other concerns are now secondary."

"But Rome wasn't built in a day, Thorn. How can he expect us to move any quicker?"

"He just has a lot on his mind. You must calm yourself, my friend. We'll be successful soon."

Kazar sighed and relented. "I suppose you're right, and complaining is only going to slow us down. Sometimes, he just burns me up inside." Kazar started mixing some chemicals into a dish in front of him.

"I know, but such is the way," Thorn said, opening up his notebook to the correct page, where earlier he'd scribbled a set of incantations essential to their work. Within moments, the pair were well under way, working in tandem, as if they'd never been interrupted.

Gawain sat with Bloodstone and Skalus at the bottom of a tunnel that had been set aside for the wizards' labours. Out of all of them, Gawain had been chosen as the intermediary, as it was thought Thorn would no doubt have the most to say about Bertilack's constant interruptions.

As Balnase plodded forwards into view, Gawain could tell by his movements that all had not gone well.

"They're not ready," the dragon stated flatly.

"Well, it was to be expected," Gawain said, his armour creaking as he rose. "Fear not, I'll explain to Bertilack." The red knight climbed onto his dragon's saddle and bid them farewell.

Balnase felt somewhat relieved at this statement, and watched as Gawain and Bloodstone departed.

"He doesn't look so happy," said Skalus, coming up to stand by his clutchmate.

"No, but we can't let it worry us too much. Do you think we may be of help to our wizard friends?"

"Perhaps," said Balnase. "After all, our ancestors were masters of that magic. It's in our blood. We may be able to help make it work."

The dragons both smiled and turned to go back towards the wizards when there was an explosion from the laboratory, followed by Thorn's frantic cursing.

"Hmm, perhaps not now," Skalus said to Balnase, as plumes of smoke billowed forth from the doorway to the lab.

***

Gawain heard an explosion from afar and despaired, hoping that this time, unlike the last few, neither wizard had been injured. He wandered through the passageway of the cave that the dragon and wizards had extended for the dragon riders to use, lost in thought.

Bloodstone walked with his friend, his mind also preoccupied. They arrived at Bertilack's quarters, but the knight was strangely absent.

Gawain called out to him, called out to anyone, yet no one answered. This was very peculiar. There should be at least someone in the cavern.

"Bloodstone, can you detect where they've gone?" he asked.

The dragon reared up and sniffed the air. "My dragon brothers are close. At the end of the cave, I think," said the dragon. He sniffed again. "I can't detect the warriors, though. None but the wizards and you are within the cavern."

This was a confusing conundrum. The knight walked down the main passageway that led to the outside, the same one he'd used on his trip here.

"Why would they leave without saying anything?" Gawain asked Bloodstone.

"Perhaps it was an emergency," the dragon replied.

But if that were so, surely it would've been even more important to take Gawain along.

They came to the end of the tunnel to find

Charlock, Argast, Sharos, and Khrishaw, all shrunk to miniature size, staring fixedly at the tunnel entrance.

"Hey, guys! What's the matter?" the big knight yelled.

Each dragon froze, and turned as one to Gawain before all hissing at him.

"What's the matter?" said Gawain, backing up a bit.

The red Khrishaw sighed and slapped a clawed hand to his face, as the others beckoned the pair forwards in hushed tones.

Gawain immediately crouched to the floor, and Bloodstone shrunk sizes so he could follow.

"What's the trouble? Where is everyone?"

"Up there," Charlock pointed out. The dragon cupped a clawed hand to his ear and beckoned for the knight to listen to what went on beyond the hole.

Getting comfortable, the knight attempted to do just that. Obviously his hearing was nowhere near that of a dragon, but he could make out two groups of voices. One belonged to the dragon riders, but the other was unknown to him. They appeared to be talking about the hole in the floor.

"Stand aside, human. Our master has business with the ones beyond," said a voice. It was deep and hollow, like the wailing of the wind or the moaning of the dammed. It spoke good English but had a threatening manner.

"There's no one here but us," yelled Mark's voice.

Why had the knight not changed? If they were being threatened, why had he not acted? Then Gawain considered that perhaps he couldn't act. Perhaps their hands were bound and they couldn't change. The knight drew his sword and smiled with glee, whoever it was they would regret coming here.

Mark sat across from a robed individual, flanked by his brothers and Tristan, and they were in trouble. Somehow Baudrous's warriors had tracked them down, but clearly the dark dragon's minions were not the smartest on the planet. Mark hoped he could talk his way into convincing them they were mistaken.

"Come, come, human. Your loyalty to them is surely not worth dying for?"

The dark figure in front of Mark hadn't come alone. Two other robed figures stood either side, staring out at him through dark cowls.

"I tell you, there's no one here but us. We

come here often. It's our favourite meeting spot."

The central robed figure laughed, a hacking, wheezing laugh like someone who wasn't well. "How unfortunate for you," the figure said. "Because now you've seen us and there can be no witnesses to our master's scheme."

The figure held up his hand, allowing a globe of energy to form. "Goodbye, humans. You may perhaps take some solace in the fact that you'll be the first test subjects of my new spell."

Mark, strangely enough, took no solace in that statement. As Bertilack he could easily deal with these sorcerers, but as Mark he was vulnerable. He fingered the ever-stone, fully aware now he wouldn't have enough time to use it. His mind raced for an answer as the creature raised his hand to strike.

The orb grew brighter, his fingers stretched outwards, and the air crackled with energy.

Suddenly, Gawain leapt out of the hole. Sword drawn, he charged at the robed figures.

The lead creature recoiled in shock but had enough magical knowledge to maintain his spell. Recovering, he changed his target and Gawain caught the blast full in the chest, sending the knight spiralling to the floor. Injured, Gawain laid still as the sorcerer moved closer.

"Not quite as alone as you said, boy. We knew at least one of our enemies dwelled here," said the creature, emitting the same harsh grating laughter as he and his fellows moved closer. "We may have only found one but perhaps we can use him to flush out the rest."

"Oh, I don't think that'll be necessary."

The sorcerer turned to face the voice only to find the steely face of the green knight staring back at him.

"We don't take kindly to trespassers. Take your travelling magic act elsewhere."

Their attention was now fixed on the knight and his companions, momentarily ignoring Gawain who managed to get to one knee using his sword as a prop.

Mark and his comrades had used Gawain's surprise attack for time to change into their alter egos.

"So," the lead sorcerer rasped. "The boy was actually the green knight in disguise. A clever ruse, but it will avail you not. Warriors, attack!"

All of a sudden, the area around came alive as hundreds of skeletal warriors poured forth from seemingly out of nowhere to face them. Attacking in droves, the undead horde set about their task, yelling silent screams from tongueless throats.

However, the ever-stone had furnished Bertilack's men with near superhuman reflexes. In a flash, their weapons were drawn, and they were fighting skeletons, fifty to a man. Back to back and side to side, the heroes fought for their survival against insurmountable odds.

Against this foe, each one knew there would be no mercy asked and no quarter given, they would win this battle or die trying.

The three sorcerers seemed content to simply observe their minions at work, but Bertilack realised quickly that wasn't the case at all. Each one was staring straight ahead, as if in deep meditation. Almost as if they were asleep or casting a spell. That was it! That was how they could win this. Evidently the wizards had to concentrate to maintain their creatures, or they would likely crumble to dust. If Bertilack could somehow break their concentration, they may yet carry the day.

"Keldon, Batras," he yelled over the din, after beheading a particularly irritating assailant. "I'm going after the wizards. Cover me!"

Batras nodded and used his giant bulk to plug the gap in their lines. Keldon himself became a whirling ball of death. Everywhere his axe fell, another skeleton turned to dust. Seeing that his men were all right, Bertilack barrelled forwards, Gawain casting him a questioning glance as Bertilack came on. Using his sword, Bertilack indicated his direction.

Gawain understood his meaning and whispered a silent prayer for the knight's success. If Bertilack could kill those three, perhaps they stood a chance. Now he only had to get there.

One skeleton fell to his blade, then another, then another, and still on he ran.

Fortunately, the sorcerers were concentrating on their creations and didn't notice the knight heading towards them.

Further forward he moved, skeletal forms weighing him down like an anchor as more fell to his blade. He had almost reached the edge of the horde, just a few more feet and he'd be on them.

It was then that the lead sorcerer chose to look up. His eyes registered great alarm as he realised how close the knight was. Uttering a curse, he levelled his hand at the knight, throwing a lighting bolt in his direction.

The magic struck the ground, creating a crater at his feet as the knight leapt into the air. Soon the other sorcerers broke concentration, far more worried about saving their own skin. They too levelled their hands and directed lightning bolts at

Bertilack.

The knight dodged this way and that, as concussive blasts struck the floor all around him. He'd almost reached his goal when a stray bolt struck his shoulder, and he was sent spiralling to the ground.

The sorcerers laughed again before hearing a great roar from the direction of the dragon riders. In their haste to stop Bertilack, they'd neglected to keep up the spells controlling their skeletal horde. Now, the others were free to move as they liked, and they came in a great wave, rushing forwards, and shouting cries of vengeance for their fallen leader.

The sorcerers never knew what hit them. Each one fell, screaming at the riders' blades. Their bodies crumbled to dust, and their robes fell to the ground, empty.

Bertilack picked himself up off the ground as the others came to his side.

"Anybody want to tell me what the hell just happened?" Gawain said, scratching his head.

"Somehow the enemy has discovered our hiding place," Bertilack answered. "We've got no choice. We must move our headquarters or face this kind of attack as a regular occurrence."

The faces of all assembled dropped instantly.

All were aware of the difficulty involved in building a new base at this time, and this was a trouble they could ill afford.

"Is there no other way, lad?" Keldon said. "Nothing else we can do?"

"I fear not, my brother. We must begin packing and preparing for mass evacuation. We'll separate into two teams. One shall remain here to pack, and the other will search far and wide to locate a new home," said Bertilack.

"Hold everything," Thorn yelled, trying to squeeze out of the hole behind Bertilack at the same time as Kazar. "We've done it! We've finally done it!"

"Do you mean the portals? You've completed them? Well done, my friends! Your timing is impeccable."

It was at this moment that the wizards thought to look around. It seemed strange to them that all the warriors were above ground and in armour. It was also peculiar that the ground was covered in bones, their last bit of confusion came upon seeing the three smouldering robes lying on the floor.

"What happened here?"

"That doesn't matter," Bertilack said. "Show me the portal, we've no time to lose."

Kazar and Thorn soon found themselves being herded back down the hole without another word. The entire team descended past the dragons as the wizards relayed to the group how they had accomplished this miracle.

"You see," Thorn began. "Once we had steadied the flux rate—"

"And added the right intermix to the formula—" Kazar continued.

"We had only to speak the correct incantations to open the gate."

Bertilack and many of the others in the group had no idea what the pair were on about, but it didn't matter. What mattered was the end result—the doorway was open. As they walked through the corridors and passageways of their subterranean base, Bertilack felt a great swell of hope again.

The two wizards led the entire party—including the now shrunk dragons—into their laboratory and beheld the glorious sight.

Suspended at the far side of the room, between a set of stalagmites and stalactites, was the doorway. The amazing aperture was circular in shape, its edges coloured in a deep blue hue and its centre a multitude of greens and red.

"At the moment, the portal is only small,"

Kazar said. "In its present state, we cannot move a great deal. Given more time, this tear in space will be big enough for even a full-size dragon."

Both wizards were ecstatic and with good reason, they had accomplished a miracle today and ensured the survival of the dragon riders.

Bertilack snapped out of his revelry to ask how long it would take to ready the portal and make it safe for humans.

Thorn answered that if calculations were correct, a full-size man could pass through immediately. "The only trouble is," the elf continued. "We've not tested it yet."

"That's a problem," Bertilack said, his mind already working towards a solution. "We'll send a small group to make sure it's safe. I trust you two but wisdom counsels on the side of caution."

All the dragon riders agreed, but there were some disagreements as to who would go. Of course, all wished to be involved, but only a few would be going. Bertilack volunteered to be the first, but the others wouldn't hear of it. He was needed far more desperately at headquarters.

Caldor was placed at the head of the team, accompanying him would be Thorn in case the portal went wrong, and Gawain, who complained so much that no one wanted the big knight left behind.

Bertilack requested that Keldon return to their home in Kingston. They'd been gone too long, and before they left this dimension for parts unknown, their mother should know they're safe.

"Tell her as little as possible, brother. Just make sure she's aware that we'll return safe and sound."

Keldon nodded. Both knew that their fate was anything but certain or safe, but what choice had they? With that settled, they turned to face the trio that would make the crossing.

"Take care, brother," Bertilack said, shaking Caldor by the hand.

"I'll see you on the other side," the elf said, smiling.

"My friends, you've nothing to fear," Thorn said in high spirits. "I wouldn't be going on this trip if I thought there was the remotest chance we could be harmed."

"I only wish I were going too," said Kazar. "But for now I shall monitor the portal on this side. Stay safe."

"Thank you, my friend," Thorn replied. "We'll compare notes upon my return."

Gawain grumped at them. The knight had already had enough and was walking towards the portal, his sword drawn. "Are we going to stand here all day, or do it?"

"Calm down, Gawain," Caldor said. He moved in front of the knight and fixed him with a withering look. "We know not what lies beyond. We must go as a team, and you must do everything I command. Understand, this is no time to be foolish."

"Don't forget who saved your hides earlier. I've proven I can handle myself," the big knight growled.

"Bravery can only get you so far before it gets you killed. Remember that," the elf scolded before turning to face the portal. "You must have wisdom and insight to carry the day." Caldor inhaled and crossed the threshold, entering the portal.

Grumbling to himself, Gawain shouldered his sword before following.

Last was Thorn, who approached his creation as if it were made of glass and could fall apart at any moment. He placed a hand on its surface and felt the warmth of the magic flow through his fingers. Steeling himself, he stepped through the door.

There was a rush of speed, and the elf found himself thrust through a gigantic tunnel. The tunnel's exterior was made up of a multitude of colours—purples, blues, greens, and reds, flooded past at all angles as he headed for a beacon of light located at the tunnel's end.

All seemed exactly as the two wizards had predicted it would. He was speeding along at a great pace, and soon found himself flung out into a different world. The portal spat him out with the force of a gun. He erupted forth and sailed clear over the trees to land in the mud alongside two very irate looking warriors.

"Wasn't that fantastic?" the mage said once he had extracted himself from the mud. "Complete molecular transfusion from one dimension to another in a matter of moments!" The wizard seemed impressed with himself, quite pleased indeed.

The others seemed less sure as they dusted and cleaned mud from their clothing.

"Cheer up, fellows. I can work on the end process. Next time we should find the end results a bit more desirable," the elf said cheerily.

The others were still not inclined to be in a good mood. Being catapulted into another dimension at the speed of a bullet had put them both at a very ill temper.

"How are we to return, Thorn?" Caldor asked.

"Through the portal, of course," the elf replied

genuinely.

"And then what you pointy-eared fool?" Gawain yelled. "We left the other portal in a cave. If we return at that speed, we'll fly straight into a stone wall."

The elf placed a hand to his chin in contemplation. "Fear not, my friends. I'm sure I'll think of something before we return."

"Well, you'd better," Gawain said. "Or you'll be going headfirst back!"

A brief look on the knight's face showed he planned to carry out his threat.

"Calm down, you two," Caldor scolded. "Gawain, I've every faith in Thorn's abilities to get us back, but until then, we're to explore this land. The important thing is that it worked."

Of course, Caldor was correct. For all intents and purposes, they'd achieved their objective and had crossed the barrier between worlds.

Caldor's first instruction was for all to climb the nearest hill and get a look at the lay of the land.

Gawain grumbled and continued to complain about the mage's spell, but Caldor was in no mood to continue to listen. The elf set off at a quick pace up the slope nearest them, with Thorn coming up quickly after. Despite Gawain's prodding, Thorn was still in a good mood. He wandered up the hill, a spring in his step, and wasn't disappointed by what he saw.

Before them, the vista was stunning. They'd come out on what appeared to be a verdant and green plateau. Life was in abundance here, as if the world had never known the hand of man—an unspoilt world.

"This is truly excellent," Thorn said, awed. "The power lines are everywhere here. If given an opportunity, I'll ask him to make this the spot of our new home."

"Well, we'll worry about that when you manage to get us back," Caldor said.

"If you get us back," Gawain grumbled. The beauty of this place was lost on the knight. He turned and made his way down the incline.

"What's the matter with him?" Caldor said.

"Gawain and I have always had our differences," Thorn said softly. "It would seem he is unwilling to give up on our old rivalries."

"It's a wonder he came along," Caldor said.

"Perhaps he didn't want to be left out, still wishing to prove he is greater than me."

"You could be right. I haven't known Gawain as long but I believe I may know him better than you now."

It was true that Thorn hadn't seen his old friend in some years. Had Bertilack not brought them back together, they'd likely have gone the rest of their existence without seeing one another again.

"Don't worry about it, Thorn. He'll forget his complaints as soon as we return and get him something else to do," Caldor counselled. "He usually does."

But Thorn wasn't convinced, it was probably more than the portal accident that was causing him trouble.

They followed the knight down the hill, attempting to catch up with the swift progress he was making towards the portal.

"Any ideas how to cushion our fall on the way back?" Caldor enquired.

"Some," the wizard replied. "I'll need to be on the other side of the doorway to affect a permanent change but I may have a spell that could work to our advantage."

"I hope so or none of us will survive the trip back," Caldor said worriedly.

***

Bertilack stood in front of the doorway. Thorn had just disappeared within its depths. He only wished he could've gone too—a fact to which Charlock was in full agreement. The black dragon perched on his shoulder and stood motionless as the three departed through the portal.

Batras exhaled a heavy sigh, as if the minotaur hadn't expected it to work.

Kazar came forwards to examine the glowing circle of light.

"What's the verdict, Kazar? Did they make it?" Bertilack asked.

The wizard nodded. "By all I can tell—wait, something's coming through! Everybody, get back!"

The wizard's tone startled the group so much that each drew their weapons, as if the portal would eject forth demons from the abyss, but all that came forth were two clouds of vapour. The mist moved up to the ceiling and became more solid. Once it had finished, the warriors were met with a huge ball of white, what looked like meringue.

"Kazar, what goes on here? What is this thing?" Batras rumbled, axe in hand.

Keldon, who'd already departed, came charging back when he heard the shock outbursts. "By my beard, what the hell is that?" the gruff dwarf said.

Kazar ran forwards and placed a hand on the substance. "It's meringue lemon," the wizard said, licking his fingers.

A great roar came from the portal as it spat forth Gawain, followed by Thorn, and then Caldor. They plunged headfirst into the meringue, which gushed out, covering all in its vicinity.

"Well, that was good," Thorn said, pleased with himself. "Better than expected actually."

"WHAT?" Gawain bellowed. "You mean you meant this to happen? You crackpot old mage, I'll skewer you for this!"

The knight had his sword out and was already wading towards the wizard before Caldor intervened.

"That's enough, Gawain. Thorn promised to get us back unharmed, and he has done so. Besides, that meringue looks good on you."

This made the whole cavern erupt with laughter, and it was then, for the first time, that the trio were aware they had an audience.

Seeing the meringue sliding off Bertilack's armour, Thorn immediately apologised.

"My deepest regrets! I'd thought the chamber would be empty or that Kazar would've warned you of the spell I was about to cast."

"How could I?" the other wizard replied. "Your

spell was almost instantaneous, we'd no time to clear the cavern."

Thorn pondered his words for a moment. "That's not possible. My spell took hours in preparation and execution, you should've had ample time to clear."

"Not so, mage," Batras said, removing meringue from his fur and wiping his horns. "No sooner had you gone than the spell came through. We thought something had gone wrong when mist issued from the portal."

The three warriors looked at each other, bewildered. "But we've been gone for hours," Caldor said. "We crossed that barrier ages ago."

"Curious," Kazar said, coming to Thorn's side. "It seems time flows differently in the other realm."

"Of course!" Thorn yelled, getting to his feet. "That must be it, what a strange anomaly." The elf smiled as his dragon flew to land on his shoulder. "Kazar, we must research this thoroughly. Imagine the advantages."

"Later, my friends," Bertilack said, walking forwards. "First, report to me all that you've found. I wish to construct the emerald spire as soon as possible."

CHAPTER NINE

The emerald spire had been in the cards for quite some time now. Bertilack often spoke of his dreams where he and Charlock inhabited a massive emerald tower that facilitated all their needs. Bertilack knew it well, the design, the dimensions, everything was imprinted in his mind, as if he'd walked its corridors all his life.

After Kazar and Thorn had adjusted the portal to accommodate safe and secure transport, the knight had personally crossed through to the other side with Charlock and the others.

"As you can see, Bertilack," Thorn explained. "The spot at the base of the hill would make an ideal resting place for our new home."

Bertilack sat on the hill looking at the spot, and watched also the dragons' aerial ballet. The great creatures were enjoying their freedom and wasting no time in making the most of the clear skies, it was nice that they didn't have to hide anymore.

"It's perfect, Thorn," said Bertilack. "As ever, your opinion is right on the money. Soon as I've finished the blueprints, you may begin."

"We may need more time," the elf said.

"Oh, and why is that?" the knight asked.

"As you can imagine, the materials required for such an undertaking are immense. It will take us considerable time to synthesise them through magical means."

"I suppose it can't be helped. I'll not allow any of this land to come to harm simply to have my tower built faster. Now that Baudrous has lost us again, we may have given ourselves a bit of leeway. How goes the research of that strange time dilation present in this dimension?"

Since the wizards had become aware that time passed much slower in their home dimension than here, they'd been trying to ascertain why.

"It appears that a ratio of a second here passes as an hour back in our home dimension. We're still not certain on the reason for it though."

"And what of Keldon? Has my brother returned from my parents?"

"I heard he'd been spotted with Argast some time ago, I'm surprised he didn't come to you straight away."

"Perhaps the meeting didn't go well," the knight said, holding up his hand. "Charlock!"

From out of the sky, riding the thermals, the great beast turned Bertilack's way, and glided majestically towards them.

"Thorn, I need you to continue constructing the spire. I won't be long."

The elf nodded in understanding as Charlock landed before them.

"Charlock, my friend, do you know of Argast's location?"

"Indeed," the dragon said. "He and your brother flew from the gateway as soon as he came into this realm."

"Can you take me to them?"

The dragon extended his wing and allowed the knight to climb on. "Certainly, my friend."

"Remember, the work is not to pause in my absence, I'll expect a progress report on my return."

The elf nodded and bowed in response.

Charlock beat his wings and leapt into the air, sailing through the clouds on his way to find Argast. And as they climbed higher, Bertilack was filled with a childlike thrill. He'd almost forgotten how good it felt to fly.

"By my sword, Charlock, I've missed this," the knight called as they soared through the sky. "We've been so busy, it's nice to cut loose."

"Agreed, my friend," the dragon roared. "It's now a time of rest, at last."

Rest, indeed. But for how long? How long until Baudrous found them again? Bertilack decided not to worry, for that was the future, and he needed his thoughts in the here and now. He was most eager to learn what had happened at his parents' home. Surely, his brother couldn't be far away.

Although Charlock's movements were playful, his course was definite. He could sense Argast in the distance, leading him straight to them.

"How much further, Charlock?" he asked.

"Ahead," the dragon answered.

Bertilack looked up from Charlock to a cliff face that stretched out into the forest. At first he could see nothing. Then what appeared to be a wing. As they closed in, the shape became more pronounced, and he saw a crimson-tinged wing, rising from the outcrop. It had to be Argast, Gawain's dragon Bloodstone would surely have no reason to be out here without the burley knight.

"Is that them, Charlock?"

"Let's find out," the dragon yelled. Shifting his immense flanks, he plunged downwards.

The shift took the knight by surprise and he nearly cried out in shock as the dragon briskly pulled up and levelled off to skim the treetops.

As they approached, Bertilack could see his brother sitting on the ground, legs crossed. He'd deactivated his dwarven form and was spinning the ever-stone in his hands. Argast sat behind him, his tail coiled in front of the young man.

"Hey, Leigh," the knight called as they landed.

His brother looked up and favoured Bertilack with a weary smile. "Wondered when you'd show up," he said, raising his hand in greeting.

Bertilack leapt from the dragon's back and came to stand by his brother, Charlock following behind.

"Why are you all the way out here?" the knight asked. "Did things with mum not go well?"

Leigh shook his head. "It's not that at all. I told her what I thought she needed to know, and said we would be away a few more days."

"And?" the knight enquired.

"And nothing. She took it in her stride, for some reason she seemed to be expecting it."

"Expecting it?" the knight said incredulously. "But how could she? We didn't know ourselves until a couple of weeks ago."

"I know, I know, but trust me, she knew," Leigh said, rising to his feet and facing the setting sun. "It makes me think that this thing is bigger than us, bro, that there's something else at work here."

"You're imagining things. Tell him, Charlock."

"I wouldn't be so sure, Bertilack," the dragon said sagely. "Stranger things have happened and all things happen within destiny."

"Thanks," the knight said sarcastically. "But you know how convincing you can be. Perhaps mum believed the story, or maybe she's fed up with us lying to her and went with it. Either way, there's no use worrying about it, for we've other matters to tend to. The spire will need building soon and we need all the help we can get."

"I suppose so," Leigh said sullenly. "What do you think, Argast?"

The dragon wasn't paying attention. He was too busy sunning himself.

"Argast!" Leigh snapped.

"What?" the dragon said lazily. "Did I miss something?"

"No, don't worry about it. Ready to return?"

"Lead the way," Argast said, unfurling his massive wings.

Leigh reactivated his armour and once again became the dwarf Keldon. He wandered towards the dragon and mounted up.

"So, Bertilack, straight back to the portal?"

"Nay, dear brother, we must find Caldor. If he doesn't know the outcome between you and mum, he's liable to worry. You know how he gets."

The dwarf smiled, recalling old memories of his brother. The man would read the back of a medicine capsule after he'd taken the medicine, and then obsessively worry about the possible side effects—at these times he could be quite irritating.

"Right you are, lad. To Caldor it is then. Argast, you think you can find that flying gecko Sharos?"

"With my eyes closed, dwarf."

"Then be about it, scale-belly, before the sun

dips and I lose all of my sight."

"I'm surprised you've any sight left, you old badger."

"Badger? Why you—"

The conversation between the dragon and rider continued on like so, and then trailed off as the duo set to the sky.

"Well, Charlock, I suppose we should follow them," Bertilack said, as the red dragon and the dwarf disappeared from sight.

"Agreed, if only to make sure Argast concentrates on his flying rather than bickering."

"You'll get no argument from me," the knight said as he climbed into the saddle. "Best speed though. I should like to reach the portal by nightfall."

* * *

Failed. They'd failed. Three promising pets and they'd failed to capture even one of his enemies. The evil dragon waited in an immense cave as another underling approached, carrying the charred robes of his ex-disciples.

"Tell me what happened," the dark dragon growled.

The man wearing purple, his face covered by a dragon-like mask, shook visibly at his master's voice. "I know not, my master."

No news was usually bad news for Baudrous.

"I scoured the area they were sent to investigate and there was evidence of a mighty battle, your Excellency."

"And?" Baudrous rumbled. "Go on."

"A-a-and I could find no evidence of the enemy, my master," the man quaked. "There was, however, much skeletal debris around, indicating that the sorcerers did not go down easy."

"You dare to make your own assumptions, do you, toad?" the dragon king screeched, his great multi-headed form looming large over his servant. "You'd think to apply your feeble brain to managing this task? Well?"

"N-n-no, Excellency, I merely thought—"

"What you thought is irrelevant to me, understood?"

The man merely nodded frantically in response.

"They fought terribly. My three most promising agents, all dead, and not a single enemy corpse?" Baudrous raised a scaled claw and clenched it into a fist.

"Perhaps they were dragged off, my liege?" said the man, trying his best to escape his master's ire.

"Do you think to give me advice now, worm?" Baudrous howled. "Very well then, if they were dragged away, I assume you found drag marks?"

The man said nothing.

"So, there were no marks on the ground? Hmm? I'm waiting, worm. Speak!"

"In truth, your evilness, I did not check for them. I was too busy—ack!"

A shard of ice leapt from Baudrous's hand and pierced the young man through the heart. He slumped to the ground, dead. Whatever information he held was now lost.

"You should've shown more restraint with that," said a black robed figure, emerging from the darkness.

"Tell me not what to do, mage," the dragon snarled. "I made you, and I can break you should I've no further need of you."

The dark figure took a polite step back and apologised. "I meant no disrespect," the mage said. He pulled back his hood to reveal his paled face. "I merely meant that he may have been useful a while longer alive."

"Your advice is noted and ignored," the dragon snarled. "Send out more agents, I want them found."

The dark mage once again placed his hood

over his head. "It shall be done, my master. What should we do once we find them?"

The dark dragon placed a claw to his chin, as if pondering the issue. "The dragons I want unharmed, they may yet be of some use to me. As for the foolish members of your kind, they're yours to do with as you wish. Try something creative."

"Thank you, my master," the mage said with glee. "I won't disappoint you."

"No," the dragon growled. "Be sure that you don't. For if you do, be sure not to return."

The mage stood shocked by his master's words, but tried to recover quickly. "As you command," he said, before hastily vacating and leaving the dragon alone in the great cavern to plot his next move.

* * *

Back at camp, the dragon riders rested by a fire. The sun had finally dipped below the horizon, the day giving way to the night.

Kazar, after a few attempts, had conjured up a bag of marshmallows for which to toast over the campfire. They'd already eaten, satiated on the wildlife of this land, the marshmallows were just a treat before they bedded down.

Around them the dragons had formed a ring of bodies, their wings folded over one another to protect the dragon riders from the elements.

Inside, they all laughed, and sung the night away. Safe, for now, from those that wished them harm.

Gawain lazed in a corner, a half-drunk bottle in his hand. Beside him sat Keldon, the pair swapping stories of their encounters with women.

"I tell you, dwarf, you've never seen such a beauty," the big knight said dozily. He took a stiff draught of his drink. "If only I could've won her over, I'd never want to go out again."

"Ha! You've never been lucky with women," said Bertilack, cutting into the conversation.

"I've better luck than you, oh, great leader," said Gawain. "Please, tell us of your stories."

The whole group cheered and hooted.

"If you have any."

"You know very well I have, but honour would never allow me to besmirch a lady's good name."

This answer did not please the big knight. "Honour be damned! You know no ladies!" Gawain belched, and laughed finding his joke uproariously funny.

Bertilack however didn't find this at all funny,

he rose to his feet and slugged Gawain in the chin.

Much to everyone's amusement, the knight fell over and landed on the ground. Always quick to see the funny side, Gawain laughed before he got up, and rugby tackled Bertilack.

The two fell to the ground, locked in mock combat as the spectators cheered on their favourites.

"Get him, brother!" Caldor called.

"Keep your guard up, Gawain!" Kazar yelled.

Through all this, the dragons merely watched the spectacle. Such battles were all but unknown in their culture.

On the two friends battled, knocking clear the contents of drinks and plates as they tumbled about. Not to be left out, other members of the group soon joined in, one after another. Each of the warriors engaged in combat until the whole camp was in an uproar. Brother fought brother, and wizard fought wizard, some even taking the time to team up on the minotaur.

A few bloodied noses later, the group sat back, exhausted, each laughing, and applauding their efforts. Afterwards, the night passed quietly. All the dragon riders snored and slept, watched over by their dragons.

The next day, work began on the spire at first

light. Bertilack roused his men as the sun rose and instructed them on what he wished to be completed, but not all of the dragon riders were so eager to join the workforce.

Batras the minotaur still slept soundly. Keldon had tried in vain to rouse him, but to no avail. Eventually it took Thorn's magic to get him out of bed. The mage thought it amusing to make a jug of water appear over the beast's head. Tipping it forwards, he gave the minotaur a very cold shower, and as the water splashed down on his head, Batras let out a feral moan. He got to his feet and set off at a run after the mage, knocking over anyone and anything that got in his way.

A distance away, Caldor—the self-appointed foreman of their grand work—was spending the majority of his time telling people what to do with Sharos assisting. Gawain, however, was far from happy with the situation. He constantly challenged Caldor, and would then mumble under his breath about the arrogance of pointy eared elves.

Bertilack himself watched the entire group's actions from the hilltop. He could see Batras attempting to wring Thorn's neck, he saw Keldon and Kazar making their way to the building site with their dragons in tow, and he saw Caldor and Gawain, breaking into another debate about the spire's construction.

Bertilack fancied that he should probably go down and sort it out, but he'd promised to leave the instructions to his brother. One individual he couldn't see was his own dragon, Charlock. The black dragon had set off through the portal just after morning to collect the last of their belongings from the cave and had not been seen since.

Bertilack got to his feet and descended the hill towards the swirling mass. If he had to go and find the dragon, it could cause more delays, and he did hate to be delayed. He crossed the open expanse of grass between the portal and the hill at a run, and then stood to admire its surface. Unchanged since its original construction, the swirling circle of light stood in all its glory. The knight had been amazed by it when it was first created, and over time, it had lost none of its wonder.

He was just about to step through when the portal pulsed suddenly—a failsafe Kazar put in to let others know someone was coming through. He backed up a ways to give whoever it was space to enter, and then, low and behold, Charlock emerged looking in a terrible state.

The dragon had shrunk down to cat size and was out of breath by the time he fell into

Bertilack's arms.

The knight looked at his friend worriedly. "Charlock, Charlock, my friend, what happened to you?"

The dragon took a few laboured breaths before responding. "Skeleton warriors ... the forest."

"Where?" said Bertilack, shocked.

"Not far from the hole. I raced here as fast as my wings could carry me. I dared not change to full-size."

The dragon had been through much and Bertilack felt great relief when Batras the minotaur came stomping round the corner, carrying Thorn under one arm.

"Yo, Bertilack! Caught a rat for dinner, let's roast the pointy eared freak before eating him."

Thorn struggled in his grasp and hurled insults at the minotaur.

"Knock it off you two. Charlock needs your help, Thorn. Take him back to camp now!" Bertilack commanded, the tone of his voice brokered no argument as Thorn hurried forwards to carry out the knight's request.

Batras could see by Bertilack's face that trouble was afoot and unslung his axe. "What happened?"

The knight reached out and handed the dragon to Thorn. "Charlock was hurt fleeing a band of skeletons in the forest. I'm worried they may have poisoned their tools. Had Charlock achieved his true form, I'm certain the enemy wouldn't have stood a chance."

"What're you going to do now?" asked the mage, accepting the dragon.

"Batras and I will venture into the forest and find them. Once you get Charlock some help, send the others after us. We'll hold out for as long as we can. Ready, Batras?"

The minotaur merely nodded, his hands tightening around the shaft of his axe.

Bertilack took a step towards the portal. "Thorn, we're counting on you."

"You have nothing to fear, Bertilack. I have him."

Bertilack smiled then offered Thorn a salute before he and Batras crossed the barrier.

They experienced the same sense of displacement as always as they passed through the portal before being deposited roughly on the other side. Thorn had addressed the problem so that they'd no longer catapult out but the ride was still hardly luxurious.

Both warriors hit the ground running, moving

with all possible speed towards the exit of the cavern. It was dark inside, the group had put out all the lights prior to leaving but Bertilack and Batras had no trouble negotiating the path out.

Eventually, with a burst that bordered on an explosion, the two emerged into the cold air. The forest was quiet as they drew their weapons and looked around for their unseen enemies. Both warriors had expected to be set upon as soon as they'd left the cavern, but strangely, none emerged. Bertilack wondered if they'd all left, but he remained cautious. He motioned with his hand for Batras to spread out and check the area.

Both warriors moved out to either side of the clearing and advanced slowly forwards. Bertilack could see nothing. He searched high and low, but in the dimming light his own eyesight wasn't very good.

Batras fortunately didn't have this problem—a minotaur's senses were naturally much better than humans. He stomped this way and that, peering into every bush and shady spot before sniffing the air for a trace of their quarry.

He detected nothing at first, but then a scent assailed his sensitive nostrils, the scent of decay, and rot only found on something long dead. In the verdant forest, this was, to say the least, an unusual smell. He wasn't at first sure that the smell belonged to the creatures they hunted, but it was all he had to go on. Holding his axe aloft, he silently got Bertilack's attention, and motioned for him to come over.

The knight complied quickly, and was soon at the minotaur's side. Batras proceeded to explain his find in coded sign language. Bertilack motioned his acceptance and the two set off in pursuit of the odious smell.

Soon, however, the trail inevitable led them out of the forest, where the sight of a huge minotaur and an emerald green knight would attract unwanted attention. The two were forced to become humans again in order to move freely. This, however, made them more vulnerable. Mark had never been much of a fighter, so Tristan would have to hold them up if trouble brewed. Mark would fight though, he only wished he was in his armour with his sword in hand, but some things were unavoidable.

The pair crossed the road at the forest edge and into the main area of the forest. Both had walked these paths a million times in their youth, and they knew them well. Each path, each tree, and every leaf, was familiar to the young men, so they were surprised to find a trail that did not belong.

Tristan was ranging ahead of Mark and noticed the anomaly first. "This wasn't here before," the big man whispered into the gloom.

Mark came up and examined the path. "No animal made this, that's for sure."

"What do you think then?" Tristan asked. "The stench is definitely more potent here."

It could only be the same undead horrors that they'd witnessed before. The question now was how many of them were there and how far down the path had they travelled?

Mark stood for a moment deliberating on their best course of action. He wondered whether to wait for the other warriors. Surely by now, Charlock and Thorn had roused them. They couldn't be far behind, but would they be able to find them in time?

The light around the forest was swiftly fading. Soon the trail they'd trodden would be unidentifiable and the smell of the undead would be all but gone.

The decision was then abruptly taken out of their hands as a young lady's scream erupted from the forest depths. She seemed in great distress, the voice appeared to be coming from the trail ahead.

Mark and Tristan needed no more

encouragement. Steeling themselves, they charged through the trees. Mark took the lead with Tristan behind as they moved down the surprisingly clear pathway.

The forest around them seemed almost still, no creatures made any noise, and the warriors fancied that not even the wind was blowing through the trees.

Before long, the pair reached a clearing and found the source of the scream. A young girl sat huddled at the far end of the expanse, a huge tree to her back, surrounding her stood five unknown figures.

Mark couldn't exactly make out her attackers but from the stench of the place he could guess what they were and he didn't like the way things were going.

He formed a hurried plan and relayed it to Tristan, who nodded his agreement before charging forwards. Mark hoped the big warrior could get their attention. Tristan held a stout branch in his hand and used the crude implement as a club. His battle cry surprised the creatures that turned as one to face this new threat.

With that taken care of, Mark positioned himself behind the battle line. At this range, he could see what they faced, and they were indeed the skeletal warriors from before. Their gleaming white bones and grisly grins were all on display as they battled with Tristan at the clearing's centre. The big man was having a hard time of it but seemed to be holding his own.

Mark came around the tree and tapped the girl on the shoulder. She turned to face him, her eyes wide with fear. Mark clamped a hand over her mouth to stifle her screams and then motioned for her to be quiet.

"It's okay," he said. "I'm here to help."

The young girl was too shocked to reply verbally but nodded that she understood.

"Run that way into the forest. After about a hundred metres, you should come to a road. Follow it and get help."

The girl got shakily to her feet and did as instructed.

Watching her form retreat to the trees, Mark wished a silent prayer for her safety. He then turned to the battle at hand. Tristan was losing, the skeletons had him trapped in a corner and were preparing to deliver the killing blow.

In a flash, the ever-stone was out of Mark's pocket. Activating it and allowing the power to flow through him, he ran and leapt among them as the green knight and let his sword do the talking. His steel flashed this way and that, tearing through the bones of his surprised attackers with ease. The fight didn't last long and the two stood in the grove, their breathing heavy.

"Where's the girl?" Tristan asked, his hands still tightly clasped around his stick weapon.

"Hopefully halfway home by now," the knight said. "Are you injured?"

"Nothing a bit of rest and relaxation won't fix. You?"

"I'm good," Bertilack said, resting on his sword. "I wonder what that was all about?"

"Maybe they were looking for us again?" Tristan offered. "Trying to finish us off."

"With five skeletons? No way. Last time they sent much more. They couldn't possible think we could be undone by such small numbers."

Just then, they became aware of a figure in the woods who stepped forwards, clapping. He wore a heavy robe and a hood to obscure his features.

"Very astute, knight. However, your revelation comes too late. Welcome to my trap."

CHAPTER TEN

"You took the bait, just as I knew you would," the dark mage chuckled.

Bertilack stared across the clearing. He recognised the voice, they'd met before. "Remove your hood, mage. I know who you are."

His suspicions were confirmed when the sorcerer revealed himself to be the mage from the museum.

"So, we meet again, coward. After you fled from me, I didn't think I'd see you again."

The sorcerer's face contorted in rage for a moment before disappearing behind a calm demeanour. "I admit, when my powers didn't work on you, I was a bit surprised, to say the least. For my failure I was punished considerably by my master."

The mage clenched his fist and shook visibly at the memory. "But this time, oh yes, *this* time will be different. You see, I've learned some new tricks, and failure is not an option," said the sorcerer, moving closer with his arms outstretched.

"Oh yeah?" Tristan said, stepping in front of Bertilack and removing his ever-stone. "Well now you face two of the dragon riders."

Tristan attempted to place the stone to his chest.

"Oh no, we can't have that," hissed the mage. His hands glowed briefly, and all of a sudden Tristan was catapulted against the wall. "It would seem not all your warriors are immune to my abilities," the sorcerer crowed. "My spell will ensure that we're not disturbed."

Bertilack turned and ran to Tristan's side.

"Tristan, can you hear me?"

The big man groaned as his head lulled from side to side with blood dripping down his neck.

"Hold on, I'll get you out of here," said Bertilack. He bent down and tried to lift the warrior onto his back.

"Ah, but I do insist you stay," the mage growled, raising his hands, and casting another spell.

Bertilack felt the earth shake beneath his feet, walls of shimmering light erupted from the ground, and purple barriers looped between the trees, cutting off all hope of escape.

"Those walls will stay in place until I'm defeated."

Bertilack looked over his shoulder at Tristan. "Coward, I won't fight you whilst my friend is injured," he yelled. "Drop this shield now!"

The mage merely smiled and shook his head. "Why, Bertilack, I'm surprised. You're being so stubborn when your friend's life hangs in the balance. You beat me easily last time, what fear have you now?"

"Regardless, cur, I won't fight you. Now, release us!"

"Get it into your head, you simpleton. Neither of you are going anywhere until we're done."

The sorcerer was starting to lose his temper and aimed a lightning bolt at the pair. Bertilack managed to dodge out of the way. Past experience had taught him that the sorcerer's magic couldn't harm him but he doubted the same was true for Tristan.

The sorcerer aimed another bolt that struck near the knight's foot, and again forced him to leap out of the way, taking Tristan with him.

Realising he wouldn't be able to keep this up, Bertilack resigned and said, "If I agree to battle, will you leave Tristan out of it?"

The sorcerer smiled and placed his hand over his heart. "Of course! Of course! I'm a man of my word!"

His words rang falser than his expression, but Bertilack had no other choice. He knelt down and laid Tristan on the ground. "Be well, my friend. I'll beat this fiend and we'll have you home before you know it."

Tristan groaned in pain, remaining unconsciousness.

"Oooh, you sound so confident! Strong enough to back it up?" the dark mage mocked.

"Let's find out." Bertilack got to his feet and drew his sword. "Make ready, sorcerer."

The mage started chanting. The words were

strange, and in the language of magic. The sorcerer was all of a sudden veiled in a bright pink light as his words increased in noise and tempo.

"My master gave me this ability," the mage cackled as his body changed. "We realised that simple spells wouldn't affect you, so we changed tactics. Hoping to overcome you with strength rather than magic."

The sorcerer's body continued to change, growing in size and tearing free of the sorcerer's robes. Fur appeared over his skin as his face grew elongated, becoming almost vermin-like in appearance. Corded ape-like muscles bulged out his arms and legs, and his chest became huge and swollen. Now the mage towered over the knight, with the vestiges of his robes hanging around his neck like some sort of ridiculous cape. His face had mutated out of all recognition, and great horns had sprouted from his back.

"As you see, my master's gifts are plentiful," said the creature, his voice having changed with his body, sounding almost alien. "You should join us, knight. Master could make use of you."

The beast moved unsteadily towards him.

"Becoming a monster is no gift, sorcerer. Leave now and I'll show pity on you," said Bertilack. Seeing what the dark dragon had forced this poor individual to endure, he couldn't bring himself to harm him.

Despite this, however, the creature seemed unwilling to listen, and instead laughed. "That can never be, this is an all or nothing battle."

Bertilack lowered his sword. "Explain yourself."

"Foolish knight, the form you see before you takes a great deal of energy and concentration. If it isn't reversed in three days, I'll be no more, and only my master knows the cure."

"You fool!" Bertilack yelled. "You seriously believe he'll turn you back? He cares not for you or anyone else. You're means to an end, surely you know that?"

"All I know is I stare at a dead man."

The creature lunged forward suddenly with a speed that belied its size, impacting a heavy claw in the ground and forcing Bertilack to jump clear. The knight sailed high in the air, but the beast wasn't finished. Moving with great speed, it swung again, catching Bertilack off guard and sending him into a stout tree.

"You see, weak knight, you're no match for me. I'll take your remains back in pieces and claim my reward from my master," the creature laughed again and roared in delight.

"If that little love tap is the best you can do, think again," said Bertilack, getting to his feet. The blow had injured him more than he liked to admit, but he dared not show weakness now. He put his sword on defence and motioned for the beast to come and get him.

"You dare mock me? I'll feast on your bones!"

The beast again came on, its sights set on the knight, but having seen its speed, Bertilack was ready. He leapt aside, delivering a blow to the beast's arm. As he went, the knight flew through the air to land in a crouch on the ground. Unfortunately, Bertilack's blow hadn't done as much damage as he'd hoped, for the beast was on him again. Grabbing the knight by the throat, it lifted him off the ground and flung him across the glade.

"Ha," the beast cackled. "Impressive displays but all for naught. Just try getting up from that."

Across from the beast, Bertilack stirred. His armour had taken most of the blow, but he couldn't take much more like that. Using his sword as a prop, he got to his feet. "As you wish, monster. But before continuing, let me ask you— why are you here instead of your leader?"

"Filthy mortal! He needs not waste his time with insects, he has more important things on his mind!"

"Or he's afraid," said Bertilack, hoping to stall the beast in favour of a plan. If he could make the beast lose its focus, it would lose control of the spell.

"Master doesn't fear you. Your world will be destroyed, and I'll laugh amidst the ashes," said the beast. There was hesitation in his voice, and it lashed out in anger towards the knight.

"Then why isn't he here? Face it, he fears me. He knows one day I'll destroy him. It's destiny."

"Liar!" the beast roared, uprooting another tree in its efforts to get to the knight.

"Am I? You don't seem so sure. Where is your master? Get him to show himself if he's so powerful."

"Shut up!" the beast roared, holding its head in its claws and roaring at the sky. "I'll silence you! No one talks about my master that way!"

The creature flailed about again, missing the knight completely. The spell appeared to be having an adverse effect on the mage's mind. Bertilack realised this could make him more dangerous. He'd have to end this soon. A little more, and the beast would lose its control. He just had to keep going.

"Give it up. You've lost your humanity and

your soul to something that cares nothing for you."

The creature swayed from side to side, unsure of itself. The animalistic instincts of its new form had almost completely taken control.

Bertilack rationalised that this was always what Baudrous had intended. Never meaning to restore the sorcerer, this kind of evil was typical of what he knew of the dragon—willing to sacrifice his own for his own sake.

"Can't you see?" Bertilack continued. "Baudrous is using you. Even now, you feel your mind slipping."

"No!" the beast yelled. "You're wrong! I'll prove it."

Again, the giant beast lashed out, racking the earth with its claws. Its strikes were getting even worse as the two halves of its mind struggled for control. "I am the greatest of his sorcerers!" said the beast, drooling. "I can command this power. I just need to eliminate all other distractions ... free my mind."

The creature went quiet for a time. Placing its claws together, the sorcerer chanted once more, and the purple border around them disappeared.

"How's that? I've eliminated the barrier. You can't leave without your friend as it is, and now I can focus all my attention on you."

"A foolish mistake!"

Bertilack's heart jumped as he recognised the voice, both he and the sorcerer turned to find the dragon riders had been waiting behind the barrier, unable to breach it. The sorcerer's spell had kept them invisible to Bertilack, but now there was nothing to stop them. All the dragon riders and their attendant dragons stepped forth from the woods, weapons drawn and armour equipped.

"Bertilack, my dear brother, who said you could start without us?" Caldor said.

"Believe me, brother mine, normally I'd never dream of such a thing, but it was hard to refuse," the knight said gravely, indicating the tree closest to the warriors where the wounded Tristan lay.

"You'll pay for that, demon," Keldon yelled. The stout dwarf rushed forwards, axe held high.

"Keldon, no!" Bertilack yelled but it was too late for the dwarf had already closed the gap between himself and the creature.

Swinging wildly in hope to maim the beast, Keldon leapt into the air, but as he did, the mage-monster dug its claws once again into the ground, flinging dirt and debris all over the glade.

Its initial strike missed the dwarf, with Keldon landing on its arm and rushing toward the beast's head. But the dwarf misgauged the creature's speed, and with one mighty claw, it sent the dwarf flying.

Keldon landed with a bump and flipped into a crouching position. Axe at the ready, he looked viciously at the creature. "That's my friend you hurt there, monster. Big mistake."

The sorcerer removed its spade-like fist from the ground and grinned manically at Keldon. "Please, dwarf. If you seek oblivion, do come and try. I'm untouchable. Even your ever-so-great Bertilack couldn't harm me."

Keldon looked to the knight to confirm this.

"It's true, Keldon. This mangy beast is strong. I barely laid a hand on it," Bertilack said. "But I doubt it has the strength left to fight us all."

The beast stood uncertainly, as if realising its predicament. Its current position left the beast greatly outnumbered, but it endeavoured to remain boastful. "Fools! My strength is superior to you all!"

The creature lurched forward, intent on battering the group. Each of the dragon riders deftly moved out of the way as it thundered past.

"Bertilack," Caldor said from his crouched position. "What's the plan?"

The mage had got himself stuck in the ground

and was struggling to break free.

"That won't hold it for long," Bertilack said. "We must find a way to subdue it. After all, it used to be human."

Caldor gasped and stared across the glade.

"That thing was human?"

"Yes, brother, one tricked by Baudrous. He came here to destroy us, but I believe he deserves compassion."

The mage-beast had extradited itself from the earth and once again advanced towards the group.

"Thorn, any ideas?" Bertilack said.

The elf stood braced against a tree, his wizard staff at the ready. "Difficult to say. This spell is unknown to me, it may be irreversible."

His answer provided Bertilack with no solace. During their battle, the knight had felt great anguish within the creature. Perhaps Baudrous had bewitched them somehow, or lured them in with false promises or hope. Whatever the case, it was still human inside and needed their help.

"Is there nothing we can do? What about you, Kazar? Any thoughts?"

The dark-skinned wizard was up close to the beast, but pulled back to hear his leader's words.

"Unfortunately, dragon sorcery has had no precedent for interracial transmogrification. I'd need time to study him, and I'd be mighty surprised if he'd stand still long enough."

In the creature's current frame of mind, that didn't seem too likely. It was then that Bertilack became aware of the beast laughing at him. From across the glade, its guttural laughter bubbled forth like some maniacal frog.

"After all this, you wish to help me?" the creature bellowed. "Surprised? Not only my strength but my hearing has also increased. I've heard every word."

Bertilack got to his feet. "Then you know I seek to save you," the knight said, approaching the beast.

"Fool," the beast snarled, thrusting a claw at the knight. "I wished for this. Baudrous brings power! Power and wealth!" The creature had gone quite mad and lunged about erratically. Bertilack managed to avoid most of the attacks, but a backhanded swipe caught him off guard, and sent him sprawling onto the ground.

Dazed and confused by the hit, the knight couldn't defend himself as the creature prepared to end him. But then, from across the glade, a torrent of fire erupted. Impacting against the creature's skin, the hair on its body burst into flames and it howled in rage, seeking its attacker.

It stared through heat-scarred eyes at Kazar and Thorn, the two wizards had combined their powers and were directing the fire at the beast.

Its main quarry forgotten, the creature lurched towards the wizards using its arms to shield it from the blistering heat.

The other dragon riders seized this opportunity and dragged Bertilack out of harm's way. Caldor and Keldon stood over their fallen brother, and Charlock hovered nearby.

"Mark, my friend, can you hear me?" said the dragon, hoping that mentioning his original name would bring the knight around. The dragon looked at the knight's broken body and through tear-stained eyes at the beast, as it battled towards the mages. "No more," the dragon growled. "I will have vengeance!"

"Wait, Charlock, stop!" Caldor yelled after the dragon. "You can't fight him."

The dragon riders had agreed that the dragons becoming full-size would attract too much attention, so whatever they faced, they'd do so in their smaller forms. Although they'd not had any witnesses as far as they knew, the introduction of a giant dragon to the mix could change all that.

Charlock's emotions had gotten the better of him, and he discarded reason. He shot skywards, his form elongating and morphing to its full-size. In the air above, the dragon blazed with rage as it spat its hatred at the mage-demon below.

The creature turned its attention towards its new foe. It was here that fear captured the creature's black eyes, for it knew that whilst enraged, even the noblest of dragons gave way to their feral side. It was a side that the ancient dragons had learned to dispel, but this was control that Charlock did not posses. The mighty dragon had great anger in his heart. From the start, he'd been charged with protecting Bertilack. Looking upon his prone form from above, the dragon felt he'd failed. The safety of this chosen one had been left to him, and he'd not been up to the challenge.

Well, no more. This creature would get no closer to any of the dragon riders. He would ensure it. Deep within his breast, fire grew. His fury stoked the flames, and his jaws opened to belch a fiery death.

Far below, the mage-beast tried to get clear, hoping to get into the trees where the shadow of night would hide it, but it wasn't to be. Just short of the tree line, the crimson blaze erupted to engulf it.

Dragon fire was one of the strongest flames. No sorcery or technology could replicate its ferocity, and the beast was witnessing this first-hand.

The riders fled in all directions. Even through their magic infused bodies, they still felt the heat.

Within the torrent, the beast writhed in agony, yelling a plea to its master to save it. But of course, no answer followed.

The dragon continued the blaze long after the creature had expired, waiting for his rage to subside, and in time, it did. The haze that had fallen over his eyes lifted, and the dragon changed and sailed back to earth once again to meet his comrades.

"What the hell are you playing at, Charlock?" Caldor scolded. "We agreed you weren't to change forms. You could've risked the exposure of our group to the outside world."

Around him the dragon riders looked away grim-faced whilst the other dragons merely stared in shock. Out of all of them, Charlock was the last one they thought would succumb to dragon rage.

"You quibble over such things whilst Bertilack lies broken on the floor?" the dragon spat back, residual traces of the rage still in him.

"You know very well this isn't how he would've handled this or how he would've wanted you to handle it. You should've used more restraint."

It was then that the party heard sirens in the distance. It seemed someone had called the authorities.

"Police. No sense taking any further risks. This little tete-a-tete, will have to wait," Thorn said, helping Tristan to his feet—the big warrior was still unconscious. "We must go now, lest we be discovered."

Keldon helped Bertilack to his feet.

"Mark me, dragon," Caldor said as he took Bertilack's other side. "This isn't over."

CHAPTER ELEVEN

For a time, Bertilac's life seemed more like a waking dream. Images faded in and out before him at sporadic intervals. Visions of being carried on broad shoulders and down a long dark tunnel. His friends and brothers talked in hushed, worried tones, discussing the knight as if he weren't there.

But he was there. He could see them, hear

them, if only briefly. Yet they couldn't hear him. Every now and again, he was aware of himself. Speaking, asking questions he got no answers for. No one seemed to be aware of him. And then it was dark, and time passed, but how much, he was unsure.

He awoke to a bright morning. He had no idea where he was for he had never before seen this place. He looked around. Still clothed in his armour, he lay on a cushioned mat on the floor. Around him a tent had been constructed, and it was then he remembered, this was his little brother's tent. Leigh, now Keldon, had bought this tent with a friend from his workplace some years ago to go camping.

Being a two-man tent, it was small, and enclosed, but since Bertilack was the only one occupying the space, it wasn't a concern. By his side was his sword. The knight reached for it and used it as a prop to get himself to his feet. He noticed he wasn't exactly alone in the small confines of the tent. At the foot of the mat, a small black dragon lay dozing.

Charlock had stayed with the knight since his injury, and was only now taking a break to rest. Bertilack didn't want to disturb him. The knight's side hurt where the mage-beast had flung him earlier, but he resisted the urge to cry out in pain and made his way outside quietly.

As he emerged, the light of the new day hurt his eyes, and he felt a chill in the air. The morning dew had formed like small crystals in the green grass, and he could smell the scent of the summer trees and wood life.

He raised a gauntleted hand to his face to shield it from the sun, and what he saw next took his breath away. Standing before him, just beyond the tree line, was an immense spire of emerald green.

It was just as he had imagined—a finger of emerald, its top in the clouds, reaching for the heavens. Small balconies and towers were seamlessly moulded into the sides of the structure, with its base appearing to grow from the earth like some great tree.

A tear graced Bertilack's face for he had never before beheld such a beautiful sight. He was amazed his warriors had finished so quickly, he couldn't wait to congratulate them.

From within the tent, the dragon stirred and called for him.

"I'm outside, my friend," Bertilack said in response.

Charlock searched for the tent flap before

moving out into the sunlight. "Bertilack, my friend, you're well!" the dragon said merrily.

"Yes, Charlock, and none the worse for wear."

The expression on the dragon's face changed as he viewed the knight leaning on the sword. "Are you sure you're ready to be up and moving?"

"Of course," the knight said. "Fear not. Where is everybody? I expected more of a greeting."

The dragon continued to look at him sceptically. "You've been asleep for many days. The others stayed with you in shifts. They would've all stayed, but your brother Caldor counselled that they should finish the spire as soon as possible. It's what he said you would've wanted."

"And he was correct!" said Bertilack. Caldor always had a good head for strategy and leadership. "Please, Charlock, take us to our new home. I want to go there. I want to see it."

The dragon hesitated, weighing the decision. "I suppose you would be more comfortable, but Thorn asked not to move you in case we did more damage than good." Charlock still looked at Bertilack worriedly, as if expecting him to keel over at any moment.

"I'm fine, Charlock. Please, indulge me."

Seeing that Bertilack wasn't going to change

his mind, the dragon complied with his request. He closed his eyes and looked inwards, performing the spell to return him to his full-size.

Bertilack sat on a nearby rock in wait. The knight wouldn't admit it to the dragon, but he was more tired than he realised. He looked around more closely at his surroundings—he appeared to be on a hill, the very same one he'd used to view the spot for the spire.

The dragon had stopped changing and stood to attention, waiting for Bertilack to finish his appraisal.

"Charlock, how long was I out?" the knight asked as he boarded the dragon. "I mean, the spire is finished. Surely it would've taken more than a few days for the work to be done."

The dragon nodded his head as he prepared for flight. "You've been asleep for a week since your injury. Caldor and Keldon kept the boys running non-stop until it was complete. They hoped it'd be a surprise."

That was an understatement, but a whole week? That monster must've hit him harder than he thought. Had he been in his normal form, he was sure he'd now be dead, and he may yet have been without the wizard's healing magic—it was a sobering thought.

Both dragon and rider flew over a lush green landscape and alighted softly on one of the spire's many dragon ports. It yawned massively before them, like some medieval helicopter pad, and fit Charlock's mass comfortably.

"Well, here we are," the dragon said as its claws scraped the stone. He folded in his wings and got as low as he could for Bertilack to dismount.

Bertilack slid delicately from the saddle, making sure not to make his wounds worse, and beheld his new surroundings. The majority of the tower was made of a shimmering emerald, but the floor itself was constructed of more mundane beige stone that disappeared off into the tower's interior. Ahead he could hear voices and music. Whoever was beyond this tunnel seemed to be enjoying themselves.

Charlock shrank back to his smaller form and caught up with Bertilack and landed on the knight's shoulder.

"Sounds like a party," the knight said.

"Yes," the dragon answered. "I wonder why?"

Both knight and dragon left the tunnel and entered a circular room that appeared to be the main room of the tower by the décor. Around the edges, the doorways to the various dragon ports yawned wide, with one archway leading to a flight of stairs. Upon the top of each was a dazzling portrait, each one depicting a dragon rider and their respective dragons.

The room also appeared to be a form of banquet hall, for at its centre was situated a huge wooden table. And each place setting was marked by gold writing designating each warrior's name.

Each of the dragon riders were present and in high spirits around the table as drinks were toasted and served by what appeared to be clouds of air. Despite the merriment, the knight's arrival didn't go unnoticed. Kazar was first to notice, then Thorn—both wizards, speechless. The others soon after spotted him and rushed to greet him. He received many pats on the back and heartfelt gestures of welcome, as warriors and dragons flocked about him.

"Please, guys," said Bertilack, cautioning his friends not to crush him. "One at a time, I bruise easily."

"How do you feel, brother?" Caldor asked with concern as the rest of the team backed off.

"Never better," the knight laughed, patting Caldor on the back. "You boys have been busy in my absence."

The knight walked to the circumference of

the room, his hand lovingly caressing the table.

"We wanted it ready for when you awoke. We all worked extra hard, this is the first true break we've had."

All eyes watched the knight as he inspected the workmanship of the table. He noticed at the head a gigantic chair sat, emblazoned with a symbol of a sword crossed fleur-de-lis. The symbol was green, apart from the swords, which were the colour of burnished steel.

"What do you think?" Caldor said with a smile, still at the knight's side. "That seat is for you."

Bertilack stepped forward and lovingly stroked the woodwork.

"It's beautiful," he whispered, before turning around to face the group. "My friends, I know not what to say. We've finally a place to call home, where we and the dragons can live in peace."

Then a thought occurred to him. "But where do the dragons sit? I see no places for them?"

Thorn stepped out of the group. "They've no need to eat indoors and their size would be problematic, so Sharos advised us to build the tower as such."

Charlock, at Bertliack's shoulder, seemed to agree with this statement. Bertilack reasoned that he must also have had a word about the decision.

"How are we to summon the dragons in an emergency?" the knight enquired.

Kazar came forward next to answer. "Each ever-stone we've discovered is telepathically linked to the dragon its wearer rides. We believe this is due to their proximity to the dragons during their inception. If, for some reason, this telepathic link fails, the tower has alarm bells for just such an emergency."

Bertilack smiled, his curiosity satiated, and sat down in his regal chair. "You've done a great job," he said in awe, getting comfortable. "A great job, indeed. Now, let the festivities continue!"

A resounding cheer went up from the group as Kazar and Thorn used their magic to bring forth drinks in large quantities. The air clouds that had hung motionless until now floated about their business again, absorbing the beverages from bottles and containers and redistributing them around. Everything went like clockwork, every consideration catered for by the wizards' magic and the cloud attendants. It was quite a show, and a celebration that lasted far into the evening.

Across the room, Batras and Gawain engaged in a drinking contest—both warriors trying to out-do each other. Caldor and Keldon sparred with their weapons, and the wizards continued their magic display. Bertilack was left alone to talk with his dragon.

"My friend, you seem troubled. Is something wrong?" asked the knight.

"No, not really," the dragon said, his head drooping over the knight's shoulder.

"You didn't tell me what happened after I passed out. How'd you best that creature? Was he spared?"

"Not all of us have your compassion, my friend," the dragon said, taking to wing.

"Charlock?" the knight called as the dragon flew off. "Charlock!"

The dragon paid Bertilack no heed and flew from the chamber. Bertilack moved to Kazar's side—the wizard being the one closest to the knight.

"What happened that night after I was laid low?"

The usually jovial wizard grew very calm then. "Caldor asked us not to say. He believed it was best between you and Charlock."

The pair stared after the dragon as he flew towards the dragon ports.

"I'd better have a word with him then, hadn't I?" the knight said. "Tell the others where I've gone. Hopefully, this won't take long."

The wizard nodded and watched as Bertilack disappeared. Kazar hoped he could cheer the dragon up, he'd been most sombre recently.

"He's gone to talk with Charlock?" Skalus said, snaking up from under the table. The serpentine dragon had been coiled around a chair leg, devouring a nice piece of meat when he'd heard Charlock's voice.

"Yes, but I doubt there'll be harsh words between them," Kazar said, smiling. "Their bond is strong."

Skalus looked unconvinced and shrugged before diving under the table again. If they did argue, he'd face any harshness on a full stomach.

Bertilack found the dragon grown to full-size and crouched on the very end of the port. The knight removed his helmet and walked into the night air.

The dragon's tail twitched as he approached, but he didn't look around.

"Penny for your thoughts?" Bertilack asked, facing the great lake on the spire's north side. The sun had set and was now replaced by its reflective brother, the moon. The pale orb threw down its light onto the water's shimmering surface, and gave it a magical looking quality.

"What do you wish to know?" he said sullenly.

"Well," the knight said. "That expression warrants a response on your thoughts and feelings."

The dragon said nothing and continued to lazily sweep his tail from side to side.

"Come on, Charlock. If you killed that creature when I tried to give him a second chance, I won't be angry. You're my friend and I know that anything you did, you did out of fear for my safety."

"No, you don't understand," the dragon said finally. "I killed him because I was enraged. I let the animal in me get out and took the easy option when I could've probably thought of something else to do." The dragon clawed at the port with his front paw. "I endangered us all with my actions and risked exposing us to the rest of your race."

"You made a mistake, Charlock. It happens, neither of us are perfect." Bertilack walked to the end of the platform so he could see the dragon's face. "But you can't continue to blame yourself for past actions. You must learn from them and move on."

The dragon turned his face away from the knight. "Look at the way the others see me now. Before we hatched, we were told that a cardinal rule of our society was to never allow the beast within control over us. Suppressing their baser desires was the reason my race became so great in the first place."

The dragon was clearly more disturbed by the issue than Bertilack had first thought. For the knight it was an open and shut case. For the dragon and his race, it wasn't as straightforward.

"Listen, Charlock," Bertilack said, sitting on the platform. "The others will forgive you in time, they'll realise that it could've happened to any one of them."

"But it didn't happen to any one of them," the dragon said. "It happened to me. I was supposed to be the leader, the calm and cool one. What would my parents think?"

"They'd think as I do. That you did what you had to do to save lives. And besides, you aren't in that world anymore. Here and now, we've a chance to make our own destiny. You don't have to be bound by the rules of your ancestors."

"What if I mess up again? What if my actions cause the death of another because I wasn't strong enough to control my anger?"

"It won't," the knight said sternly. "I won't let you. You're my partner, Charlock, and there's no one, dragon or human, that I'd rather have in the skies with me. Now, come back to the party or I'll get enraged," the knight finished jokingly.

Charlock smiled. "Well, we wouldn't want that," the dragon said mockingly. "Where would it end?"

The two friends laughed, and Bertilack clasped the dragon's neck warmly.

"So, ready to go back in?"

"Not yet," the dragon said, looking up at the moon "It's such a nice night, it seems a shame to waste it."

"Aye," the knight agreed. "If you like, I can stay out with you."

"No, return to the party. I'll be in momentarily."

Bertilack did as he was bid, and got to his feet. "You okay though, yeah?"

"Yes."

Bertilack walked back down the platform. He hoped his words had helped Charlock, he hated seeing the dragon upset.

Ahead, he could hear the noise of the party continuing. The music was peculiar, a sort of rap meets medieval. It appeared that some of his friends were even trying to sing, and the results were not encouraging. He entered the hall, and the noise abruptly stilled as all assembled stared his way.

"How is he?" Caldor asked, putting his weapon away to come to Bertilack's side.

"He's fine, brother. He still hasn't forgiven himself but I'm afraid I still don't understand what exactly he did that was so terrible."

Caldor went quiet, and none of the dragon riders could meet his eye.

"You know, don't you, Caldor? I know you do. Just tell me whatever it is I need to know."

The elf motioned for Bertilack to sit at the table, and the others crowded around to hear Caldor's retelling of the events that had befallen Charlock and how he torched the glade and disintegrated the creature. Behaving like a wild beast and putting the rest at risk.

Bertilack didn't consider it to be such a big deal, for no one got hurt and Charlock managed to save them all. In truth, the knight wasn't sure if he could've overcome the creature, even with all his warriors helping. He opted however, to stay quiet about his opinions on the matter.

"Thanks for telling me. At least I know now."

"Are you going to tell him that you know?" Gawain asked.

"If he wants to tell me, he will. But for now, I thought we were having a party, let's get it going."

The others needed little encouragement, all

eager to get off the topic and back to what they were doing.

Bertilack himself sat still at the table a while longer, mulling things over in his mind before drinking more than his usual share that night.

CHAPTER TWELVE

Bertilack had retired from the party early and left to examine his new quarters, only to find himself missing his old room. The new bed was a little lumpy and he couldn't figure out how to warm the place.

After a good rest, he returned in the morning to survey the aftermath of the party and found two members still present. Gawain was asleep in his chair, and Batras passed out on the floor. All around lay debris from the night's event.

As he stood in the doorway, he heard footsteps behind him and was soon joined by Kazar and Thorn. The two wizards entered the hall and couldn't believe their eyes.

"Some party," Kazar said.

"Truly one to remember," added Thorn. "And how are you this morning, Bertilack?"

"Head's a little groggy. Just glad I left when I did or I'd probably have shared Batras's fate."

The three looked on at the minotaur's sleeping form woefully.

"He did drink a lot," Kazar said, righting a chair that had been overturned near the table.

"You think we should wake him?" the knight asked.

"Why bother?" Thorn said. "As soon as my elementals get breakfast ready, they'll come around."

"True," said Bertilack, he knew how much Gawain especially enjoyed his food. "Well, while you're doing that, I think I'll go out for a ride with Charlock. After that, I could use something to clear my head."

"Have fun," Kazar said, conjuring up a small

goblet of ginger ale from the air before proceeding to take a sip.

"I've always found that a bit of the hair of the dog works wonders," said Thorn as he summoned the cloud beings that had served them the night before. "Don't be long, Bertilack. These guys may not look like much but they can sure move fast."

"No worries, Charlock's pretty fast too," said Bertilack with a smile before leaving the two wizards to their business. He walked to the end of the dragon port and summoned Charlock by ringing the platform's bell.

Within no time at all, the dragon's great form was speeding along the treetops in answer to the knight's summon.

"Good day!" Charlock said as he landed upon the port.

"And to you. I trust the day finds you well?"

"That it does, my friend, but then I didn't drink last night. How's the head?"

"Fine, Charlock. That's why I called you. I want to go for a morning flight."

The dragon smiled and nodded. "So, had the same idea as your brother, did you?"

"What do you mean?" Bertilack asked, puzzled.

"Keldon left the tower with Argast this

morning."

"You don't say," said Bertilack as he mounted Charlock's back. Perhaps he'd see him out there then. "Let's head to the mountains, Charlock. Everybody knows that's where you get the freshest air."

"You're the boss," the dragon said, before spreading his wings and taking flight.

∗ ∗ ∗

Keldon had landed within sight of the tower and witnessed Bertilack's departure. The dwarf was still a bit shaky from last night's activities and couldn't keep his axe straight as he chopped wood in the forest.

The work was doing his head some good, and he enjoyed being outside. He figured his brother must've thought the same.

Bertilack had left the party much earlier than he or Caldor, but had never been one to stomach his drink. Out of the three, Keldon figured he'd done the best, drinks wise. With Bertilack gone, he and Caldor had spent the night in each other's company, drinking and telling stories. His brother's constitution as an elf, however, hadn't been up to the task, and had passed out.

With no one left to drink with, Keldon had

retired to bed with his brother over his shoulder. The sleep would do them both a world of good. He hadn't slept well, however, and had gotten up at the crack of dawn to do some wood cutting. It wasn't like they needed firewood, the wizards' spells kept the spire warm, but Keldon had needed something to do, and wood chopping was as good an idea as any.

He had selected the glade he was in because of its proximity to a fresh water stream. The water from this area was cool and fresh, properties that the still hungover dwarf needed. Across from him, Argast lounged, watching his friend as he chopped back and forth with the axe. He had watched last night as the dwarf consumed vast amounts of brown liquid. The repugnant brew had done nothing for the dragon when he drank it, but it seemed to have quite a debilitating effect on the dwarf.

All morning the stocky warrior had complained of having a headache, so much so that the dragon was quite put off drinking the foul liquid again. If the aftereffects were this bad, he wondered why anybody would partake of it. But in the end, all these concerns mattered little to the dragon. He'd been awake when the dwarf had summoned him, and was now using this chance gloriously to sun his wings. The natural rays had the capacity to make his scales change to a healthy shine—a fact the dragon was more than willing to take advantage of.

He was still sunning his wings when his finely tuned senses heard movement in the forest. A sharp crack in the air, whatever had caused the noise moved closer.

Keldon hadn't sensed the movement, but he'd heard the crack in the trees and now stood to attention watching Argast. The dragon scanned the trees with his eyes intensely. Had Keldon been alone, the dwarf probably would've dismissed the sound as regular forest noise, but Argast's expression told him there was something dangerous out there.

Without taking his eyes off the dragon, Keldon backed up to where he'd left his war axe. Placing his wood chopper on the ground, he picked up his mighty axe, the familiar grip comforting in his hands.

"Argast," the dwarf whispered, moving towards the dragon. "What's the matter?"

The dragon remained motionless, continuing his vigil. "I sense we're not alone," the dragon growled.

All of a sudden, there was a flurry of

movement and a dragon burst from the trees. It was an ice dragon, and it darted skywards before turning and hovering above the pair like a spectre.

The creature's name was Shard, and he was among the first to be brought into the new world by Baudrous. The dark dragon had personally sent him on this mission—a mission to find the dragon riders.

Some days previous, after the disastrous failure of his top sorcerer, Baudrous had sent his beasts into the different material realms in an attempt to find Bertilack and his friends. He'd figured that they'd change realms, and had his own mystics prepare a portal.

After much searching, Baudrous had sent Shard into a little used dimension called Kallisx, and it was here that he'd finally found them. But he'd need proof of his discovery, for his master wasn't the trusting type. So, the dragon elected to give him the charred remains of this dwarf. Surely, then, there would be no doubt.

One problem—the irritating dragon of light that'd been sunning himself like a fool barely moments ago had gone, but where to? Probably in fear of Shard, no doubt. He must've sensed the white's power and fled. No matter, the dwarf was plenty for his master. He'd hunt the gold dragon at a later date.

"Say goodbye, dwarf," the dragon snarled as it drew back, preparing to belch white hot flame onto the dwarf. Many of his species couldn't breathe fire as he could, the act required a lot of energy on his part, more so than if he just froze the little wretch, but Shard wanted to make a good first impression.

He felt the heat building in his chest and forced his lungs to swell accordingly. Any moment now, and the dwarf would be no more. It was then he felt a great weight land from behind. Powerful claws raked his back as Argast, the gold dragon, attacked from the skies.

Shard turned in rage and unleashed his flame upon his assailant, but most gold dragons were immune to fire breath, so it did little more than singe Argast.

It did, however, surprise him. Argast hadn't realised ice dragons could spit fire, enough for Shard to flee to a better position. The gold dragon gave chase and an aerial battle began.

Keldon watched from the ground as the two mighty dragons shot into the sky and disappeared from view. He continued to watch, hoping to see where they'd gone, but neither dragon reappeared.

The dwarf was about to let his guard down, but became aware of a sudden movement to his right. He turned just in time to deflect a clumsy blow aimed by an undead warrior. As he battled this new threat, a small group emerged from the woods and headed towards him. He counted an additional four skeletons emerging from the tree line.

Freeing himself from his current entanglement, Keldon managed to get a stout tree to his back. Raising his axe, he prepared to meet his enemy.

Argast had underestimated this dragon, for it was a much more formidable adversary than he'd originally thought. The white was much faster than him. Time and again, the villainous monster avoided his attacks, but it didn't stop Argast from trying. All Argast needed was one good hit, just one, and he could end this.

Turning from the battle, Argast climbed into the sky, hoping to get the drop on his smaller opponent, but Shard matched his moves, and followed.

Argast noticed another form approaching, Charlock and Bertilack were speeding towards him. Shard noticed the pair also, and soon realised that with Charlock and Bertilack's help, this would be a battle he couldn't win, so he fled.

A mistake. That moment's hesitation was all that Argast needed. He swiftly moved to gain the upper hand. The gold dragon delivered a huge blow across the dark dragon's snout and sent his white counterpart reeling.

Shard lost his balance and fell, but still managed to rake Argast across the chest as he tumbled, trying to right himself. Argast was momentarily stunned by the blow, allowing the white dragon to get its balance back.

High in the sky, the two faced each other. Shard's snout was covered in blood, whilst Argast had merely scratches on his scales.

"So, ready to surrender?" said Shard.

"You can't defeat me."

Shard dived at Argast and the two clashed together in the sky. Shard tried to get in an early death blow to the neck, but Argast's mighty arms kept him at bay. The white dragon's jaws snapped shut scant inches away from the gold's face as Argast wrestled to keep him in place. Seeing this fail, the white kicked out with his hind quarters and managed to catch Argast in the chest, making him lose his grip on Shard.

However, their proximity to one another meant Shard couldn't make good on the breathing space with Argast on him. Enraged by the last strike, Argast was in no mood for talking. He slashed at the evil dragon, delivering blow after blow against the enemy.

Shard found himself on the losing side of the fight and tried to flee, but couldn't escape his tormentor. Argast caught hold of his tail and dragged him towards him, unleashing a torrent of lethal flames. Unlike the gold's and other devout fire breathers, white dragons had no immunity to flames. The inferno washed over him and Argast held his tail, keeping the flames going until the other dragon lay still. Then he released his grip, and the white spiralled to the ground, smashing the trees beneath.

***

Keldon was still engaged in battle with the skeletal warriors, the fight for his life made more difficult by the splitting pain pounding in his head. Two of the skeletons had already been laid dead, but they hadn't fallen without a fight. Keldon's right arm was bleeding from an injury taken earlier, but the dwarf tried not to let it affect his performance. If he'd been in top condition, the fight would've been no contest. However, the beasts had caught him off guard and his hangover wasn't helping.

The two remaining skeletal warriors were closing in, trying to use their greater speed to their advantage. Luckily, the dwarf had managed to keep his back to the stout tree so the skeletons couldn't get around him. It was then that the dwarf noticed movement to his left, and a huge group of skeletons appeared. It seemed that these four had been just the advance group of warriors, this next lot was the main force, and a group of this size probably meant there was a sorcerer nearby.

This was a fight Keldon knew he couldn't win. Outnumbered and wounded, they'd easily overcome him, his only option now was to retreat. He'd have to make it to the spire. Once there, he and the others could easily overcome them. The dwarf parried the blow of the closest warrior to him and ended the existence of the other. Clutching his arm, he fled into the trees with the skeletons hot on his heels.

As he moved, Keldon changed his form back to Leigh. His human form was much quicker, and since he didn't plan on turning around any time soon, he believed this to be the best course of action.

Behind him he heard the stomping and crashing of tree branches as his pursuers intensified the chase. With luck, they'd be unable to move very well on this terrain and he'd have the advantage.

Running full tilt, he turned a left and could once again see the tip of the spire rising above the treetops. He hadn't far to go. He slid down the rocky slope connecting to the ledge he was on. As he reached the bottom, the first skeleton crested the verge and searched for him. A good sign, in Leigh's opinion. If those bags of bones kept stopping like that, he'd be miles out in front in no time. He hit the ground running and swiftly climbed the other side of the hill, but the skeletons finally spotted him and he couldn't resist showing them how impossible it would be for them to catch him.

He turned around and laughed at the creatures. He wasn't sure if these things had any concept of humour or taunting, but it made him feel good to think he was safe.

The skeletons, however, had other ideas. Each one walked a few steps back and then leapt straight off the edge of the hill. Falling a distance of some thirty feet straight down, each warrior emerged unscathed. Then, with implacable determination as one, they continued the chase.

"Damn." Leigh promptly wheeled around, and once again, pumped his legs in the direction of the spire. The skeletons may have outwitted him on the downhill, but it would still take them time to get uphill, and by that time the gates of the spire would be in sight. He reached the edge of another glade and quickened his pace on the open ground. In school, Leigh had been a long-distance runner as well as a gymnast, little did he know these skills would one day save his life.

He was almost across the glade when he stopped in horror, for on the other side of the glade was another skeletal band, smaller than the first, but still enough to be a problem. And there was still the matter of the skeletons behind him. In a few moments, they'd be on him.

The boy did the only thing he could, grabbing his amulet, he powered up to his dwarven form. Grabbing his axe from his back and still favouring his right arm, the warrior prepared for an attack from both sides.

The skeletons in front advanced just as his pursuers came crashing through the trees. It was then that their sorcerer controller made himself known. From the first group, a nearly transparent figure appeared, which Keldon guessed wasn't a real person, merely as illusion. It seemed that the dark mages had learned their lesson from last time and were now less willing to battle the dragon riders in person.

"At last," the spectral apparition said. "We've found you, but where are the rest of your friends?" The mage looked behind the dwarf, above the treetops to the spire. "Ah! So, you've built a home for yourself here. My master will be pleased, oh so pleased he may even make me head mage."

The dark sorcerer hovered before the dwarf, his body virtually translucent, wearing black robes and a silver neck chain. "But first you're in my way."

The dark sorcerer extended his hand and the skeletons charged.

Keldon prepared for the crush and brought his axe to bear. Blood pumped in his head and his wound weakened his body, the skeletons were all around. He battled harder than he had ever before. Slashing, hacking, and trying to dodge each skeletal strike before the next.

And for a moment, he believed he'd survive, but the sorcerer had other intentions, and the dwarf watched in horror, as with the merest flick of his hand, all the skeletons that'd fallen returned to the fight.

From then on, no matter how hard he battled, no matter how many fell, moments later, they returned to normal. He knew when he was beaten, there was no way out for him. He'd begun to feel himself grow faint, but he couldn't give up. He was the only force between these beasts and the spire, he couldn't just quit.

"You won't take me demons! Though I may fight you with my dying breath, you will not take me!" he roared, and once again gripped his axe with a look of stern resolve on his face.

"Excellent, I was rather hoping you'd say that. My master had instructed me to keep some of you alive, but if you give me no choice . . ." the dark mage trailed off with glee. "Well, I'll have no choice but to dispatch you."

"I don't think so," said Bertilack, exploding from out of the tree line. Sword drawn, he plunged it through the image of the sorcerer. The magic of the sword reacted with that contained within the image of the mage, and it shrieked before disappearing into vapour. The knight then ran through the skeletons, clearing them away, and coming to his brother's side.

"What took you?" Keldon said.

"Well, you're so short you were hard to spot," Bertilack said with a smile.

"Funny, bruv, funny, but you won't be laughing when you see what these things can do."

Bertilack saw, to his surprise, that the dwarf was right. Even without the sorcerer's magic, all the skeletons that Bertilack had chopped through returned to life.

"I see what you mean," the knight said as the undead creatures renewed their attacks. "Luckily, I've got a plan." Bertilack stood back-to-back with Keldon and reached within his armour to touch his amulet. "Charlock, it's time. We need you."

"We're here," the dragon boomed. Bertilack's voice reached across the trees and brought the dragon forth. With Argast at his side, the two mighty dragons erupted into the glade, and landing, shielded the two combatants with their wings.

"Why call us just for these?"

Both dragons looked at the skeletal horde. Like automatons, they continually battered themselves against the dragon's armour, all the time seeking a way through.

"They may not seem like much, but they're very hard to bring down," the knight said.

Argast looked on unconvinced, raising a claw, he brought it down on a pair of warriors, and they shattered beneath it. "Seems easy enough to me."

"Just wait," Bertilack said. "They're not done yet."

Both dragons looked to the ground, and sure enough, within seconds the skeletal warriors were on their feet, already renewing the assault.

"Well, isn't that special?" Argast remarked. "So, what now?"

"We incinerate them," Bertilack said. "Keldon and I will hide with you, Argast. Your body's immune to the flame. Charlock, you take to the sky and deal with them but be careful not to burn the trees, we don't want a forest fire on our hands."

"Good plan," Keldon muttered weakly.

"Some dragons get all the luck," Argast grumbled.

"Just keep them safe," Charlock answered. "And don't worry, you'll get your chance to fight. We still have a sorcerer and perhaps more skeletons to find."

"Yes, well, let's just hope that sorcerer's spell was a one-off," Bertilack said. "I don't fancy fighting many more invincible skeletons."

"And the only way to do that is to find him," the dwarf grumbled. "So, let's stop chatting and do it."

"Negative," Bertilack said. "You're injured.

Argast will return you to the spire. Charlock and I will search for the sorcerer."

"But—"

"No buts, brother. You're no good to us like that. You must return."

"You can't do it alone," Keldon said, struggling to remain upright.

"Charlock is with me. I won't be alone."

"Keldon is right," said Argast. "There's no telling how much of an army the mage has brought with him. You may be outmatched."

"Very well," Bertilack said. "If it will make it any easier, we'll ask some of our warriors to accompany me. Now get going."

Reluctantly, the dwarf climbed aboard Argast. "As soon as I'm well, I'll be back. I've a score to settle with that mage."

"We'll try to save you some," Charlock said. "But we make no promises."

Mollified, Keldon allowed Argast to take him into the sky, and off to the spire.

Bertilack boarded Charlock.

"Any idea how we're going to find this sorcerer?" the dragon asked. "He's not exactly going to roll out the welcome mat and announce his presence."

"I've been thinking about that," the knight

answered. "We gave him a fair beating a moment ago, stands to reason that he may try to establish the portal again to get some help. If we're lucky, we'll be able to see it from the air, but we must be quick."

The dragon gave Bertilack a disapproving look.

"Hey, if you have any better ideas, I'm all ears."

The dragon didn't, so in the absence of a better plan they were forced to try Bertilack's. Still standing in the glade, Charlock rapidly beat his wings and took flight into the sky. In moments, the pair were soaring over the treetops. The forests of this world stretched for miles, coming from a city, Bertilack had never seen the like.

"He couldn't have found a better place to hide," the knight yelled into the wind. "That forest is intense."

The dragon nodded in agreement and swung his head back, so that he could better converse with the knight. "Even with my superior eyesight, I can barely penetrate that foliage."

It seemed to the knight that this was a losing proposition. It was still early in the day and the sun was high in the sky, even if the mage activated a portal in this light, and with this distance to cover, there was no guarantee they'd see it.

"We'll never find him like this," Bertilack admitted. "He can't be this far out, we must've missed him."

"Perhaps we should return to the spire? Many heads are better than two," the dragon counselled.

"Maybe I made the wrong decision. Turn us around. Let's get back to the guys."

"Right," the dragon said, but as he tried to move he found he was stuck. "We seem to have a problem." Charlock's feet and wings refused to obey his commands.

"What's the matter? Why aren't we moving?"

"I don't know. There's an invisible barrier of sorts preventing me from moving, it's pulling us back."

Indeed, he was right. They were moving backwards.

"Not sure where this thing is pulling us, but it's a safe bet we don't want to be there."

Bertilack tried to struggle out of his saddle, but found the same force affecting him as it was Charlock. They were almost on the tree line and still descending. Bertilack managed to free his head enough to look behind them. Below was a flurry of activity. Skeletal warriors stumbled together in a clearing below, gathering around a central figure. As they got nearer, the knight managed to make out details on the face of this figure. It was the sorcerer from before! His arms outstretched, he seemed to be literally pulling the dragon and rider down.

"Looks like tall, dark and gruesome found us instead of us finding him," Bertilack said.

With great effort, Charlock craned his neck back enough to see what Bertilack was talking about. "Hmm," the dragon growled. "He's got quite a welcoming committee down there, what should we do?"

"I'm open to suggestions," the knight returned. "But I don't think there's much we can do. Hopefully, this will work to our advantage somehow. At least now we've found him."

Bertilack's cheerful position left Charlock with little comfort. If the mage could bind them with one spell, then who knew what else he could do.

"Don't look so worried, my friend. What can he possibly do against us both?"

By this point they were almost on the ground and well within earshot of the mage.

"Oh, I can do much," the sorcerer yelled. "You'll soon see that your paltry fighting skills are nothing compared to me."

Charlock's feet had just about touched the

earth, and the dragon was in a very ill temper. No sooner had his claws touched the ground when he attempted to lunge at the wizard. Unfortunately, his efforts failed, and the force field still held them tight.

"You see, knight? You cannot break free!" the mage crowed. "My master's magic is far greater than anything you possess."

"You're a riot. How about you release us and we'll see how your magic helps you." Bertilack tried again to unsuccessfully escape his seat.

"Oh, I don't think so. My master knows of your invulnerability to our magic, so he designed this spell with you in mind. Using me as a conduit, he was able to channel this awesome power through me."

Bertilack smiled at this news. "So, it's as we suspected. You're just some two-bit conjurer, a puppet with Baudrous pulling the strings."

Bertilack sought to anger this mage as he had the last, knowing full well that their concentration on a spell was crucial. If he could wind this one up enough, he'd lose control of the spell holding him.

In response to his barbed insult, the mage's face contorted with anger, but only briefly, he was soon back in control. "Commendable. You seek to goad me into losing control as you did my predecessor, but it won't work for not only am I wise to your rouse, I'm also not the one controlling the spell."

"If not you, then who? I see no other."

"Oh, he's not here. My master is merely feeding power to the spell via the portal gate. Observe."

With a wave of his hand, a small group of skeletons brought forth a platform from out of the trees. "Behold my master's greatest invention, the portable portal!"

The skeletons removed a sheet from the platform to reveal a portal doorway beneath.

"This gateway relies on its own unique power source to keep it open, and doesn't drain the mage controlling it. I can keep it open indefinitely, allowing my master to constantly feed the spell that holds you prisoner. You're trapped like a rat in a cage."

Bertilack considered his options and the situation did indeed seem hopeless. He could think of nothing to do to free them from the net. His only hope was that his brother and Argast had made it to the spire, and that even now, a force was on its way to assist.

"Now, my guests, we don't wish to keep my master waiting," said the mage. At his signal, a team of skeletons made their way to Charlock's rear. The group then proceeded to attach a rope to the dragon's tail.

The mighty beast tried desperately to move, to flick out his tail and crush these offenders, but couldn't. "Bertilack, it's no use. I still cannot move. It galls me to think that they're this close and I can do nothing."

"Don't worry, help should arrive soon. If I know Keldon and Caldor, half the spire is out looking for us."

The dragon nodded, but his face still looked grave. "They'd better hurry for I can think of only one reason they'd be attaching such a sturdy restraint to my flanks."

"And that'd be?" Bertilack said stupidly.

"They intend to drag us through the portal."

CHAPTER THIRTEEN

"Where the heck is he?" Gawain shouted as he and Kazar soared above the clouds on their dragons. "How long do we have to be out here?"

Kazar could tell that Gawain was getting impatient, but more than that, he was tired of the big knight complaining. He admitted that this job in theory should've been an easy one. Keldon had been in bad shape when he'd landed amongst them at the ports and sounded the alarm but all they were told, was that the land was under siege by a small invading force, thus the task of defeating them minimal.

Despite the fact that they'd fought many battles already against marauding skeletons and the odd white dragon, Bertilack's fate was uncertain, for they'd still been unable to locate him.

Luckily, Keldon had allowed Kazar to borrow Argast for this mission, as Skalus would've never been able to keep up over land.

Gawain glared into the distance, hoping to catch a glimpse of Bertilack. "This is hopeless. What if he's already back at the spire and we missed him? He's probably enjoying a nice bit of steak and an ice-cold drink as we speak."

"And what if he's not? If he was brought down somehow, and we've left him to die?"

"Why can't you just cast a spell?" Gawain moaned at the wizard. "Surely you've got something in that bag of tricks that can help?"

Kazar pondered this for a moment as the dragons skimmed the treetops. "I've never tried to find a person before, I've only used that ability for objects."

"Damn it, man. Look for his armour, his sword, or even his watch for crying out loud, just something."

"Okay, okay, calm down," Kazar soothed. "We'll stop here and try the spell but I make no promises."

"Good. No offence, Bloodstone, but your saddle was starting to chafe."

The red dragon looked back at the knight on his back. "If you lost a few pounds, it wouldn't feel like such a weight," the dragon laughed. "Kazar, where should we land?"

"Wherever is best for you, I just need to be still so I can concentrate."

The dragon pair chose a patch of clear land in the forest canopy and headed for it. As they neared, the dragons used their eagle-like eyesight to scan the area for any remnants of enemy forces. The grove below was quiet. A dragon's sharp eyesight could tell if even a single blade of grass had been disturbed. And fortunately, there were no signs that the forces of darkness had reached this area.

The dragons landed in the clearing with all the grace inherent in their species, allowing the warriors off. The two great beasts stood and remained on guard.

Kazar moved to stand in the centre of the grove.

"So, how does this spell work?" Gawain asked, seating himself on a nearby stone.

Kazar positioned himself accordingly, searching within himself for the power needed to work his magic. "First, I must picture the object I desire squarely in my mind. Once I have it, I must hold the image, draw from it, and make it a part of myself."

The wizard closed his eyes and chanted.

In his mind, the spell took shape. He could see Bertilack's sword, the emerald blade spun slowly before him. With an ethereal hand, he attempted to reach, but on the plane of his mind, the blade continued to move just out of grasp. Before him, on this barren scape, erupted a mighty forest, into which the sword fled. His ethereal body gave chase.

Down winding trails and over lakes it went, eventually coming to a halt about six miles south. Kazar felt a great power in this place. Not knowing what was about apart from the aspects of nature, Kazar tried his hardest to gauge and memorise his position.

It was then that he saw it, off to the right, and drawing the sword towards it was the ethereal energy—a portal. Usually portals couldn't give off enough energy to make an impact on this world, but something was different about this one. Its energy was enormous, and appeared to be coming from the portal itself.

Kazar advanced and stared within the vaguely circle shaped cloud. How was this being accomplished? The portal he and Thorn had built was nowhere near as powerful. Reaching out with his mind, he touched the energy, and within his subconscious he felt a jolt. Something was trying to gain access to his head.

"Who?" demanded a dark voice.

Kazar didn't answer. He moved his hand away, but found it stuck.

"Who?" the dark voice demanded again.

Fear took hold. Kazar tried unsuccessfully to extradite his hand from the cloud.

"Who?" said the voice, getting increasingly more insistent. Then something else happened. A claw appeared from the portal. A giant, all-encompassing hand that gripped the wizard's very soul, draining his life essence.

Kazar struggled and kicked before shrieking in anguish at the pain coursing through him.

But just as soon as it started, it stopped, and the mage came catapulting back through the ethereal realm, like he'd been attached to a spring. Reaching his starting place in the forest, his mind reconnected to his body and he opened his eyes to find Gawain standing above him, helmet off, a worried look on his face.

"You okay, mate? Thought we lost you for a moment there," said Gawain.

He seemed genuine in his concern, and Kazar was surprised to find himself flat on his back.

"What happened?" the wizard enquired.

"You looked a little far out there. Had to slug you to bring you out of it."

The wizard looked at the knight and rubbed his jaw ruefully. "I suppose I'm grateful," he said, bringing himself to his feet. Then he remembered the portal and the terrible clawed hand with Bertilack's sword being dragged towards it. He rushed to Argast. "We must hurry. I'm afraid Bertilack may be in grave danger."

"From what?" Gawain said, keeping up.

"There's no time," Kazar stated as he clambered aboard the dragon. "We must fly quickly. I'll guide us."

***

The skeletal warriors had almost managed to drag Charlock to the portal. The pair had tried to escape every which way they could, but to no avail.

"There's darkness coming from that portal, Bertilack. I can feel it. I know what lies beyond."

Bertilack was still finding it hard to look in that direction, let alone see directly into the magical gateway.

"Dare I ask?" said the knight, continuing his struggle against their confines. For a moment, he almost believed that his hand gave a little. It wasn't much but enough for him to consider that the bonds may not be as unbreakable as first thought.

"It's him, Bertilack. It's Baudrous. The energy's the same as that which I felt at the museum." Charlock was clearly distressed. Though he ached to battle the slayer of his family, in this prone position, he had no real chance of success. "I won't go to my grave like this," said Charlock. With great effort, the dragon managed to sink a clawed hand into the earth, halting their progress momentarily.

"Well done, Charlock. Don't look now though, but I think you've upset gruesome over there."

Towards them the sorcerer marched, an angry scowl on his face. "You heroes," he said, getting to his knees and looking the dragon straight in the eye. "Face it, you've lost. Why won't you just accept it? Why must you make my master's life so difficult?"

"Oh, don't say it like that!" Bertilack smiled. "Admit it, you love us really."

It was the mage's turn to smile now, a cocky arrogant affair that displayed his weasel-like character. "I'll miss your bravado when my master parades your helmeted head before your friends," he said with a wicked sneer. "How well do you think they'll fight, hmm? When they see their leader slain, they'll crumble and fall, and thus will end your irritation to my master."

After ordering some of the skeletons to quit their work and remove the dragon's claw from the earth, he returned to his accustomed distance.

"Damn, he pisses me off," Bertilack growled. "If I could get just one hand free . . ."

"I'd settle for a claw," Charlock complained. "My tail itches."

This last comment made Bertilack smile despite himself. It felt good to laugh under these circumstances.

They were almost at the gate, the skeletons hefted the dragon's tail to take it through the portal.

As they did, the dark mage threw his hands up high and yelled at the sky. "Baudrous! Baudrous, my master! Hear me now, I bring you an end to all your troubles. May you destroy this villain and finally reunite the world beneath your taloned hand!"

"Not so fast!" cried the voice of Gawain.

From behind, out of nowhere, the mage was struck down. The force of the blow sent him tumbling across the ground to impact a number of feet away.

"Who dares?" cried the mage. He was livid and shook visibly as he got to his feet. He turned to lock eyes with Gawain's helmeted face. "You'll pay dearly for that."

"Do tell," said the red knight. He had his sword in hand and brought it up to the mage's eye level. "Free my friends and keep your hands where I can see them."

The mage said nothing and smiled at the knight. Behind Gawain, the skeletal host gathered.

"Release me, knight, and I'll make your end brief. My master has no need of you."

"See, now you've gone and hurt my feelings." Gawain let out a sharp piercing whistle, and the dragons alongside Kazar, appeared over the treetops. Seeing the situation, and wasting no time, both dragons unleashed their breath attacks and incinerated the skeletons, leaving none standing.

"You were saying something about threatening me?" Gawain encircled the mage's neck with his hand.

"It makes no difference," said the mage, gasping as the knight tightened his grip. He then smiled and broke into manic laughter. "My master controls the energy flow to the capture device. You must destroy the portal to free them, but you'll never succeed! You're all doomed! Doomed! Doom—"

Gawain's gauntleted fist came up and connected with the mage's face, sending him sprawling and knocking him unconscious. "What an irritating guy. Kazar, get your brightly coloured buttocks down here. We've got an emergency."

Kazar leapt off Argast and ran to the knight's side.

"That portal thing needs to be destroyed to free those guys," explained Gawain.

"Did he tell you how?" asked Kazar.

"Well..."

"Well, what?"

"I sort of knocked him unconscious before that."

Kazar fixed Gawain with a stern glare.

"He just wouldn't shut up, he was pissing me

off, and anyhow, how difficult could it be?" Gawain called Bloodstone forth. Clambering aboard, he instructed the dragon to rush towards the portal gate. Having no fear, the pair catapulted themselves at the gate, only to be instantly repelled. They flew backwards through the air and impacted onto the ground near Bertilack and Charlock.

"So, Gawain, how's it going?" Bertilack said as the red knight got to his feet.

"Shut up. I'm trying, aren't I?"

The big knight stomped past Charlock and Bertilack as Bloodstone got shakily to his feet.

"Let's not try that again," the red dragon winced. "I don't think that my scales could take it."

Gawain wasn't listening. He was too intent on the portal. "There must be a way of destroying this thing, even if I have to pull it down with my bare hands."

He promptly drew his sword, and swinging it above his head, he brought it crashing down on the gate. There was a brief spark of energy as his sword met the barrier that protected the gate. As he pushed down, the others started believing he could do it. A little more, just a little more strength, but it appeared he didn't have a little more. The barrier flashed brighter and the sword was repelled, flinging Gawain with it, and forcing him to impact against Bloodstone who was standing nearby.

"Fantastic effort," the dragon said sarcastically.

"I was close," said the knight. He once again drew his sword and approached the portal.

"He is persistent," Charlock said as he positioned himself to get a better look at Gawain.

"I for one have always wondered when Gawain crosses that fine line between bravery and stupidity," said Bertilack. "We used to say that when we were kids, Gawain could either break things or build things. He had an uncanny knack of doing both."

The group again watched as Gawain struck the portal, which promptly sent him flying across the glade. He got to his feet in a foul mood. "Don't just stand there, you stupid wizard! Help me!"

"And how do you propose I do that?" Kazar asked.

"Surely if we both strike the portal at the same time, we should be able to destroy it."

"Or send the pair of us shooting across the glade."

"Fine, I'll do it myself."

Gawain attacked the portal again with similar results causing Kazar to chuckle briefly.

"You think this is funny, spangle pants?" Gawain said menacingly. "I don't see you doing anything."

Kazar smiled again before dismounting Argast.

"Could you two please hurry this up," the gold dragon complained. "I wish to return to the spire to see how Keldon is faring."

"Very well, I'll see what I can do." Kazar approached the portal and placed his hands in front of him. "I can feel the power of the gateway," he said solemnly. "It comes not from here, but from the other dimension. With luck, I should be able to close it like I would one of my own."

Gawain came to his side. "Why didn't you just say so earlier?" said the red knight, fuming.

"You didn't say the magic word," the wizard replied.

Gawain nearly lost it again. He struck out and missed the wizard, connecting once again with the portal and sending himself sailing over Bloodstone's head. He was still fuming when he got up and went to go for the wizard again, but the dragon blocked his way.

"Out of the way, Bloodstone. That warlock needs to be taught a lesson."

"Grow up, Gawain," Bertilack said. "Let him

work to free us, and then the two of you can have this out."

"Fine," the knight grumbled. "But as soon as he's done, we settle this."

"I can't wait, genius," said Kazar.

Gawain fumed even more, but Bloodstone held him back, allowing Kazar to return to his work unmolested. With some intoned spells, and the help of a few choice magic instruments, the portal was soon closed, and the spell holding Bertilack prisoner severed. Both knight and dragon were much relieved to be moving again.

Gawain glared at the wizard. "I hate you," the knight spat as Kazar passed by.

"Well, the feeling's mutual, you metal studded oaf."

"Why you—"

"That's enough!" Bertilack admonished as he dismounted from Charlock. "We must return to the spire and warn the others of what we've seen. We don't know when the next attack may come."

The two warriors simmered down at their leader's command and stood begrudgingly side by side.

"What do we do about our sorcerer problem?" Gawain asked, staring at the prone form on the ground just starting to awaken.

"Charlock and I have a score to settle with that one," Bertilack said. He summoned the dragon forth so that he stood claw poised above the mage's head.

The robed figure moved as the shadow hit his face, and he opened his eyes to see his fate and the dragon's claw. "What? How'd this happen? How'd you get free? When my master finds out, you're all doomed."

Bertilack had had enough of this one's words and clasped his neck harshly. "I'd choose my words carefully if I were you, mage," he said menacingly. "We wouldn't want Charlock to slip."

The mage once again glanced up at Charlock's suspended claw and the dragon's toothy grin.

"Now, tell us where you're from. How did you come into Baudrous's service?"

The mage kept his eyes on the dragon, but his expression remained defiant. "Do as you wish, you'll get nothing from me."

"Very well," Bertilack replied. "Perhaps you'd like to play with Gawain some more?"

The red knight cracked his knuckles, but the mage remained silent. Then he advanced on the mage with a menacing glint in his eyes.

"Okay, I'll talk, I'll talk!" cried the mage. "Just keep that thug away from me!"

"Damn," said Gawain. "I was hoping he'd resist."

"Talk, dark one," Charlock said, his claw coming down hard inches from the mage's head.

The mage was visibly shaken and Bertilack thought he may faint this time.

"I was recruited from Earth," the mage stammered, his attention flitting from the red knight to the dragon. "I came from—"

Suddenly, the sorcerer went into convulsions. His body shuddered and foam flecked his lips. "Master Baudrous . . . *no!*" he cried, and with that last weak call, the mage died and went cold.

"What the hell happened?" Bertilack said to no one in particular. "Kazar?"

Kazar looked as shocked as them and hesitantly approached the corpse feeling for a pulse. "It seems he wasn't as free as he thought. Somehow Baudrous must've been keeping tabs on him and took him out when it looked like he'd betray him."

"Not much of a redundancy plan," Bertilack commented. "And we were so close to getting that information. Damn."

"And I was so close to knocking some sense into him," Gawain said moodily, shaking his fist.

Bertilack and Kazar continued to examine the

body.

"Unfortunately, my knowledge is more magic than health," the wizard said. "Not much good here."

"Everyone, mount," Bertilack instructed. "We're going back to the spire."

"What of the corpse?" Kazar asked "If it's left out here, it may invite disease."

"We'll have Argast incinerate it before we leave, his fire will leave nothing but ash."

Each rider mounted their steeds, Kazar again rode with Argast. Gawain hoisted himself into the saddle and immediately instructed Bloodstone to take wing. The pair hovered above the clearing, waiting for the others to depart. Bertilack sat in Charlock's saddle and watched as Argast unleashed his flame to forever cleanse the mage's body. Both dragons and riders remained in the clearing until the whole body was smoke and ash.

At the spire, the other warriors were having trouble keeping Keldon from charging forth in pursuit of Argast, citing that he demanded revenge against his attacker. Caldor and Thorn had spent much time in vain explaining to the dwarf the folly in his actions.

"You think I give a damn about a wounded arm?" he yelled in fury. "Take this bandage off and give me my axe and I'll best any one of you."

Thorn had bandaged the dwarf's arm to give it support whilst it was healing. Thanks to the elf's magic, it wouldn't take more than a day or so to heal, but that was still a day that Keldon would have to stay and rest.

"Sit down, you whiney whinge bag!" Batras finally yelled, losing his temper. He had sat idly at the main table whilst the two elves did everything in their power to keep the dwarf within the spire, and could sit still no more. "Do you really want to go out there and waste their sacrifice?" said the minotaur, slamming his fists on the table and awakening the assembled dragons that slept at the far side.

"Gawain, Bertilack, Kazar, and the dragons, one of which is your *own* dragon, are even now fighting out there. If you go out in your injured state you could end up making a bad situation worse, so just sit down."

Keldon fixed Batras with a steely glare and slowly advanced on the minotaur. "You big shaggy carpet," the dwarf spat. "Don't you think I know that? I know what they're doing, and I know the stakes, but I can help them, I know it!"

No one in the room would've doubted the dwarf's bravery, but neither would they've put much faith in his common sense. Despite his words, none among the dragon knights were willing to let him go out to help Bertilack, and eventually, sullenly, he gave in.

Fixing the three with a steely stare, the dwarf plonked himself down at the table. "Fine, if I'm stuck here, then one of you pointy ears can fix me up some grub. Wounded soldiers need to eat. And don't you be giving me any looks, Batras. Your words mean nothing. I'd be gone now if not for them standing in my way," said the dwarf, before snorting like some great wild boar, a gesture that Batras promptly chose to ignore.

On Caldor's request, Thorn made food for the dwarf appear with his magic, placing in front of him roasted chicken with potatoes and gravy.

"Ah, now that's more like it," Keldon smiled. "But where's the drink?" he said imperiously. "Heroes need to quench their thirst as well, you know."

Thorn bit back the acidic remark that'd been forming on his tongue, and complied with the dwarf's request.

Batas, meanwhile, requested a drink for himself, allowing Thorn to pour a second flagon.

"You? A hero?" Batras fairly spat, taking a sip. "And what heroic feats have you performed, dwarf?"

Keldon nearly lost his chicken all over the table. "What heroic feats have I performed?" the dwarf repeated. "Did you not hear my tale? Battling against the odds, wounded and outnumbered, fighting for my very life! All to get to here and warn you lot of impending doom. You should be thanking me."

Batras scoffed at this and took another long pull on his drink. "Oh, shut up. As if that was a heroic act," the minotaur bellowed. "Why, I could've taken them on with one hand behind my back."

"Oh really?" Keldon said. "Then why is it you were a first-round knockout in the last fight you fought?"

"How dare you?" said Batras, rising to his feet, the sting of losing to the mage when he was fighting with Bertilack was still fresh in his mind, and despite the fact that it wasn't his fault, he still hadn't forgiven himself. The minotaur drew out his axe. "If you want to fight sunshine, I'm right here."

"Any time, bovine, any time," said Keldon, noticing his axe by the table and reaching for it in response.

On the other side of the room, both Thorn and Caldor watched patiently. Caldor knew from years of experience that the two friends would never fight. Both were just blowing off steam, worried about the others as he was. Thorn, however, didn't know them so well, and as they squared up, he moved to intercede. Using long graceful strides, he crossed the chamber only to be stopped by Caldor's hand. Thorn turned to break Caldor's grip, but the other elf's expression told him not to interfere, so he stopped and waited.

Despite knowing the outcome, Caldor had no wish to see if he was correct. He collected his sword and walked towards the dragon ports in the hope that he might see his brother and the others. Selecting Charlock's dragon port as the most likely point of return, he left the room and headed down the passageway. He'd not gone far before Sharos caught up with him. The dragon had been awakened by the minotaur's earlier outbursts and had seen Caldor slip out.

"Come to keep me company, Sharos?"

The dragon was in his miniaturised state and alighted easily on the elf's shoulder. "Beats watching your brother and the minotaur argue."

Caldor was glad he had some more sensible company. Thorn could be a bit strange at times, and at the moment, the other two seemed completely off the walls. It was no surprise, then, that he should turn to the dragon for comfort. They left the tunnel and strode out onto the landing platform of the port itself, taking in the view. Caldor had never been to this side of the spire before. Sharos's own port was on the far side of the building, so he'd never seen this vista before.

"Beautiful, isn't it, Sharos? A man could lose a day simple staring out from here."

"That he could, my friend. That he could."

CHAPTER FOURTEEN

It was late in the day before Bertilack and company flew back into sight of the spire. They'd travelled far during the day, and none of them realised the distance covered.

Through the air the trio flew, watched all the time by Caldor and Sharos waiting upon Charlock's dragon port. He'd been there since the argument between Batras and Keldon, all the while remaining confident that his brother would return.

Sharos was still in his miniaturised state. Using his excellent vision, he alerted Caldor to the knight's coming.

"Just as I said, Sharos, no skeletal force could best our boys," said the elf, waving his hand enthusiastically at their approach.

"Never doubted you for a moment," the dragon replied earnestly. "Hopefully now, that gruff brother of yours will be a bit more bearable."

The three warriors returned the wave and swooped low over the treetops. They appeared to be racing, which was hardly surprising. By now, Gawain was probably getting hungry and Argast would be getting very eager to see how the dwarf was faring.

The group crested the ports individually as they arrived, with Charlock landing on his accustomed space in front of Caldor. The dragon alighted onto the platform with regal grace, his wings beating up a torrent of wind as he slowed down. The result nearly blew back both Caldor and Sharos, as the two headed for the relative safety of the ports connecting tunnel. Shortly, Charlock's wings stopped beating, coming to a halt at the dragon's side. Charlock braced his legs, allowing Bertilack to dismount.

The knight landed on the stone with a clashing of armour and patted Charlock's flanks affectionately. The dragon responded with a smile and then shrunk in size. It was then that Bertilack noticed his brother.

"Caldor, my brother, we thought you'd left the port to notify the others of our arrival! Why are you hiding?"

Caldor realised how he and Sharos must have looked like they were cowering in the dark. He stepped forwards with a sheepish look on his face. "We weren't hiding! We merely forgot how powerful Charlock's wings could be. He nearly blew us off the dragon port."

Caldor strode forwards, regaining some of his elven dignity, and clasped his brother's hand warmly. "You've been sorely missed. We half thought Keldon would tear the spire apart waiting for your return. Good day to you too, Charlock." Caldor favoured the dragon with a bow as he landed on Bertilack's shoulder, shadowing Sharos on Caldor's.

"And a good day to you too. I trust the day finds you well?" Charlock was in good spirits, and smiled toothily. The day had taken nothing out of the dragon, and he was still in the mood for some fun.

"Indeed. How went the quest?" Caldor asked, refocusing his attention back towards Bertilack.

Bertilack's face fell. He raised a gauntleted hand and placed it on Caldor's shoulder. "Though we were victorious, I fear for the worst," Bertilack said ominously. "Come inside, I'd like to talk to the entire group, there's much to be discussed."

The elf was surprised by his brother's serious mood, but said nothing and merely nodded his agreement.

Bertilack turned, leaving the cool daytime air behind with Charlock still on his shoulder.

They strode down the tunnel, Bertilack striking a regal gait. Behind him, Caldor wondered inwardly what could've happened that had his brother so worried that he would think it more prudent to wait until all were assembled before revealing the news.

Ahead of them, the noises of laughter and celebration could be heard. Clearly both Kazar and Gawain had left the ports before Bertilack and were even now talking of their adventures. During the flight, it had been Bertilack's command that neither warrior fully divulged the day's events until he had time to discuss the problems with the entire team. He didn't want any unnecessary questions or undue panic amongst his friends before he had fully prepared them. He was especially concerned about Kazar's experience with the disembodied claw in the sprit world. Surely whatever had commanded such power was a force to be feared, but hopefully, something that could be conquered.

As they stepped forth into the brightly lit interior of the spire's main chamber, Bertilack still wondered what he would say to his friends. He needed them to see the danger and urgency of the matter at hand and how best to fight it. Soon all thoughts of the coming speech fled his mind as Batras came forth, and imprisoned him in a tight embrace.

"Welcome back!" the minotaur roared, pulling Bertilack off his feet like a rag doll. Swinging him around, and allowing Charlock to fly clear, Batras brought Bertilack into the rest of the group.

In front of him the others sat, talking and chatting. In the corner, Kazar and Thorn whispered to each other whilst Keldon just seemed happy to have his dragon back with him. Gawain was busy explaining his own part in the saga, each time over embellishing his significance in the battles.

Batras put Bertilack down and allowed him to find his seat. Upon viewing his grim countenance, the others ended their merriment and took their own seats at the table. A deathly silence hung over the room. Bertilack was puzzled over what to say. For long moments, he had anguished over this. Now the time was upon him, and he still couldn't find the right words.

The knight was glad that the dragons had chosen to stay. Charlock returned to Bertilack's shoulder, his presence lending Bertilack much needed support. All the warriors of the spire continued to sit before him, each one looking to him for guidance.

Bertilack got to his feet. "My friends, as you know, the enemy has found us again. We must prepare countermeasures. Hopefully, closing their portal device has brought us some time to do so."

Mutterings amongst his warriors followed.

"I've been thinking of a plan, and with your help, I believe we can pull it off. It'll be dangerous but I'll think no less of any of you if you wish to back out."

Caldor stood up, the elf's face was dour, but he seemed resolute in his actions. "I think I speak for all present when I say that none of us would shy away from the fight now."

"Hear, hear!" said Keldon, banging his fist against the table. "In for a penny, in for a pound. One for all, and all for one!"

With these words the table erupted in cheers.

"You see, brother?" Caldor said. "We're all with you. Now, what's the plan?"

Bertilack smiled. Though he'd assumed this would be their answer, there was always an outside chance some would say no. "Very well, this is what I propose, in order to get the desired result, two things must happen. First, we must send a team through the portal device. Kazar believes that as he was the one who closed it from this end, it must be he who opens it again. Correct?"

Kazar shifted uncomfortably as Bertilack fixed his gaze upon him.

"In theory it should be just a matter of tracing the portal's origin before reopening it, but we're dealing with unfamiliar magic. I can't be certain of anything."

Bertilack nodded before he continued speaking. "We're going to have to guarantee it. Thorn, I want you to work with Kazar, this is one of the most crucial parts of the plan and we can't afford for it to fail."

Thorn smiled warmly at Bertilack and

immediately started making calculations in his mind for the portal.

"When Baudrous comes, we'll need to be ready, and our defences at the moment are decidedly less so. Whilst the wizards work, we'll fortify the tower."

If Baudrous attacked whilst they were unprepared, they'd be in serious trouble, it was a lynch pin in the plan but now came the part of the plan that Bertilack had dreaded—the explanation of the most dangerous role. His voice dropped noticeably as he began.

"Finally, loyal comrades, it pains me to say but we must send someone through the portal in order to ascertain the enemy's strength, and sabotage it, if possible."

This last sentence sent the whole table into a frenzied discussion.

Was he mad?

Could it be done at all?

Bertilack allowed it to continue for some time before butting in. "Silence, all of you!" he yelled. "I wouldn't have decided on this course of action if I didn't feel it was appropriate. We need knowledge of the enemy, and this is the best way. I volunteer myself to go and one other."

Again, the room erupted in complaints, with

Caldor standing up in protest. "Enough!" the elf said. "Bertilack's plan is correct. However I ask for one change, that I should go in his place."

"No, brother," Bertilack said. "It's too risky."

"Nonsense, this task is mine. Your place is here, leading our forces. Should Baudrous pass my team, then you'll be forced to protect the spire, we need you to do this, not I. Let this responsibility be mine."

Bertilack could see the wisdom in his words, but he couldn't bring himself to agree. "I could never forgive myself if something were to happen to you."

The elf laughed and smiled at his brother. "You've nothing to fear. For me, and for whoever is chosen to accompany me, there can be no failure."

"But—"

"No buts. I'm going, and that's final."

Bertilack felt like he was ten years old again and his brother had just told him off for doing something stupid—a silly notion but old habits died hard. He remained seated, and eventually gave his approval to Caldor being the one to go in his stead, but that still brokered another question—who else would go? Bertilack stared hard around the room at all his friends. He looked at them each in turn, though he'd already chosen who would accompany Caldor.

Each warrior returned his gaze with a mix of fear and excitement. Whoever went would return to the spire as heroes, but death awaited if they failed.

Caldor took his seat. The elf seemed quite pleased about winning the argument. It wasn't often he managed to out-talk his brother. "Who else will accompany me? Any takers? You, Gawain? Or how about you, Batras?" Caldor pointedly didn't ask Keldon for the same reasons he hadn't wanted Bertilack to go, to protect him.

Gawain stood and drew his sword. "Be it food or fighting, you can count on me for both," he said proudly, laying his sword on the table for all to see.

"Oh no, you tin-plated moron. I'll not let you have all the fun," Batras rumbled. "Sending Caldor off to fight alone with a clumsy oaf like you as his backup? I think not!" Batras leaned across the table menacingly. "Clearly, Bertilack, I'm a much better choice."

Gawain was incensed by Batras's words and snatched his sword off the table. "You great shaggy carpet! How dare you insult me? I'm twice the fighter you are and I'll prove it!"

Batras unslung his axe and waved it threateningly. "Any time you're ready, dough boy."

The two friends squared off. Each warrior at the table cheered on their favourites, except for Bertilack who simply despaired. He thought they would've matured a bit by now, but the more things changed, the more they stayed the same. Under different circumstances, Bertilack himself would've probably stood as referee, but this was a serious matter. The spire could ill afford a schism between its strongest members.

He got to his feet and banged his heavy mailed fist on the table. "Stop this, both of you! You're behaving like children, for God's sake! It just so happens that neither of you will be going."

This statement brought proceedings to an abrupt halt as all eyes stared at Bertilack.

"But why, Bertilack?" Gawain asked.

"Yeah, what gives?" Batras chimed in. "You need the strongest guy for this and I'm it."

"Says you, you big shaggy carpet," Gawain said, starting the fight all over again.

Bertilack scratched the table with his fingers to keep himself from exploding entirely. "Neither of you'll be going," he said in a raised voice, to get over the ever-encroaching din. "Thorn will go."

Everyone was surprised, including Thorn himself. Caldor turned to Bertilack with a look of worry on his face.

"With all due respect to Thorn, he's not exactly the best fighter. Taking him along is folly."

"Brother, can you explain how to open a portal gate? If you can, I'm all ears," said Bertilack.

Caldor fell silent.

"Kazar and Thorn are the only ones who know how, and for this mission we'll need at least one of them. Once you go through, the portal will close behind you, trapping you in whatever world awaits you on the other side. To escape, you'll need someone who can reopen portals under pressure, can either of you do this?"

Both Batras and Gawain shook their heads.

"Maybe he could teach us?" Gawain said. "How long could it take?"

"Long," Bertilack said. "And neither of them has time to teach you, they'll need every spare moment to work on opening the portal."

"But—" Gawain protested.

"No buts," said Bertilack. "If you need something to do, the pair of you can take your dragons and guard the portal until the wizards are ready. I know Kazar said it's sealed but Baudrous has powers beyond our comprehension, we can ill afford a mistake now."

***

The sun had set many hours ago. The great orb slipped into red, and then into nothing before the eyes of the warriors and their dragons. As instructed, Gawain and Batras lay in wait, guarding the portal, both Bloodstone and Khrishaw at their side. As the light waned, the warriors had decided to make themselves comfortable in the bows of a nearby tree, and happily the dragons had fallen asleep at its base. The tree they'd selected stood poised on the edge of the grove in which the portal still stood, and as far as Gawain could see, no one had moved it since he'd been here earlier.

Before they left the spire, the wizards had retired to their indoor laboratory located at the base of the tower. Meanwhile, Keldon and his brothers had begun planning the spire's defence. Upon thinking about this, Gawain believed that perhaps he'd gotten a good deal after all. The knight had managed to sneak out a small keg of ale with him, and the warm liquid was indeed helping to make the night go faster.

"Think we'll get any action tonight?" Gawain asked Batras as he took a long draught from the keg.

"Doubt it. Hey, stop hogging that! There are two of us here, you know." Batras made a grab for the ale, which Gawain kept just out of reach.

"Calm down, just give me a minute, and a few more sips." Gawain, true to his word, drank a little more before passing the miniature barrel to the minotaur.

As the pair drank, Khrishaw awoke and glanced up into the tree. "Batras, my friend, what is that you're drinking?" the dragon asked, feeling thirsty after his nap.

"This?" the minotaur said, indicating the miniature barrel.

"Yes, what is it? I could use a drink."

"It's some of Thorn's best magically produced ale, procured for us by Gawain." Batras took another gulp, as if the mere description of the drink had made him thirsty. "Want some?"

"Yes, please," the dragon said eagerly. "I'd like to see what effects it'll have on my kind."

Though the dragons had seen some of the other warriors drinking the noxious liquid, none of them had yet to try it for themselves.

"Very well, shrink on down and hop up here," the minotaur said, patting a tree branch. "You'll see the effects on you much quicker in that form.

Usually the smaller you are, the quicker you get hammered."

Khrishaw shrank down and leapt onto the tree branches. As he did, a branch came loose, and struck Bloodstone on the head. The red dragon awoke with a thunderous roar, thinking himself under attack. He opened his teeth-lined maw and belched sheets of flame forth into the clearing.

The other warriors watched, dumbfounded, before bursting into tears of laughter.

The red dragon stopped his raging and looked at the ground, and at the branch laying broken on the floor. Seeing his mistake, the red dragon hunkered back down and folded his arms in a sulk. "I don't know what you're doing," he grumped, spying on the beer keg. "We're supposed to be guarding, not getting drunk."

"Settle down, my friend," Gawain said. "This is merely to alleviate the boredom. There's not nearly enough drink in there to get us drunk, not with Khrishaw drinking as well," the knight said plainly. "Besides, after the beating I gave that sorcerer, I bet they're all running scared!"

Gawain leaned back in his seat and nearly fell from the tree. He wasn't happy with the situation, just sitting here not knowing was too difficult for him. What he wouldn't give for some action. The darkness around them closed in and the knight felt a chill in his armour. "Damn, it's getting cold out here. Batras, let's go. We won't see any action tonight."

Batras was still sharing the beer keg with Khrishaw and looked upon Gawain. "Where would we go? We can't very well return to the spire, can we?" he said, pouring more ale into the dragon's mouth. "Besides, it's not so bad here. The dragons get fresh air, and the minotaur side of me prefers the great outdoors."

Gawain glowered at Batras, inwardly swearing at the pig-headed minotaur. "Yeah, but you got all that fur, and the dragons were born in a cave," he said, repositioning his weight in an attempt to get more comfortable. He wondered if he could start a fire with Bloodstone's flames, at least then he'd be warm.

Just then the dragon reared up below him, and even Khrishaw sniffed the air before him.

"What is it, Khrishaw?" Batras asked. "Do you smell something?"

The dragon continued to sniff the air suspiciously. "Not smell but I sense something comes this way."

Below, Bloodstone appeared even tenser. "I feel it too, like electricity running through my scales."

The group scanned the surroundings before them. Nothing moved, the forest was just as quiet as it had been. But that was the problem, nothing was stirring, no animals moved, no owls hooted, nor crickets chirped. An uneasy calm had fallen upon the place.

"What's going on?" Batras asked no one in particular.

"Beats me," Gawain answered. "But something sure feels wrong."

The big knight drew his sword from its scabbard as Batras unslung his axe from its harness. The ground shook beneath them. The warriors leapt from the tree and positioned themselves for battle along with the dragons, with Khrishaw returning to normal size.

None of them knew what to do. The tremors were increasing.

Batras put his hand to the ground and felt the shocks run up his arm. "The tremors are coming from the portal," he exclaimed.

"But how is that possible?" Gawain queried.

"Someone is trying to break Kazar's hold over the gateway," Bloodstone said. "Dragons are specially attuned to magical currents, and it'd take a fairly immense power for us to feel it like this."

And so they stood, stunned as Bloodstone's words came true. The holding spell on the portal burst asunder, and a gateway was formed in the device. No sooner had it been established when an ice dragon crossed over the void. Having prepared itself for a fight before it arrived, the beast let out a sheet of bright cold fire. Due to its haste, the creatures aim was off and the blaze impacted the ground, knocking both Batras and Gawain off their feet. They fell to the ground, stunned by the sudden attack, with Gawain striking his head hard as he fell. The dark dragon sneered and took to the sky, leaving the heroes inert in the glade.

"Bloodstone, what do we do?" Khrishaw asked.

"Wait here and guard Gawain and Batras from harm. The blast wasn't much, so they should be up in a short time. Follow me when you're able."

"But where are you going?"

"I've got a dragon to catch. If Baudrous sent only one warrior, he must have a mission. I must see that he doesn't complete it."

With a nod from Khrishaw, Bloodstone took to the sky, intent on his prey, leaving Khrishaw to stand protectively over the fallen warriors. All Khrishaw could do was hope Bloodstone knew what he was doing as he charged off into the night.

Bloodstone contemplated his next move as he

gave chase. This dragon had to have a mission, especially if it had come here alone, but what was it? The spire and its warriors desperately needed information, and Bloodstone considered hanging back for a short time in the hope that the dragon would lead him to whatever it sought. But this plan didn't show much promise, as the ice dragon had already spotted him. Bloodstone resolved to bring his enemy to the ground and pump for information. He just had to catch him first.

His dark counterpart was swifter than he was, so he'd have to use guile to bring him down. Positioning himself directly behind the ice dragon, Bloodstone unleashed a torrent of flame. The incinerating jet thundered forwards and narrowly missed its target.

The white retreating form turned briefly, risking a look behind itself. It could see how close Bloodstone was and hastened to quicken its pace.

As luck would have it, however, this brief stop allowed for Bloodstone to get nearer. Thus his next release of flame came even closer.

The turn of events had the dark dragon worried, it tried to ditch Bloodstone by making a steep dive and losing itself in the tree canopy.

In a straight race, Bloodstone would've never caught his opponent, but since it had dived amongst the trees, he now felt he could catch him. Manoeuvring himself so that he was directly above where the other dragon had gone, he pierced the gloom of the night with his excellent vision to locate his enemy.

Unfortunately, it wasn't as easy as he had thought. Bloodstone knew from experience that a dragon on the ground could move startlingly fast, and he didn't even know which direction his quarry had taken. He resolved then to land and pick up the trail. Once he had the direction he needed, he could follow again, and in the skies, he should be able to catch up. He sniffed the air, and the taint of the creature's evil was unmistakable. The creature's claw marks in the dirt led away from him in a northerly direction and disappeared into the trees.

"Well," said Bloodstone. "No rest for the wicked." He positioned himself for a leap and jumped skywards, hoping to find his prey before it got too far away.

CHAPTER FIFTEEN

More creatures from Baudrous's realm crossed through the portal. The first entity to emerge was a skeletal warrior. Its bony protrusions slipped free of the portal followed by a number of its brethren. Their birth in this world was short-lived for they were turned to ash by Khrishaw's flames. More shapes materialised on the heels of the first, and Khrishaw continued his attack. There was no end to the creatures as they poured forth.

It was then that the dragon felt a force coming through the gate. An ethereal clutching force that seemed to tug at the dragon's soul. Briefly, he was shocked and stopped his attack. The force was evil, and the young dragon had never beheld anything like it. He stood mesmerized as the skeletons came forwards and began to overrun him like a tide of bone.

From beyond the gate, a face appeared and coalesced in its smoky form before his eyes.

"Who are you?" asked the face. Its features became more pronounced, and resembled that of a dragon. "I don't recognise you. You're not Charlock. Neither are you the entity I felt in the spirit world."

The ethereal face seemed to ponder this point. Its face was now fully formed, and Khrishaw could see it was the face of Baudrous.

"Ah, you're another of his followers!" the tyrant said viciously. "Another one of the sheep, kept ignorant of your true powers by Charlock and that human germ."

At this last statement, Khrishaw finally found a voice and managed to shrug off the dark dragon's power. "No, you're wrong. You're a murderer ... you killed my family." Khrishaw's words were weak as he struggled to form them, and the dark dragon laughed.

"Such a minor incident was unavoidable, I'm afraid. Had they listened to me, perhaps they'd have lived."

Khrishaw was gaining strength, and he railed against his capture. "You wished to destroy the world! You're a monster!"

Baudrous grew angry and flew into a rage. "You, a mere hatchling, dare call me a monster? Your parents were fools! They couldn't grasp the brilliance of my plan. We could've done great things. Worlds would fall, plebeians would cower, and all would've been ours, but no!"

An ethereal clawed hand appeared near Baudrous's face and pointed at Khrishaw accusingly. "No, your family, yours and all the rest, couldn't see my vision. They were blinded by their own virtue and didn't see what was right before them—me!" Baudrous drew closer, and fairly spat these words out. Clearly, the fact that more of the ancient dragons hadn't joined his cause infuriated the dark dragon. He believed he was right, that all non-dragon life was inferior and should hold fealty to them. For their denial, Baudrous had killed any that opposed him. His actions had ensured the downfall of the dragon race and brought them all to this world.

Khrishaw wondered what his life could've been like, who his parents had been. Had he any brothers or sisters? Were they scientists or magicians? All these questions now would go unanswered because Baudrous couldn't accept one little rejection.

"Damn you, monster!" Khrishaw yelled. He noticed Batras moving slightly as his mind struggled to wakefulness. A promising sign for Khrishaw, all he had to do was keep Baudrous distracted until Batras was on his feet. "You killed them all, just because they knew you were mad!"

"*Mad*? You dare call me mad? I was to be their saviour, their hero! Only I could see what was best for our race! They couldn't!"

Batras's hand moved up to clasp his axe reassuringly. Gawain too stirred, but if the dark dragon were to turn now, the results would be disastrous.

"*Saviour*? *Hero*? Really? And what were we being saved from? Ourselves? Some otherworldly threat that only you were aware of?" Khrishaw's temper was hot now and he continued to wail at his opponent. "And who would've led this new era? You? You who used your undead creatures to remove all opposition to your rule? But it wasn't enough, was it? They still wouldn't follow you in the end."

"They were sheep," Baudrous sneered. "They weren't worth letting live, but perhaps you're different?"

Khrishaw flinched visibly at the other dragon's expression. He looked like a lion eyeing up his next meal. Khrishaw wished for the nightmare to end and soon got his wish. From beyond his field of vision, came a great bellowing as Batras brought his axe down through Baudrous's ethereal head. The minotaur gasped as his strike failed to connect and impacted the ground.

"Damn," Batras gasped.

Baudrous turned slowly. "You're awake," said the dark dragon, keeping his vision locked on him. "Good, I was getting bored. Perhaps you'll provide better sport."

With the briefest nod of his head, the skeletons holding Khrishaw disengaged and attacked Batras. As one, they unhooked their bony appendages and drew their weapons.

Batras drew back, befuddled, his mind hadn't yet cleared, and he'd hoped his first strike would end the dragon. In retrospect, it was a bad idea. To think that a strike from his axe could harm one of the most terrifying and powerful beings on Earth was laughable, but in his hazy state, he was convinced it would work. He continued to stumble back, shaking his head, and nearly dropped his axe.

Seeing a moment's weakness, the creatures attacked. Batras swung out in defence but his aim was off, and the skeleton got under his arm, injuring him with its cutlass.

Blood burst from the wound and Batras roared in pain, using his hand to staunch the flow. As the red liquid flowed through his fingers, it seemed to excite the skeletons, who came on again in full force. Once more, Batras defended himself against the blows, parrying and swinging, trying to keep them at bay. It soon became apparent that the creatures were toying with him. Whatever reincarnated intelligence governed them was making them act malicious and dangerous.

What were they waiting for? Was there a plan, or were they putting on a show for their master? He pressed his back up against a tree and glanced about the glade for help. Khrishaw still hadn't moved. Batras reasoned that he must've been under some kind of spell, but where was Gawain? The red knight was no longer lying prone on the ground.

Baudrous followed the minotaur's gaze to where Gawain had sat. "Interesting, where has your friend gone?" At another nod of his head, more skeletons erupted forth from the portal.

Exact to the others in every detail, the undead creatures swayed uncertainly on necrotic feet, their eyes glowing green.

"Find the red one. Make sure he doesn't reach the spire," Baudrous ordered.

Whether or not they understood was unclear, but each skeleton shuffled off in different directions, apparently intent on finding Gawain.

As they moved, their ancient limbs gathered pace, fairly running in all directions. Those that had Batras against the tree stayed put, hovering, and unable to move until their master spoke again. The dark dragon was distracted, using his dragon senses to scan for Gawain.

The minotaur reasoned that if these creatures were inert whilst Baudrous controlled the others, he could use this to his advantage. He hoped he was right. Slowly pulling his axe up, Batras prepared to strike. If he failed, his injury meant he'd be unable to defend himself. But so be it, he would rather die fighting, than continue on like a trapped animal.

He waited some more to be certain that the dragon wouldn't turn, and then he struck. Leaping off the tree and propelling himself through the air, he brought his axe around to cleave a skeleton through the head. The blade came down in a chopping motion, as if from that of an executioner, but was stopped short of its target.

The skeleton's cutlass had erupted forth to deflect the blow and now the green soulless eyes glinted at him, the creature's face a rictus grin.

Then he heard the chuckling, malevolent chortle of Baudrous as the vile creature's twin heads turned around to view the startled minotaur.

"Oh my, did we think that would work?" the dragon said sarcastically. "Really minotaur, I'm far too powerful for that. It amused me however to give you a glimmer of hope."

"Why are you doing this?" Batras yelled. "Finish it and be done!"

"My, we do have a flair for the dramatic, don't we? Very well, if death is what you seek ..."

Baudrous motioned to his skeletons. There'd be no reprieve this time, no pause. Batras had no way to defend himself. His life was forfeit. But just as his tormentors closed in to deliver the final blow, Baudrous once again stopped them.

Batras looked up, but the dark dragon was no longer looking at him. His great scaled eyes scanned the sky, as if the beast had sensed something that had disturbed him.

"So, there you are," Baudrous muttered. "I knew there'd to be another dragon out here aside from this weakling," Baudrous said, indicating Khrishaw. "You must've come with the red knight. Now, come to me! Come to your new master."

Batras stood staring. Once again he'd beaten the odds and survived, but what was the dragon talking about? Could he sense Bloodstone? Had Gawain's dragon returned? If so, it'd be disastrous. Bloodstone wouldn't know about the dark dragon's mind powers. He'd be walking into a trap.

Sure enough, within moments, the other red dragon crested the tree line to come hovering overhead. Bloodstone billowed flame as he went and took the whole scene in with eager anticipation.

Batras knew however, what was to happen if the other dragon touched down and couldn't allow it. The minotaur thundered forwards and tried to warn Bloodstone of his impending doom, but Baudrous's skeletal warriors barred his way.

Bloodstone saw Batras from where he was and

realised the minotaur was in considerable danger, and so, flew down to help. "Release him, creature!" Bloodstone growled at the ethereal visage of the ancient dragon. If Baudrous's presence there bothered Bloodstone, he didn't show it. The great red merely repeated his demand through gritted fangs.

Baudrous, however, was unmoved and continued to stare at the other dragon. Then his eyes went red and glowed with an unearthly light.

Bloodstone suddenly found himself captivated by those eyes. His anger slipped away, to be replaced with only calm. Calm, and the voice of Baudrous in his ears, calling him forwards. The dragon's spell was powerful and despite his strength, Bloodstone found himself powerless against the ancient magic.

Batras watched from afar and reasoned that this was what must've happened to Khrishaw. The dark dragon had hypnotised him and made him weak. If Bloodstone too, fell to magic, their end would be a forgone conclusion. He had but one chance to snap the dragon free of the spell, but he'd have to be quick.

As Bloodstone moved forwards in a trance, Batras hefted his axe and took aim. With luck, there was enough strength in his arm left to make the throw. Bracing himself and leaning back, he sprung with all his might and sent the weapon soaring. Into the air it flew, and then came crashing down on the dragon's snout.

Baudrous shrieked in rage as he saw the arcane weapon land and felt his hold on Bloodstone break. Cursing the minotaur, he once again tried to establish a link but Bloodstone's mind was now closed to him and he yelled again as the red dragon's head snapped upwards, releasing a gout of flame to incinerate his ethereal body. Luckily for the dark dragon, he couldn't be harmed in this form, but it didn't stop Bloodstone from trying.

Unable to see through the sheets of flame, Baudrous summoned his skeletons, both the ones attacking Batras and the ones engaged in finding Gawain. The entire troop turned as one carrying out their master's wish and attacked the red dragon, giving Batras some much needed breathing space.

Whilst the skeletons fought Bloodstone, he needed to figure a way out of this. "If only Gawain hadn't left us," he muttered.

"Who said I did?"

Batras turned groggily and saw Gawain at his back on the other side of the tree. "Gawain?"

Batras said, wondering if his injury was causing him to hallucinate.

"In the flesh," the red knight said, coming round the tree and helping the minotaur to his feet.

"You coward!" Batras spat. "You left us to die."

"What?" Gawain said, aghast. "Just because I wasn't stupid enough to take on that transparent nutcase by myself?"

"At least it would've been more honourable than hiding in the trees," Batras growled.

"Yeah, your way worked so much better," Gawain said, indicating the minotaur's injuries. "Look, just shut up for once and let me help take you somewhere safe."

Batras merely glowered sternly as he allowed himself to be taken away, while before them, the fight began in earnest.

Bloodstone stood alone, battering skeletal warriors left and right. The undead apparitions were no match for his skill, as they constantly battered themselves against him. The dragon had become like a great rock in an unfriendly ocean, determined not to yield to the waves. For a long time, it looked as if he would weather the storm, but then Baudrous himself, in his ethereal form, intervened in the battle.

It seemed that the old dragon still had some tricks to cast even in his spectral form, and used his mind to blast at Bloodstone. Bolts of energy welled up before the face of the ancient dragon and struck forth to impact against the noble dragon.

Seeing this, Batras strained against Gawain's grasp. "Release me. I must help your dragon, even if you won't." The minotaur flexed his muscles, which even in his weakened state, were nearly strong enough to break free of the knight's grip.

"You're not thinking straight!" Gawain scolded. "You stumble out there like that and you'll not only get yourself killed, but you'll also get in Bloodstone's way, so just stay put."

The minotaur met Gawain's gaze with a hard stare, but finally relented and sat down in the thicket that Gawain had found for them to hide in.

"Once Khrishaw is free, I'll enter the fight, to do otherwise is suicide."

Batras nodded his agreement but was clearly unhappy about it. "You come back safe, knight," Batras said with a hand on Gawain's arm. "I wouldn't like you to die before I've a chance to best you in battle."

"What you wish for is impossible, my dear friend but fear not, I shall return."

The two friends smiled before Gawain launched himself through the trees and towards an uncertain fate.

* * *

Back at the glade things were not going well. In his current state, with his magic stretched between holding his ethereal form and keeping the portal open, Baudrous was unable to fully focus his attention on harming Bloodstone. The blasts hitting the young red were only at partial strength. They still caused pain, but not enough to kill or do permanent damage. The skeletons, however, were the main problem. Their numbers and strength made things much more difficult.

Bloodstone felt tears in his wings as the vicious creatures slashed at the soft membrane. He placed a claw in front of him to try and block Baudrous's spell and roared in pain. This action to defend himself was costly. However, it meant he had one less tool to strike at the skeletons threatening him on the ground. In desperation, he unleashed a gout of flame at the creatures and turned many to ash, but not enough. He needed help and fast.

He risked a glance at Khrishaw, the other red lay motionless on the floor. He'd no idea what fate had befallen his friend and deeply regretted leaving him alone. Just then, out of the corner of his eye, he spied Gawain moving through the underbrush. The knight was making his way towards Khrishaw, attempting to stay hidden.

Gawain looked to the clearing where the battle was taking place and saw Bloodstone glance his way. At least the dragon now knew he was unhurt and hopefully realised what his plan was. As if on cue, Bloodstone redoubled his efforts to keep the other skeletons and Baudrous at bay.

Mouthing a silent thank you for his continued good fortune, Gawain stepped into the open and rushed to Khrishaw's side. It appeared for the time being that he'd got away with it. The battle continued unabated, neither side seeming to take an interest in the lone knight. At first Gawain lay with his back to Khrishaw, resting against the dragon's flanks. Unfortunately, he couldn't reach the dragon's head. Khrishaw had fallen facing the battle. In order to talk to the dragon, Gawain would have to risk revealing himself to Baudrous.

Drawing his sword, Gawain tenderly jabbed Khrishaw in the back. The great beast flexed as he felt the sharp point on his skin, but didn't move any more than that. Gawain replaced his sword. He'd have to do this the hard way. Making himself as small as he could, Gawain clambered onto the dragon's neck.

As he came into view of the battle, he allowed himself a brief glance at how Bloodstone was faring. Most of the skeletons had already been defeated, and the red's main problem was now the magic of Baudrous. With Khrishaw's help, it wouldn't be a problem for long, if only Gawain could rouse the dragon into battle. Gawain looked down into the face of Khrishaw. The dragon's face was ashen and pale, his eyes wide. He didn't seem aware of Gawain's presence.

"Khrishaw, Khrishaw, wake up. Move, come on ... do something!" Gawain saw the dragon's eyes twitch, but he still didn't move. "Damn it."

Gawain glanced up again to make sure that he hadn't been discovered before slipping over Khrishaw's neck so he could face the dragon. He was still in a near comatose state, and even Gawain's movement didn't rouse him. He wondered what he would do. Drawing his sword, he tried to get the dragon to follow it with his eyes, but to no avail. "Khrishaw, wake up . . . come on." Gawain even resorted to slapping the dragon, but nothing seemed to reach him.

Unfortunately, his work hadn't gone unnoticed, for Baudrous had turned his attention towards him. The great dragon ceased his attack to look upon the warrior. "So, there you are, insect. And here I thought you'd run away." Baudrous aimed a mental blast at the knight and sent him flying across the glade. "You can wait there until I finish with your friend."

Baudrous turned his attention back to the battle and found that Bloodstone was no longer there. The red dragon had dispatched the remaining skeletons whilst Baudrous's back was turned and had fled to the portal. Baudrous prepared another thought blast.

"Hold, cur! If you fire again, I'll destroy the portal and leave your mind trapped here!"

Baudrous stopped for a moment, unsure of himself, not knowing if Bloodstone would make good on his threat. "You bluff."

"Do I?"

"If you could've destroyed it, your friends would've no doubt already done so."

"At that time you had your evil influence upon it, but I'm guessing now your wards of protection are decidedly less powerful. The battle has taxed you, old one. You aren't the sorcerer you once were."

"You're mistaken," Baudrous snarled. "I will destroy you."

"Try, and I'll carry out my threat." Bloodstone's confidence in his idea was growing as he saw Baudrous waver. "You can't, can you? Your power is fading the more you're away from your body. Soon it will be gone, and you'll be unable to maintain that form."

Baudrous looked about worriedly momentarily before setting his face to its usual calm demeanour. "Well done, young one, well done. It would appear that you've bested me. Curious though, I wouldn't have thought you'd be bright enough to come up with such a plan. We are full of surprises, aren't we?"

Baudrous left where he'd been floating and manoeuvred closer to Bloodstone. "I could use a warrior like you. Your friend Khrishaw turned me down, but how about you?"

"Never, sorcerer!" Bloodstone said acidly. "My only hope is that when next we meet, you're at least corporeal so that I may kill you."

"Until we next meet then," Baudrous said mockingly, his ethereal form beginning to fade. "Until we next meet ..."

Soon the dark dragon had all but disappeared, but Bloodstone waited where he was until he'd completely gone and the gateway had closed. He then tore across the glade to be beside Gawain and

Khrishaw.

Gawain was only just getting to his feet after Baudrous's attack and allowed Bloodstone to help him the rest of the way. "Where the hell have you been?" Gawain said, feeling much more like himself now that he was in no immediate danger.

Bloodstone let the hot-headed knight drop to the ground again. "I was trying to catch that ice dragon, if you remember," Bloodstone growled. "It's not my fault you couldn't handle a few skeletons and a decrepit old sorcerer."

"Why you—" Gawain had almost got to his feet when he aimed a poorly directed swing at Bloodstone. His attack went wide, and Gawain found himself face down in the mud again.

"If you're quite finished making a fool of yourself, I suggest we help Khrishaw to his feet."

Behind them the other red dragon was beginning to stir, his mind free of the spell now that Baudrous was nowhere in the vicinity.

Propping himself up, Gawain muttered something incoherent about the arrogance of dragons, before fully righting himself and following Bloodstone.

Khrishaw was already up by the time they walked over to him. Though he'd not yet gotten to his feet, the dragon remained sitting staring at the portal.

"Khrishaw," said Bloodstone. "Why do you stare so?"

Khrishaw was evidently shaken up by his experience with Baudrous, and his face was still pale.

"He was in my head, Bloodstone. He used me. You, you were strong enough to resist but I wasn't."

"You're mistaken, my friend. Were it not for the timely intervention of your minotaur I would've been in the same fix as you, dear boy."

"Batras," Khrishaw suddenly said, as if for the first time, realising the minotaur wasn't present. "Where is he?"

Gawain overheard and cursed. He'd forgotten about Batras. "Don't worry, I know where he is."

They heard a mighty bellow from beyond the tree line. "Gawain, Gawain, where are you, you fat tin-plate monkey?"

"See? He's fine," Gawain said sarcastically. "Bloodstone, let's let Khrishaw deal with him. We should go to the spire and tell Bertilack what's happened."

Bloodstone gave Khrishaw a sympathetic look as Batras roared again for Gawain.

"Good luck, my friend," Bloodstone said.

"Gee, thanks," said Khrishaw. He watched Gawain mount and disappear into the sky, before heading into the bushes by himself in search of the furious minotaur.

CHAPTER SIXTEEN

Gawain flew through the night, intent on the emerald spire. Beneath him, Bloodstone panted from the exertion. The dragon had had a difficult time, and his battle with Baudrous had taken more out of him than he would admit. In the darkness, they could see the lights of the spire burning brightly. Many of the spire's warriors must've been working even at this late hour to finish their respective roles in the mission.

Bloodstone was almost on top of the dragon port. His wings beated slowly and laboured. It was a testament to the dragon's strength that he'd made it so far. With a bump they landed, the dragon's claws gouging great furrows in the port's masonry.

Gawain leapt from his friend's back and placed a hand on his scales. "You okay?" he asked.

"Just need a minute to catch my breath. I haven't the energy to transform."

Gawain was acutely aware from his past experiences that magic took a lot of energy. "Worry not, my friend. Wait here while I go and kick those wizards into touch."

Gawain turned and stalked down the dragon ports, thinking that if those two wizarding hacks had done their job, Bloodstone wouldn't be in this position.

"Gawain, wait! We need more than the wizards," Bloodstone gasped. "That white dragon is still out there. Charlock is the only one I'd trust to track him."

Gawain had completely forgotten. "Don't worry, I remember," he lied to put the dragon at ease.

The great beast stopped being so rigid and slumped to the ground to rest.

Gawain ran down the corridor, joining the port to the spire, and all the while calling the names of his friends. He came to a halt in the spire's main chamber, and was aware that he was no longer alone.

"Who's here and why didn't you answer?"

Over in a secluded corner of the spire, a figure moved—it was Kazar.

"I was trying to take a nap," he scolded, giving Gawain a disapproving glance. "Why are you running and shouting at this hour? You drunk or something? You know how important this leg of the plan is, for you to compromise it—"

"Be silent!" Gawain had completely lost his temper. "All you do is talk. Where's Bertilack? I must speak with him immediately."

Gawain advanced on the door to find Kazar blocking his way. "Remove yourself right now," the knight growled.

Kazar remained firm. "What're you doing here? Bertilack told you and Batras to remain on guard at the portal until summoned." The wizard placed a restraining hand on the knight.

"I told you to remove yourself!" The knight raised a mailed hand to strike at the mage, but found his hand barred by another mailed fist.

"Gawain," Bertilack said, the leader of the dragon riders had come up another entrance with Charlock sitting on his shoulder when he'd heard the commotion. "What's the matter with you? Tournament bouts are all well and good but I won't have bad blood between my warriors."

Gawain removed his helmet so that Bertilack could see the look in his eyes. "Bertilack, it's not what you think. I came here to warn you all. Baudrous came through the portal. He sent his minions forth and one of them is still loose in this dimension."

Bertilack released his grasp and regarded his friend with a worried look. "Where are Batras and the others?"

"Batras is in the glade, healing from his wounds. He took a pretty bad beating, but Khrishaw is administering aid. Bloodstone brought me here and is on the ports. He wants Charlock to go look for the dragon that escaped."

Charlock looked to Bertilack, who nodded that it was okay, and without a word, he took flight, and headed to the ports.

"Kazar, head to the laboratory and get Thorn," commanded Bertilack. "I'm afraid we're out of time."

The wizard agreed and went in the opposite direction to the dragon.

"Bertilack," Gawain said. "What should we do?"

"We'll rouse the others and head to the glade but then I shall ask you to stay here with Bloodstone."

"But Bertilack—"

"You've done your job. We'll take it from here. If this other minion of Baudrous gets past Charlock, we need someone here to guard the spire. Besides, Bloodstone is tired and wouldn't be able to keep up with the others. For this mission, we must make haste."

Gawain, though not convinced, agreed to remain behind to guard. With any luck, he thought to himself, as the pair broke off to wake the rest of the spire's warriors, that white dragon would attack, and he'd get to fight him himself.

***

Bertilack and the others took flight from the spire. Since Charlock had left to hunt down the white dragon, Bertilack doubled up with his brother Caldor on Sharos.

With Khrishaw out in the field and Bloodstone on the injured list, they were woefully short on airborne dragons. Both Kazar and Thorn rode aquatic dragons which would be too slow for the current endeavour. Speed was of the essence, and neither wizard could afford to be left behind.

It was decided that Keldon would have to give up his seat on Argast and ride either Balnase or Skalus. On the dragon ports, Keldon waved off his friends and watched his dragon depart again without him for a second time. Turning, the dwarf strode down the corridor of the dragon port and descended the stairs that led to where the aqua dragons were at rest.

From his vantage point, atop the mighty Sharos, Bertilack watched him go, hoping all the while that they'd not need his younger brother's strength until they were once again reunited.

"So, you ready for this, brother?" asked Bertilack.

"As ready as I'll ever be," said Caldor. "I only wish we had more hands with us."

Bertilack was inclined to agree, this particular mission was going to be hard enough without the added fact that only two spire warriors were going.

"We need you to be successful, brother," Bertilack called into the wind as Sharos dove towards the tree line.

"Fear not. I've a good head on my shoulders, and with Sharos with us, we cannot fail."

"His sheer size, however, may prove problematic," said Bertilack. "Remember, until you strike, Baudrous must not know you're there."

"Sharos will be shrunk until we hit a problem."

"How soon I forget. I suppose then having this big bruiser along couldn't hurt," Bertilack said.

At this he felt Sharos buck beneath him.

"Hey, who are you calling a bruiser?" Sharos scolded, turning his head to regard Bertilack.

"I mean it as a compliment, Sharos," said Bertilack.

"If that's a compliment, I'd hate to hear an insult."

Bertilack had forgotten how testy the haughty dragon could be. It was strange how different he and Charlock were.

Their course now took them over the final feet of trees, and Bertilack could see the clearing looming ahead. From his vantage point behind Caldor, he studied the layout of the glade.

The portal itself stood unmoving to one side of the clearing, its grey surface belying its evil nature. Around the ground were scattered various bones of the dead opponents defeated in the last battle.

The knight searched the area for the whereabouts of the dragon and the minotaur. At first there was no sign, but as Sharos landed, he detected movement from the tree line. Emerging were Batras and Khrishaw, the minotaur was still weak and was using Khrishaw's shoulder to prop himself up.

"Batras!" Bertilack yelled, jumping from the saddle as soon as Sharos's claws had touched the ground. He ran forwards and embraced his friend. "I see you're none the worse for wear?"

"Yes, no thanks to that red suited moron, Gawain. Fairly left me for dead, that coward."

"Gawain left to get us," Caldor said, coming over to join the discussion. "Bertilack asked him to wait at the spire for Bloodstone was in bad shape."

"Ah," the minotaur said. "Bloodstone is a true warrior to whom we all owe our lives, unlike his partner."

Batras was clearly unwilling still to forgive Gawain for what he'd assumed to be cowardice on the knight's part, and at this moment, Bertilack didn't feel it was a good idea to get involved in the discussion.

"That aside, how have things been here?"

"Quiet, too quiet," said Batras. "That cursed

thing hasn't moved since we sent Baudrous packing with his tail between his legs."

Bertilack was pleased. He imagined the dark dragon was busy licking his own wounds and wouldn't stage another assault just yet. He turned from the minotaur to address the wizards who'd already begun to examine the gateway. "Kazar, Thorn. Batras says there hasn't been movement from the artefact in some time. We must hurry and use this window. The dark dragon mustn't know our intent."

Both mages nodded and busied themselves around the portal's edge. They attached charms and wards to the sides to ensure the gate stayed closed until they were done, and then began their chants and incantations.

"Do they know what they're doing?" Batras growled. "I've no wish to battle Baudrous again until I'm well enough to deal with him."

Bertilack smiled inwardly, for none of the spire's warriors could match the devilish dragon, and they were all aware of it. Batras's bravado was appreciated, however.

"Worry not, my friend!" the knight said. "The wizards have been up all night preparing."

Bertilack realised all too well that his words probably wouldn't inspire much confidence, but it didn't matter, for Batras wouldn't be going through. That task was reserved for his older brother and Thorn. He only hoped they were up to it.

"I don't want you getting in their way, Batras. As soon as this is done, you're returning to the spire for some much needed rest."

The minotaur looked at him quizzically. "What're the rest of you going to do?"

"We're going to hunt down that ice dragon loose upon our world. It's why Charlock isn't here, he's out looking, and we'll soon join him."

The minotaur wasn't pleased. His mind was torn between fighting alongside his friends and returning to rest. "I'll do so this time, but I'll be kept out of no fights in the future. And what of Gawain? Where is he to be?"

"Gawain will assist you and Khrishaw, should the dragon get past us to the spire."

"I'll work with him this time, if it's your wish," the minotaur snarled. "But I'll have my reckoning with him when this is over."

Bertilack smiled and placed a hand on his friend's shoulder. "Dully noted. Kazar, how's it going?"

The wizard turned from his work to regard the knight. "Almost finished. Thorn is just calibrating it so that we don't come cannoning out the other side and then we're done."

"Good," Bertilack said, and crossed the glade to stand at his brother's side. "You okay?"

"Of course, brother. With Sharos at my side, how can we fail?"

Bertilack held back his reservations. The diabolical dragon had many weapons at his disposal, and the party didn't have any guarantee they'd reach the other side alive. All they could do was pray to God for their safety and do the best with what they had.

Over by the portal, Kazar and Thorn stood back and announced they were done. Seconds later, the portal opened in all its glory, and it was time for the mission to begin.

***

Gawain sat with Bloodstone, staring out of one of the spire's many windows. The pair were still a little upset at being left behind, but both knew and understood the reasons behind Bertilack's decision.

Unknown, however, to both of them, their movements weren't going unnoticed. On the edge of the forest, watching intently, the ice dragon observed everything.

His name was Ice Slayer, and he was a particularly vicious dragon. Sent through the portal to sabotage the spire from the inside, Ice Slayer had a savage predisposition to his work. This sneaky, vindictive streak, as well as his tendency to even turn on his own friends, was why Baudrous had chosen him.

"Oh," said Ice Slayer, his tongue curling. "This job is so easy."

The spire was almost undefended now, its only guards being the red dragon that'd pursued him and the vermin of a human it called friend.

Baudrous's instructions had been to observe and destroy, and with the spire so ill-guarded, he was in a position to deal them a decisive blow. Baudrous would be thrilled, this one act would secure Ice Slayer a place at his master's side for eternity. Thinking all the time about the horror he'd unleash, Ice Slayer wove his way through the trees, intent on his target.

Far above, still in the spire, Gawain lounged backwards in his chair, a flagon of beer in his hand. Bloodstone lay across from him, shrunk down to size, and given a comfortable bed in which to heal. Gawain had already drank a large portion of his drink and was speaking to the dragon about how wrong the minotaur was in his estimation of Gawain's actions.

"How dare he call me a coward?" the knight slurred. "I risk life and limb keeping his furry posterior safe, and what do I get? I get told I'm a coward."

"Why'd he call you a coward?" Bloodstone had been absent for much of the fight on the ground and was unaware of events.

"Well, you see," Gawain went on, "I saw that twin-headed nightmare emerge from the portal. He almost instantaneously had Khrishaw in his power and it soon became clear that a physical attack wouldn't work." Gawain was in full swing now, enjoying telling his side of the story. "So, I used my noggin and came up with a plan. I'd get out of sight and await the opportune moment to strike. As you know, I accomplished this part of the plan, and as soon as the moment presented itself, I acted and saved the day! Ha! See my brilliance? It's unparalleled!"

Bloodstone thought that he himself had done more than a little to help during the battle but decided that mentioning it would solve nothing.

"But do I get any respect? No! I get one ticked off minotaur who goes around and tells all my friends that I was a coward." Gawain got to his feet and paced the floor. "I just couldn't believe it, you know?"

Bloodstone nodded and tried to be sympathetic to Gawain's dilemma. However, truthfully, he couldn't see the point of such an argument. What was done was done, as Bertilack had once said. The thought that two firm friends could fall out over a clear misunderstanding was beyond him.

Just then something caught his eye in the forest below. It was only for a second, yet he was certain he'd seen something, but what? None of the others would be back yet, and whatever it was, moved back into the shadows before he could get a positive identification. One thing was certain though, they had company.

Gawain was still complaining when he noticed the dragon was no longer paying attention. He crossed over to the window and peered out. "Something wrong, buddy?" he asked.

"Not sure," the dragon answered. "I saw something shine in the trees but then it was gone."

"Huh," Gawain grunted, staring hard into the gloom. "Any ideas?"

"Either my imagination or we have a visitor, I'm inclined to think the latter."

Gawain walked to the table in the room where his sword lay and drew it forth, smiling. "The white dragon."

"Has to be. Our white scaled visitor was obviously trying to sneak in through the lower levels. If the moon hadn't been out, I probably wouldn't have noticed him."

"Think you can handle him in your condition?"

The dragon shrugged and flexed his muscles. "Perhaps, but I'm gonna need some help. He's going to have to be able to change in order to enter the spire. If he changes like me and shrinks, then we should be able to best him."

"Hop on my shoulder and we'll sniff him out."

Bloodstone complied, and the pair made for the door. Opening it a crack, they looked out cautiously to make sure all was clear.

"Which way?" Gawain asked.

Bloodstone sniffed the air tentatively. "He seems to be masking his scent," the dragon stated. "Let's make our way to the lower levels, he'll find us soon enough."

Gawain looked despairingly at the dragon. "That's your plan? What if he doesn't turn into a small dragon? What if he becomes a ruddy great Bengal tiger for crying out loud?"

"Then you'll have to fight him. Surely a tiger is no match for you?"

"You know what I mean," Gawain said through gritted teeth. "I just don't fancy him getting the drop on us, but I suppose it's better than any plan I've got."

With a stealthy approach, the pair left the room and stepped out into the corridor. Gawain's chambers were located in the shaft of the spire just below the main hall. They approached the stairs outside his room that led either up to the hall or down to the lower levels at the spire's base, where the aquatic dragons made their entrance. Logic dictated that the dragon couldn't have got past them already. There was only one way up to the top of the spire and it currently passed straight through the heroes. Gawain reached up to the wall and removed one of the torches which Bloodstone lit, and together they made their descent.

Gawain's quarters lay roughly halfway down the spire. Above his were the minotaur's, and below, the rooms of the two wizards, plus their laboratory, and the armoury and workshop. The top levels of the spire had been reserved for the meeting hall, the dragon ports, and of course, the rooms that Bertilack and his brothers occupied. This layout then meant to Gawain that the dragon would only have a few places to hide. As long as they were diligent, they should cross paths soon.

That's if the dragon hadn't already caught their scent and was waiting somewhere up ahead, but he told himself he was just being pessimistic. Hopefully, whatever was affecting Bloodstone, was also affecting the other dragon and may still give them the element of surprise.

The torch burned brightly in his hand as they came to the first door on the route. This particular dwelling belonged to Thorn, the elven wizard. Externally the door didn't look damaged and there was no sign of forced entry. Gawain placed his hand on the doorknob and turned it, but the door remained locked.

"Well," said Gawain. "One down."

"And four to go," said Bloodstone.

Neither warrior actually thought that they'd need to try each door. The dragon had come here, obviously, with malice in mind, and probably had designs on killing both of them. Thus, there was more of a chance that he would seek them out and even perhaps find them first. Sighing, Gawain turned from the door and continued down the stairs. The next door on the route was Kazar's.

"Are we sure it was the dragon you saw, Bloodstone?" Gawain asked as they approached the sea wizard's room.

"We were a fair distance up, but I'm sure that's

what I saw. I can think of no other thing capable of reflecting the moonlight like that."

Gawain felt less and less convinced of Bloodstone's conviction. Perhaps it was just nothing. He'd been so geared up for a fight he hadn't thought about it properly. He was just about to call it a night when he heard footsteps approaching them coming up the stairs.

Both warriors paused and listened to the footsteps. None of the spire's heroes would be home already. Gawain readied his sword and waited for their visitor to reach them. As it emerged, the torch revealed details. First his trousers came into view. They were white and made of an unidentified material. From his build, Gawain deduced it was a man. His suspicions were confirmed when the figure stepped fully into the light.

The man before them was clearly human, and though his skin was pale, he would've been considered handsome. From head to foot, he was garbed in white. The only difference in colour were his eyes, which were blue, and his hair, which was long and jet black.

"What're you doing here? Tell me your name!" Gawain demanded.

The man regarded him briefly, a smile upon

his face, before he turned his gaze to Bloodstone. "He knows who I am," the figure said in a deep, inhuman voice.

Bloodstone shook his head in response for he'd never before seen this person.

"It appears you're mistaken, friend," Gawain said. "This dragon doesn't know you."

At this the other man laughed out loud. "Oh, how soon you forget! You chased me over the forest today, but I escaped."

Bloodstone's eyes widened. "No, it can't be. You can't be the—"

No sooner had the words left Bloodstone's lips when the unknown human dashed towards Gawain, and with inhuman speed and strength, knocked the knight off his feet. The force of the blow threw Gawain backwards were he crashed on the stairs. Luckily, he'd been wearing his helmet or that blow could've broken his jaw. Bloodstone however, had fared much better. He'd leapt from Gawain's shoulder just in time to avoid the impact. Hovering in the air, the shrunken red dragon breathed flame forth upon his evil opponent.

In his current form, Bloodstone's flame was considerably less effective and only managed to singe his foe. His attack however, did bring Gawain some respite and the knight managed to capitalise, and get back to his feet. This time, when the attack came, Gawain had his sword ready and deflected the blow. He was stunned to be fighting sword against fists. His opponent's skin seemed to shimmer before it was hit, and looked almost scale-like in appearance.

"Who are you?" Gawain managed through gritted teeth as the pair clashed.

Again, his mysterious assailant smiled and jumped back out of reach.

"It doesn't matter who I am," the deep inhuman voice seemed to speak in Gawain's head rather than out loud. "For you'll never leave this place alive."

The white warrior attacked in a flurry of fists that Gawain struggled to parry with his blade.

"You're the white dragon, aren't you?" Gawain grunted, struggling to keep his adversary at bay.

The other fighter sighed and once again pulled back. "Why must you lesser beings always talk so?"

To Gawain, even the voice in his head sounded impatient.

"But I suppose we can play, after all, your friends won't return in time to help you."

"So, it's true. You're the dragon Bloodstone fought, but how did you come to be in human form?"

"My master's powers are far greater than yours. All of us can become this vermin form."

"Why do you follow Baudrous?" Bloodstone growled. "He's evil incarnate."

"He is power!" the white dragon shouted back. "Power for himself and for those loyal to him."

"We've seen his rewards," Gawain said, thinking about the monstrous mage creature. "He sacrifices his followers to further his own aims."

"Fool, he only sacrifices your kind. We dragons have an honoured place at his side, just as your dragons would, if they join us?"

"The dragons of light would rather die than be a part of your side!" Bloodstone snarled.

"Very well. We'll end this conversation."

With that, the fight was back on, and Gawain found himself once more being battled up the stairs. The confined stairway was preventing the dragon from using his speed to get around Gawain's guard, but it also meant that Gawain couldn't swing his blade to capitalise on this. His only hope was to allow the dragon to back him up into the main hall where he'd have more room to manoeuvre. Bloodstone was of little help, and due to their proximity to one another, he couldn't breathe fire in case he struck Gawain. Thankfully, his opponent seemed completely unaware of his ruse, and with luck, would do just as Gawain hoped.

CHAPTER SEVENTEEN

Caldor, Sharos, and Thorn crossed the threshold of the portal without problem—a fact that worried Bertilack. He was certain Baudrous would've caused some problems. Perhaps the dark dragon was so arrogant that he didn't expect an attack on home soil. If this was true, his overconfidence would cost him dearly.

Keldon had only just arrived on the scene in time to bid a final farewell to Caldor. It wasn't a tearful parting, as neither warrior was what Bertilack would consider in touch with their emotions. Instead, they'd merely clasped hands. Keldon had insisted that Caldor not say goodbye, saying that the elf had better be coming back and that goodbye sounded so final. Bertilack and the others had made similar conversation with the team before finally watching them disappear into the void.

Kazar managed to close the portal after some initial difficulty, and as one, the group mounted and prepared to move for home.

The sunlight crested the sky and Bertilack fancied that he'd find both Gawain and Bloodstone asleep when they arrived. He wouldn't blame them either, for they'd had a rough time of it fighting Baudrous and his servants. His mind then turned to the ice dragon that'd escaped Bloodstone, for it was the one decidedly loose end to be tied up. Charlock had left some time ago to hunt his quarry, and as of yet, hadn't contacted them.

Ordering his thoughts, Bertilack reached out with his mind through the link he shared with the dragon and attempted contact. "Charlock, can you hear me?"

The dragon didn't answer straight away, but after a few seconds Bertilack heard the dragon's voice clearly in his head. "Yes, Bertilack. How'd everything go?"

"Well, my friend. Caldor says he'll see you when he returns. How goes the search?"

"I'm afraid I may have bad tidings. I picked up the trail and have been following it. However, it seems to lead back to the spire. I fear Gawain may be in danger."

"This is most alarming. Continue following the trail and inform me if it deviates. We must make haste and pray we're just being overly cautious."

"As you wish. Good luck, my friend. If all is well, I shall see you upon my return."

Bertilack was currently sitting upon Argast's back behind Keldon. The dwarf had just motioned for the gold dragon to rise into the air when Bertilack tapped him on the shoulder to gain his attention.

"Yes, brother? You need something?" said the dwarf, clearly he was in a very good mood about riding his own dragon again.

"Charlock believes the white dragon that fled the portal before the attack may have doubled back and headed for the spire. It may be nothing but to be sure, we need to get back as fast as possible."

Argast had heard most of the conversation, and his head was already facing their way.

"You get that, you flying iguana?" the dwarf said.

Argast snarled at the dwarf good-naturedly. "I hear better than you do, you bearded tree stump. I'll move as fast as I can."

Argast beat his wings faster and accelerated their pace. The other spire's warriors followed suit. None of them wished to be left behind.

Bertilack hoped they'd be in time and that the spire would still be standing when they returned.

***

The dragon had almost backed Gawain to the top of the stairs, but Gawain thanked his lucky stars that he was skilled enough to be able to deflect his opponent's attacks. Despite his surprising speed, the dragon appeared to be having trouble dealing with his new shape and form. Gawain reasoned the creature hadn't had much practice as a human, which gave Gawain an unprecedented advantage. Gawain smiled inwardly, thinking of the damage he'd do to this beast once they were out in the open.

"Why do you run, knight? I thought the warriors of the spire had a reputation for bravery, a reputation that you seem to be failing," said the dragon, completely convinced of his superiority.

All Gawain needed was a few more seconds. A few more steps, and he'd be out in the open hall, but the dragon noticed the light from the torches behind Gawain, and immediately guessed his plan.

"Ah, I see. You hope to battle me better with more room to manoeuvre. Ha! Do you really think you'll fare any better up there?"

Gawain grunted from exertion as the dragon aimed another flurry of blows at his defences.

"Time will tell, lizard, if you're up to the challenge."

"Believe me, you weak fool. I'm more than ready."

Gawain finally burst into the chamber, his pursuer hot on his heels, and Bloodstone trailing behind. Managing to disengage from combat, Gawain positioned the great table between himself and the white dragon. Both fighters walked the edges of their respected table side, eying each other warily.

The white dragon still had an evil smile playing across his face, as if it were the only human expression he was capable of imitating. Bloodstone came forth to stand on the table and hissed at their dark opponent, who took no notice of the diminutive dragon.

Their aggressor seemed to take in the décor before depositing himself in the chair marked for Batras, showing his complete contempt for the knight's skills.

"Remove yourself from that chair," Gawain said, aiming the point of his sword at the man-dragon. "You aren't fit to be seated there."

"Really?" the dragon said, fixing the knight with a toothy grin. "Perhaps then you should make me? After all, was this not your plan all along? You've brought yourself into a position where you can use your feeble skills to the fullest, so let's see them."

Gawain released a bestial cry and leapt across the table to bring his sword crashing down on the chair in which the dragon had rested moments before. Briefly commiserating himself for destroying Batras's chair, the knight turned to his opponent. The dragon moved once more with speed that no normal human could posses, and stood now beside Gawain.

"Is that how fast you can move?" the dragon said, easily dodging more blows from Gawain.

"Because it's too slow." Ducking under Gawain's guard, the dragon struck the knight in the chest with the flat of his hand and sent him flying clear over the table. "Pathetic, I'd hoped for a challenge from one of the spire's best."

The dragon leapt over the table after Gawain. "My one consolation is that perhaps your fellow warriors will provide me with more sport."

As he'd fallen, Gawain had lost his grip on his sword, which the dragon now casually picked up and brought point first to Gawain's neck, effectively pinning the knight in place.

"Goodbye, knight. Ah, now don't feel bad. Your kind never truly had a chance in the first place."

The white dragon moved to strike, but before he did, he heard Bloodstone roar as the diminutive creature tore through the air to connect with the dragon. Considering Bloodstone no threat, the dragon hadn't paid him any attention, and was caught completely off guard.

Dropping Gawain's sword as Bloodstone impacted against his face, the dragon tried hard to recover. He grabbed the red dragon by the wings and promptly flung the small dragon through one of the main chamber walls.

"Fool! You think to match me in this form? As

a dragon you may be my equal, but as I am now, you're by far my lesser. If you'd stayed still, perhaps I'd have considered you beyond my notice, but as things stand now, you'll have to be destroyed."

"The only one being destroyed around here is you!"

The white dragon realised his mistake. By taking his attention from Gawain, he'd allowed the crimson knight to get to his feet. Sword in hand, the knight struck at the dragon, and severed his arm from his shoulder.

Howling an anguished cry, the dragon dodged away from the attack. Instinctively, the dragon's arm shot out to grasp the bloodied stump at his shoulder. "Damn you, you inferior lower life form. What've you done to me?" he said, staring at his severed arm in disbelief.

"I've done to you no worse than what you would've done to me, creature," Gawain spat, advancing on his adversary.

"You think this'll stop me? I'm a dragon! I posses recuperative powers far beyond your comprehension," he snapped, tightening his grip on the wound. Closing his eyes, the dragon focused his energies on healing, but soon discovered that something was wrong. The power in his body was there, but he couldn't reach it. He felt it within himself like a stone at the bottom of a pond, and yet still he couldn't harness it. Snarling, the dragon gave up and shot Gawain an angry glance. "This is your fault! What've you done to me?"

Gawain looked up, puzzled. "Aside from severing your arm, I've done little else. I posses no magic."

It was then that his predicament dawned on him—he couldn't heal himself because he was human! Only in his natural state would his recuperative powers work. "Damn you humans and your feeble physiology! Can you primitives do nothing right? It matters not, after I've defeated you, I'll return to my full-size and heal, ready to face your friends."

"One problem," Gawain said.

"What would that be?"

"Well, you see, the human body can only hold a small amount of blood, and by the look of that hole in your arm, you've lost an awful lot."

"You're lying."

"I'm sure you can already feel your body getting heavy, your limbs going weak," said Gawain. He was glad he watched so much television. He'd never call another documentary boring again.

"No, it's not true!" the transformed dragon snarled, backing away from the knight.

"It's over, dragon. You lose. Surrender."

The dragon's eyes darted backwards and forwards as it assimilated the validity of the knight's claim. His body was indeed sluggish, his movements slower, but what could he do? Surely he couldn't return to Baudrous empty handed, or the master would be furious. But he couldn't surrender either.

The dark dragon fixed Gawain with a sly look. "I believe I'll choose not to surrender."

Gawain prepared himself, thinking that the evil warrior would make a suicidal last effort, but he didn't. Turning his back on the knight, the dragon-man ran to the nearest window and flung himself through the glass.

Gawain gasped. He had expected many things, but not this. Waking himself from his trance like state, Gawain rushed forwards to stare out of the broken window.

In the brightening light of dawn, he viewed the spot from which the dragon had fallen. Straining his eyes, he looked to the base of the spire, and although he couldn't be sure, he believed he saw the outlines of an impact crater.

He wondered if his adversary could've survived such a fall, but decided he would worry about it later and ran over to where Bloodstone had fallen.

Moving aside the destroyed masonry that had collapsed when Bloodstone had impacted, the knight picked up the shrunken dragon, and brought him to the table where he could better see the dragon's injuries. His scales had dulled from a once bright crimson to a muddy red, with several small lacerations opening up across his body.

Gawain shook the little dragon slightly and called out his name in an attempt to wake him.

At first it seemed that he wouldn't wake despite the knight's assistance, but after a few moments, the dragon did indeed stir. Opening his eyes slightly, the dragon fixed Gawain with a confused look.

"Gawain?" the dragon said, puzzled. "Did you win? What happened to him?"

"Gone, flying out the window. I think he left a crater below. Are you well enough to move?"

Bloodstone gave this question much consideration before trying to bring himself to his feet. Each movement felt like his muscles were burning and his breathing laboured. Despite this, the little dragon managed to stand. Shaking dust free from his body, Bloodstone tried to flex his wings, but the effort was too painful. "I can move, my friend, but you'll have to carry me until we get outside, and I can assume my true form."

That was all Gawain needed to hear, for if his opponent had survived, he may have changed shape to heal and could be now lying in wait for the knight to descend the spire's stairs. With luck, Bloodstone would have the energy to change into his larger state, and then the white dragon would think twice about engaging.

Bending down, Gawain scooped Bloodstone up in his arms, taking special care to avoid contact with the dragon's wings where possible. Then, with as much speed as the knight dared, he retreated back down the stairs so that they could reach the exit.

Along the way he was still cautious, in case the white dragon made a suicidal, last-ditch attempt at their lives. Eventually Gawain and his precious cargo made it outside. The sun streamed over them as it rose and Gawain could feel the forest come alive. He placed Bloodstone on the ground and stepped back while the red dragon changed.

This change didn't happen as quickly as it usually would. The light that surrounded the dragon continued to flash and fade as the dragon painstakingly tried to complete the spell. Gawain watched this unfold and attributed the strange rate of transformation to the injuries the dragon had sustained. And though it took longer, eventually the dragon was finally finished and stood once again at his full and impressive size.

But only for a moment did he stand for he was still weak. Cursing, Bloodstone fell to his knees, the strain being too much to bear.

Gawain was swiftly at his side. "Bloodstone, are you okay?" the knight said, concerned.

Weakly, the dragon nodded and turned his gargantuan visage towards Gawain. "Fine, my friend, fine. I just need a moment to collect my thoughts." And with that, the dragon promptly passed out.

Gawain checked him over as best he could, but not being a man of medicine, he didn't know what to do. He then resolved that Bloodstone should be fine here, for the recuperative power of the dragons was astonishing, and besides, he had another mission.

Patting Bloodstone's flanks and promising that he wouldn't be long, Gawain set out to the other side of the spire where the crater was located. Wandering around, Gawain at first thought that he'd missed his enemy's impact site, but as he looked up, he saw the broken window and realised he must be nearly on top of it. No sooner had he thought this when he nearly tripped on the crater's edge. Looking within, Gawain saw the body of the dead dragon. The beast had almost completed its transformation, and now seemed stuck between human and dragon forms.

"Damn," said Gawain. He'd hoped the dragon had survived, for the information he could've provided would've been immeasurably valuable. Cursing again for not stopping the dragon from jumping, Gawain turned from the hole. He didn't get far, however, for the body which he'd taken to be a corpse, spoke.

"Come to delight in my agony, knight?"

Gawain immediately drew his sword and pointed it in the half dragon's general direction. "Any reason why I shouldn't?" Gawain said coldly.

"Perhaps not," the dark dragon rasped. "After all, I was planning to do the same to you."

"Of that I've no doubt, but why speak to me, dragon? Surely your last minutes should be spent more fruitfully?"

The dragon merely laughed, with blood appearing on his lips from the exertion. "If you believe I'm capable of doing anything else, do you not believe I'd be doing it? No, my body is done.

I'll die here."

Despite his last statement, the dragon didn't appear worried. Gawain thought that when his time came, he doubted he would take it so coolly. Willing to at least engage the dragon in one last conversation, Gawain stabbed his sword into the ground, and crouched by the hole so he could better hear the dying creature.

"Do you willingly embrace death, dragon? So willingly that you no longer have the will to live?"

The dragon tried to move its head to face the knight, but the act of movement was too much. "My name is Ice Slayer. I'd thank you not to keep calling me dragon."

Even in death and knowing that it was Gawain who'd bested him, Ice Slayer was still defiantly talking to him as if he were a child.

"Bit of an unusual request when you're so close to death but very well. Ice Slayer, will you answer my question?"

The dragon lay still for a moment, his energy almost spent. It wouldn't be long now.

"You ask if I should so willingly embrace death, and I say to you, yes. Upon setting out on this mission, I knew I might not return, but facing the hated enemy in battle was worth the risk. You fought honourably, a characteristic that the human germs my master employs lack. Perhaps it was a mistake to tar you with the same brush."

Strangely, at that moment, Gawain found himself feeling sorry for the dragon. Here, at last, was the more human—or dragon in this case—face of the enemy. Gawain had battled with the clear knowledge before that he was in the right and his opponent in the wrong. Still, now, staring at his dying foe, Gawain came to realise how blurred the line between good and evil could be.

"Do you have anybody to which I can tell of your passing? Any family who may wish to know your fate?" Gawain said, feeling that it was the least he could do.

Again though, this made the dragon laugh. "All my clutchmates would kill you on sight but thank you for the gesture. Perhaps one day you'll meet them in battle, and then you may retell my story. Tell them I fought with honour, that I battled to the last. That I was . . . a true warrior," the dragon said his last words and shuddered once more. However, the spasms were more violent this time.

Gawain jumped into the crater and took hold of his enemy's hand. "Ice Slayer, are you still with me?" Gawain said. "Ice Slayer?"

It was too late. The dragon had gone, passed

away into the next life, and Gawain found himself deeply saddened by the loss. Had it not been for him being born on the other side of this conflict, Ice Slayer and Gawain could've been friends in another life.

The knight climbed out of the crater and found Bloodstone walking towards him. The dragon still seemed a little shaky on his feet, but otherwise, none the worse for wear. He hailed Gawain as he approached.

"Gawain, are you okay? What has become of the enemy dragon?"

Gawain paused for a while and looked back towards the crater. "He didn't survive the fall. His body is there and unmoved. In the end, he was an honourable warrior. I believe we should bury him."

Bloodstone looked perplexedly at Gawain. He'd never heard the loud, brash knight talk like this and wondered what had happened whilst he'd slept. "Are you sure you're okay? You don't sound like it."

"I'm fine, Bloodstone. Please comply with my request and incinerate the body. I believe it's what he would've wanted."

This last statement further confused the dragon, but he did as he was told. Opening his mouth, Bloodstone belched forth as much flame as his injuries would permit.

"Goodbye, warrior," Gawain said in an almost inaudible whisper as he watched Ice Slayer's body turn to ash. "Perhaps we'll meet again in the next life."

CHAPTER EIGHTEEN

Dragon wings flew into the spire's dragon ports. Upon their approach, Bertilack spied Charlock rising above the tree canopy. The black dragon looked like an arrow or a spear of midnight black that'd been shot from some otherworldly bow or thrown from a giant hand. Seeing the great dragon soothed Bertilack's nerves. He'd pushed the others hard to reach here and hoped they were on time.

Underneath him, Argast still flew strongly. The gold looked ready to go another round, but Bertilack looked forward to getting back on Charlock. He could now see why Keldon had so wished to return on Argast, for without Charlock, Bertilack had almost thought he'd lost a part of himself.

The group alighted on their specific dragon ports, with both Bertilack and Keldon leaping from the saddle and charging headlong down the tunnel. Only they knew the danger the spire was in, and haste was of the essence.

As one, they exploded into the main chamber, weapons drawn to find the place in ruins, with Gawain resting comfortably in one of the remaining chairs.

"By the spire," Batras said as the other warriors left their dragon port tunnels. "What has happened here?"

The whole group stared around at the devastation littering their once beautiful home.

"Gawain, are you okay?" Bertilack said, walking towards the knight, his sword still drawn as a precaution.

The other warriors followed, drawing their

own weapons, not wishing to be unarmed should whatever had done this return.

Gawain looked at them as if in a trance, his eyes taking time to register his friends. "Bertilack, yes, I'm fine. Welcome home."

"Welcome home?" Batras sputtered, appearing at Bertilack's elbow. "By my axe, what've you done to the place? To even call it a mess would be an understatement!"

Gawain slowly rotated so he could face the minotaur. "We had an intruder," Gawain said without a hint of emotion. "The white dragon, he broke into the spire. Bloodstone and I battled him and emerged victorious."

Bertilack was relieved. At least that was one problem they no longer had to worry about. Still, what was wrong with Gawain, and where was Bloodstone? Surely he hadn't fallen during the fight.

"Gawain, my friend," Bertilack said, sheathing his sword. "Where's Bloodstone? I don't see him here."

From the corner of his eye, Bertilack saw Charlock approach and land on his shoulder.

"Bloodstone is fine. He rests in my chambers. I waited up for you so I could assure you that all was well, but I must now depart also." Gawain pushed out of his chair and walked towards the stairs.

"Wait a moment," said Batras. The big minotaur approached Gawain menacingly with his axe drawn. "You and I still have a score to settle."

Gawain turned and gazed at Batras with exhaustion. "Look, if this is about my apparent running away, it'll have to wait."

Yet Batras wouldn't be put off and stood before the knight. From across the room, the warriors of the spire looked on in dismay.

"Bertilack, you must do something," Kazar said. "Though there's no love lost between Gawain and myself, I don't wish to see him harmed, especially by one of our own."

Bertilack steeled himself and prepared to step between the two, but something unexpected happened.

Instead of fighting, Batras put away his axe and extended his hand. "Can you forgive me? I acted irrationally, the haze of battle was upon me, and I couldn't see the truth. You didn't dishonour us."

Gawain took Batras's proffered hand. "Took you long enough," the knight said with a smile before his strength finally gave out, and he fell into the minotaur's arms.

"Look at that. He passed out!" Batras exclaimed.

"Take him to his chambers and then return here," Bertilack said, coming to his friend's side. "We must put the final touches to the spire's defence."

Batras nodded and lifted the big knight, armour and all, as if he weighed nothing, and took him down the stairs.

Bertilack turned to the others and bid them to be seated. He took his own chair after a quick dust for masonry and regarded the group as a whole. "Well, that certainly was something," he exclaimed. "But the wheels are in motion, and we're now well beyond the point of no return. From this moment, we've no choice but to move on regardless. Kazar, can I count on you to finish the tower's fortifications with Keldon's assistance?"

The wizard curtly nodded but said nothing. Keldon was also unusually quiet.

"I understand it's a lot to take in, my friends, but now is not the time for pause. Now is the time for action."

"None of us doubt that, brother," Keldon said. "But you must admit, this seems more difficult by the minute. We started as a team, and now the team is considerably depleted."

Bertilack considered his brother's words but could think of no other choice. All they could do was hope that Gawain would soon recover and that Thorn, Caldor, and Sharos returned home safe. It was then that Bertilack and Charlock sensed a presence behind them as Batras returned to the room.

He sat at Gawain's seat, as his own was wrecked beyond use. "What tasks have you for us?" the minotaur said casually as he stroked Khrishaw, who'd just appeared on the table.

Glad for the minotaur's bright attitude, Bertilack focused himself on him. "Once you two have had enough time to rest, I wish you to patrol the borders of our territory. We must keep our eyes and ears open."

Pushing the chair, the minotaur rose to his feet, and Khrishaw took wing. "We're ready now. How should we contact you if there are problems?" Batras asked, his face a mask of grim determination.

"Ah, now that's another problem," said Bertilack. "Kazar, any thoughts?"

The wizard didn't answer right away. He placed his hand to his chin as if pondering the issue. Soon after, the light returned to his eyes as ideas formed behind them. "Thorn and I had pondered this very same conundrum, but I believe I may have come up with an answer. Give me a few hours to put something together."

With that, Kazar stood up and wandered off, muttering to himself with both aquatic dragons in tow.

"Batras, despite what you say, I believe you two could also use some rest," said Bertilack. "Return to your room and try to sleep until Kazar is finished."

Batras was about to voice his objections when he suddenly felt how tired he was. Perhaps a little sleep was in order. He didn't want to be caught unaware again just because he was tired. Excusing himself, he too exited the main chamber room, leaving Keldon and Bertilack alone with their respective dragons.

The knight looked at his brother's dour countenance, but the dwarf didn't return his look.

"Why so troubled, little brother?" Bertilack said, standing and walking to Keldon's side.

"What if he doesn't return, Bertilack? What if Caldor gets himself killed in that dark, out-of-the-way dimension, and we never hear from him again?"

Bertilack could do nothing. These very

thoughts had permeated his own mind so often since Caldor's departure. If something horrible happened to him, Bertilack would be the one to blame. He had sent their brother on this errand. Still, it shouldn't have been Caldor going. It should've been him.

"I feel your pain, brother. All the warriors of the spire do, but perhaps I'm the only one who can truly understand. But we mustn't give up on our brother, for when he succeeds, it may be very likely that he'll be coming through that gate with the very demons of hell at his back, and the spire must be ready."

Keldon looked at his brother with understanding in his eyes. "Yes, you're right," the dwarf said, thrusting his chair back and rising to his feet. "Our brother is out there risking life and limb while I sit here feeling sorry for him. What has he got to be sorry about, taking on the fight of the century and leaving me to sweep up and make the tea? When he returns, and he better, I'm going to kill him!"

Bertilack knew that the dwarf's gruff demeanour was really a defence mechanism designed to hide his emotions. He watched with a smile as his diminutive sibling stomped around the great hall.

"Summon that blasted mage, get me those elementals, and bring me my hammer! I shall make defences the likes of which have never been seen. Bring on Baudrous! His forces will break upon the steel of dwarven ingenuity!"

"Well said, dwarf. Well said!" Charlock said, still on Bertilack's shoulder. "Fear not. Should you not be up to the task, Argast and I will be there to save you." The black dragon cast his gold clutchmate an arrogant glance.

"Agreed," Argast said, taking to the air. "We, after all, will be doing most of the work."

"Why, you scaled jackals!" Keldon sputtered. "When the fighting starts, you two can take a back seat and allow real warriors to fight. I tell you now. No evil force will cross these thresholds."

Keldon spun on his heels and headed for the armoury while Bertilack and the two dragons resisted the urge to laugh at their compatriot's antics.

Once he'd gone, Argast turned to Bertilack and Charlock. "I'd better go with him. He's nothing without me, you know."

From beyond the stairs, the dwarf's voice echoed. "I heard that, you flying iguana!"

"You were supposed to, you ancient footstool!" said Argast. He favoured Charlock and

Bertilack with a wink before flying down the stairs in pursuit of his partner.

Charlock and Bertilack were left alone in the main chamber. Where once had all been chaos, now all was calm.

"We were fortunate this time, Charlock," said Bertilack. "Had we left the spire unguarded, we might've returned to find it nothing but ruin." Bertilack paused to pick up a fist-size lump of rock that'd once been part of the main chamber's inner wall.

"Fortunate we were indeed," intoned the dragon. "I'm just sorry that I didn't manage to catch the ice dragon. If I had, then none of this would've been necessary."

Bertilack smiled at the dragon warmly. "There's no need to blame yourself, my friend. It all turned out for the best regardless of your or anybody's actions."

Charlock nodded absentmindedly.

"Hey, how about we take the first patrol?" Bertilack said, smiling. "We can have a fly in the fresh air."

"Perhaps we shouldn't. The spire can ill afford to be devoid of your leadership, especially with your brother gone."

Bertilack merely sighed at this and dropped

the piece of masonry he'd been holding. "These are the precious little moments of calm before the coming storm. We should enjoy them whilst we can."

Charlock considered another objection but thought better of it—Bertilack was right. The black dragon nodded his assent, and Bertilack spun on his heels, intent on the dragon ports.

* * *

The next few days passed in a flurry of activity for the warriors of the spire. Gawain and Batras flew upon their dragons and spent the days watching for trouble around the spire. Bertilack had cautioned them both on the need for eternal vigilance at this difficult time.

Gawain himself had recovered from the injuries sustained at the hands of the white dragon but was still reluctant to talk of the incident even to Bloodstone, who'd also made a full recovery.

It had been four days since Baudrous's forces had attacked the spire, and Bertilack had sent Caldor through the portal gate. In that time, both Keldon and Kazar had worked tirelessly on the spire's defences. Kazar had also perfected his crystal communication devices to contact the different teams in and around the spire. These items were a great help to Bertilack, who often had to coordinate between his teams and give instructions. Bertilack's resting chamber had been made the official command post where Bertilack could be found at all hours of the day. Bertilack was eating and sleeping in this room, wishing every moment that he had more warriors to take care of the tasks at hand.

On today's itinerary, the knight was scheduled to talk with Kazar about his work on the dragon ports. The mage was deploying many countermeasures to protect these vital areas, but Bertilack was starting to believe he was going overboard with the amount. After that, Bertilack would be conversing with Batras and Gawain on their new patrol routes. It'd taken many days, but Bertilack now believed he'd drawn up the most efficient route possible.

Bertilack's chambers were richly decorated in colours that suited his role as the green knight and were expansive, to say the least. His bed was an enormous four-poster affair, lavishly decorated in shades of emerald green and bordered with gold. A side table lay at each side of his bed, allowing the knight to place items from his home. The team hadn't made many trips to their home dimension, but once or twice, members had gone through to collect personal belongings. In addition to the side tables, Bertilack's room was furnished with a desk against the wall, which housed the knight's only mirror in the room. Whilst he was by no means a vain man, Bertilack did enjoy seeing his own face from time to time. The rest of the room had been cleared out to make space for a great desk from which Bertilack concluded his daily business with his teammates.

Dressed at the moment only in his undergarments, he wandered to the window. Like the rest of Bertilack's room, the window was very ornate, strongly favouring medieval-style architecture. Briefly, the knight stared through the glass before taking the handles and swinging the windows wide to embrace the day.

It was a fine morning. The sun always seemed to shine in this land, brightly reflecting on the verdant greens and summery blues. Moments like this both warmed and chilled Bertilack's heart. This land was beautiful. Still, with their presence, it may soon change. The knight feared he'd never be able to view this vista in the same way again.

Turning from the window and the odd feelings it caused, Bertilack regarded the still sleeping form of Charlock at the bed's foot, looking almost like some scaled family dog. As a boy, when Bertilack had been just plain old Mark, he'd had a dog—a miniature collie called Shobey. The family hadn't had another pet since he died but seeing the dragon lying there brought back all the memories.

Silently, Bertilack crossed the room and returned to his bedside, where he stroked the dragon's head with his hand. The dragon growled softly, rolling away from the unwelcome attention, and remained sleeping on his back. Smiling, the knight moved to his bedside table and placed the ever-stone that lay there around his neck. Instantaneously the armour that he wore now as a second skin erupted forth, sheathing him once more.

As it did so, the armour created a brilliant emerald flash, moving out like a living being over Bertilack's arms and body. The light awoke Charlock from his slumber, and his serpentine head rose from its resting position to regard the knight with sleepy, weary eyes.

"How long have you been up?" the dragon said before displaying an almost cat-like yawn.

"Not long," the knight said. "Just long enough to catch the first breeze of the morning."

Charlock shook the sleep from his limbs before jumping from the bed and flying to the window ledge. "Do you think today will be the day?" he said as he stared at the picturesque scene.

"Anything is possible," Bertilack said as he buckled his sword to his waist. "Baudrous could still attack at any time. Hopefully, Kazar and Keldon are done before then."

The knight rose to his feet and joined the dragon at the window, looking down. Bertilack noted the strange expression on Charlock's face. "What troubles you, my friend? You look perplexed."

The dragon didn't look up. He merely sniffed the air hesitantly. "There's something wrong. It's a feeling I cannot describe, but beyond here, I sense trouble."

Bertilack was about to press further when the communication crystal on his desk hummed to life. Momentarily forgetting the conversation, Bertilack approached as Batras's face appeared within the orb.

"Batras, greetings. What's the matter? We're not due to speak until this afternoon."

"Something's come up. Bloodstone and Khrishaw have been acting strangely since this morning. They keep saying they feel something strange."

"Interesting. Charlock expressed the same

sensations. Any idea what's causing it?"

Batras shook his head.

"None, and the dragons seem as confused as we are. However, Bloodstone did mention that the feeling got worse the further he flew from the spire."

Bertilack wondered what could be wrong. For all three dragons to feel the same sensation, there had to be something to it. "Batras, I want you and the others back in the spire. I don't like the way this feels."

"With respect, if we can get nearer to where this sensation is strongest, we may find something."

Suddenly, the sky outside the window darkened as the brilliant sunshine was blotted out, and black lightning struck the clouds.

"What's going on? Where'd that storm come from?"

Batras moved away from the globe as he consulted someone else off-screen and then returned. "I've asked Khrishaw to use his enhanced vision to look around. He says a portal gate has opened and that it's from this that the cloud is emanating."

Bertilack's face darkened. This could only mean that they were under attack, for no other force he knew could control the portals save for his wizards and Baudrous.

"Bertilack, there's something else."

The knight quickly snapped out of his revelry to regard the minotaur once more.

"Khrishaw says he can see shapes emanating from the clouds ahead," the minotaur said urgently. "It's Sharos! And Caldor and Thorn are with him."

Bertilack breathed a sigh of relief. "Maintain your current position. I'll come out to meet you."

"Come fast! Ice dragons, lots of them!"

Batras's head was gone from the globe, and Bertilack turned to his dragon.

"It's time to teach these pale imitations what it means to pick a fight with the knights of the spire."

Bertilack and Charlock rushed out the room and headed for the dragon ports. On the way, they met Kazar and Keldon, who'd come in search of them. Keldon still wore his apron, and his face was blackened from his work.

"Bertilack," Kazar said. "The dragons are on edge, the sky around us darkens, and a foul wind blows."

"My brother and Thorn have returned with Sharos. We hope to have them in the protective confines of the tower within the hour."

"Glorious news," Kazar said. "But what causes the darkness? It doesn't feel natural."

"The dragons of darkness follow Caldor. We believe the darkness heralds the beginning of our greatest battle yet," Charlock said, speaking from Bertilack's shoulder.

"If Caldor is in danger, then by my axe, I'll go meet them!" Keldon turned on his heels to fetch his weapon.

"No, brother," Bertilack said, calling Keldon back. "You must stay here to finalise the defences."

Keldon turned his face, angry. "You ask me to tinker with weapons while Caldor's life may be in jeopardy? Do you think me a coward?"

"Nay, brother. Caldor is in good hands. Both Gawain and Batras stand with him upon their dragons. Charlock and I stand poised to meet them and assure their safe arrival."

Keldon's face remained hard, clearly unconvinced.

"Brother, this is for the best," Bertilack continued. "You must make all the defences ready, for we'll not have time once I bring Caldor and the others in."

Keldon still didn't like it. The feeling was etched into his features, but he acquiesced. He looked at Bertilack with fire in his eyes. "Make sure he comes home safe."

"Count on it."

CHAPTER NINETEEN

Bertilack and Charlock charged forth from the spire. The sky above was dark, with a huge purple orb spinning at the nexus of the disturbance. Using his excellent vision, Charlock could make out shapes in the storm. He could see the dragons of light having met up with Sharos, Caldor, and Thorn. Beyond that, ice dragons filled the sky.

The evil creatures seemed intent on their targets. Although the dragons of light were by themselves more powerful, the sheer numbers were taking a toll.

"What do you see?" Bertilack said, having noted Charlock's expression.

"Our friends are under siege, Bertilack. They're attempting to head our way, but there are many enemies arrayed against them."

"We must hurry. I told Keldon we'd bring our brother home. Let's not make me a liar."

Bobbing his head in ascension, Charlock dove through the wind, using his wings to cut through the gale. The weather had worsened since the clouds had appeared, and now the wind threatened to take the mighty dragon from the sky. Rain poured forth, and hail lashed against his scales. Still, the dragon prince would not be slowed from his present course. Flying at breakneck speed, he was soon on top of the battle.

The spire's knights raised ragged cheers into the storm as Bertilack and Charlock exploded from the clouds like a black spear.

The ice dragons had been too intent on their prey to notice them coming. The first fell defeated before them, without even raising a claw in defence. The other evil dragons flew about in momentary disarray as they struggled to meet this new threat. As they did, their movements enabled Charlock and Bertilack to take a few more of their numbers down with well-placed blasts of flame and strategically placed claw strikes.

Despite their efforts, the ice dragons still numbered greatly more than the spire's knights. Charlock and Bertilack killed many, but many more were still to come. The knight motioned for Charlock to fly closer to the other three dragons of light.

"We'll have more chance of making an effective defence whilst we stand beside the others," Bertilack yelled into the wind.

Charlock agreed. Whilst the ice dragons were forming up for another strike, the pair joined their friends who'd gathered just north of their position. Bertilack motioned a quick greeting before turning Charlock around to face the oncoming flight.

"What's the strategy?" Charlock asked as they hovered in the air.

"The only one we can make when facing a numerically superior enemy. We make hit-and-run attacks. Take them out one at a time, and then retreat for greater manoeuvrability before flying in again."

The ice dragons were likely to give chase should they start killing their friends. This hopefully would separate them in flight even more, and they could play divide and conquer.

Bertilack looked over his shoulder to his brother and just hoped that Caldor and the others would follow the same plan. For it to work, Bertilack and Charlock would have to focus on their own opponents without worrying about how the others were doing.

At a motion from Charlock, Bertilack refocused his attention on the enemy dragons. The white beasts had already reformed and were attacking again. Despite the loss in their numbers, they believed that Bertilack and his men would be no further threat.

Bertilack would prove this assumption wrong. The green knight waited until the white dragons were in range and kicked against Charlock's flanks.

The black dragon reared up and released an ear-splitting roar before diving headlong towards the lead dragon with the other warriors of the spire, forming a rough wedge shape behind him.

The closest ice dragon looked up at them in horror as he watched the mightier Charlock bearing down on him. Figuring that retreat would keep him alive longer than a head-on charge, it dived into the clouds. The ice dragon behind suddenly found itself in a very precarious situation. It'd manoeuvred itself into what it considered a safe position behind the leader but now found itself extremely vulnerable as the two sides clashed together.

Charlock caught the surprised dragon in the face with his claw and used the momentum to slice through the dragon's wing. Howling in pain, the enemy dragon spun out of control. The other spire dragons did likewise. Before the larger force of dragons could retaliate, each one peeled off and disappeared. The demoralised ice dragons cast about, looking for their opponents whilst others gave chase to the warriors they could see.

Charlock and Bertilack had flown up high by this point and were in a perfect position to get the better of the dragons that'd remained stationary. Swooping round like some great black shark, the pair hunted their prey. Bursting suddenly from cover, they impacted another ice dragon that wasn't paying attention. His life was over before he knew it as Charlock tore his throat from his neck.

The other ice dragons nearby turned quickly, but Charlock and Bertilack had already disappeared back into the clouds. This hesitation on the ice dragons' part would prove fatal. They checked the skies for Charlock, and Bloodstone and Khrishaw claimed two more of their numbers.

Few invaders remained alive. Charlock continued to glide through the mist. It was then that Bertilack noticed Caldor and Sharos were nowhere in sight. He was well aware that several ice dragons had followed them when they retreated. If they weren't chasing him or the others, then they were likely pursuing his brother and his friends.

Bertilack motioned for Charlock to disengage from the fight. Uncomprehending and unwilling to leave the battle, the dragon fixed Bertilack with a quizzical glance. Bertilack immediately saw the confusion in the dragon's eyes, but the storm around them had worsened. He could no longer make himself heard over the gale.

The knight screamed at the top of his lungs. Still, Charlock couldn't hear him, so the knight resorted to more frantic hand gestures to make Charlock leave the cloud cover.

Shrugging once again, Charlock decided that perhaps he should fly on the side of caution and follow Bertilack's instruction. Abandoning the ice dragon he had been watching, Charlock pulled a u-turn and flew at top speed outside of the cloud.

Bertilack was relieved to finally be leaving the black darkness and hoped that once they were out, he could find his brother. Already the cloud was thinning, and Bertilack could see shafts of light permeating the gloom. Soon they were outside, and Charlock came to a halt.

"The battle was in our hands. Why'd we leave so prematurely?" Charlock said, clearly unhappy.

"I'm concerned about my older brother's safety. I saw some ice dragons pursue our group into the mists, yet none returned in pursuit of us or the others. I can only assume that they followed Caldor and Sharos."

"And you believe they're out here somewhere?"

"I do, my friend," Bertilack said. "And judging by the number that disappeared, he may be in grave danger."

"I'll attempt to scan the skies with my superior vision to locate your brother or his pursuers." With that, the great black dragon stared off into the distance in an attempt to locate Sharos and his passengers. "I see them, Bertilack. Sharos is retreating towards the spire. No fewer than seven ice dragons are pursuing him."

"Any sign of Kazar or Keldon coming to his aid?"

Charlock once again starred off into the distance. "No, perhaps they're unaware of the danger."

"Damn," Bertilack said. "We have to get there."

"Even at top speed, I don't believe we'll catch them before they reach the spire."

"Just do your best, Charlock. It'll be enough."

Nodding, the dragon flapped his wings faster and sped towards the spire. Charlock was so fast that even with his super strength, Bertilack found it difficult to hold on. They swooped away from the growing darkness, heading straight towards their objective. The ice dragons were coming into Bertilack's field of vision more clearly now, and they were almost on top of the spire. If something wasn't done soon, the spire would suffer irreparable damage before the main battle began.

Bertilack prayed silently. He wasn't the most religious man, but given the current situation, it couldn't hurt. He prayed to God, asking for help in this time of need. And it was then that he saw movement on the newly constructed spire ramparts. Had his prayer had been heard? Soon Bertilack saw Keldon and Argast take off from the dragon ports. Moving at speeds close to that which Charlock was now performing, the dwarf and dragon headed towards the enemy.

Bertilack viewed the spectacle from his position on Charlock's back and noticed something different about Argast. Around the gold dragon and resting upon his shoulders were sheets of glowing black armour. Bertilack wasn't sure how it was possible, but as the gold dragon closed with the ice beasts, the armour seemed to turn aside all his foes' attacks. Sheets of ice sprayed forth from seven throats, and all vaporised before making contact. Argast seemed covered in a flaming aura as he clashed and sent the dragons scattering.

The awesome spectacle made Charlock momentarily stop mid-flight and gape. "Bertilack, do you see what I see?"

"I do, my friend. I just don't believe it."

Argast defeated three of the ice dragons by himself and sent the other four retreating back towards the ever-expanding storm front.

"Let's hurry," said Bertliack.

"Do you think they have some of that armour in my size?" the dragon said as they headed once more for the spire. Soon after, they landed upon the dragon platform.

Together, man and dragon hurried to find their companions. Before they'd left, Keldon and

Kazar had been busy in the armoury, so this was Bertilack's first stop. Diving down their adopted home's corridors and stairwells, the heroes soon came to their destination.

The armoury was well lit and was possibly the largest room in the entire spire. Gigantic furnaces and kilns pumped hot fumes into the air, making the room humid. Inside were many of the spire's assembled warriors as well as their dragons, and a great cheer erupted as the warriors recognised their leader.

Caldor approached first. The tall elf embraced his younger brother warmly. "It's good to see you again, little brother. I'm glad you didn't burn down the spire in my absence."

"We'll have several creatures knocking on our door in a few moments wanting to do just that."

"Not whilst I draw breath," Charlock growled at Bertilack's shoulder.

"Indeed. We saw Argast equipped with some form of enchanted armour that made him nigh invincible. Tell me, have they made more?"

Caldor nodded and ushered his brother towards their younger sibling. "I confess I was just asking him the same thing," Caldor said as they walked. "It would appear that our younger brother has been quite busy. He says he's almost finished making the armour for the entire dragon force."

The pair crossed into an adjoining chamber where Bertilack greeted his younger brother and Thorn.

"It's good to see you well. After we were forced to retreat from the fight, we feared the worst," said Thorn.

"No overgrown ice lizard could ever get the better of Charlock and myself," Bertilack said with a smile.

"I must confess," said Thorn. "It's partly my fault that we're in this mess so soon."

"How so?" Bertilack enquired.

"Caldor and I were busy observing Baudrous's forces over a huge number of mustering points, as well as the odd act of sabotage. Once we'd gathered enough intelligence, we headed for home. I opened a portal but forgot to hide my tracks, as it were, and that's how Baudrous's wizards traced me. Bertilack, I'm so sorry for this. Can you ever forgive me?"

"My friend," said Bertilack. "You've clearly nothing to be sorry for. If anything, you should be congratulated."

"Congratulated?" said Thorn in surprise.

"If you hadn't given away your presence, Baudrous may have waited much longer and built his forces up even more. As it stands, you've forced him to move ahead of schedule, and for this, we're all grateful."

Thorn hadn't thought of this perspective. Instead of a mistake, his lack of concentration might be the crucial element they needed to win this war. "I'd been so caught up with berating myself that I hadn't considered any good could've come from my actions."

Bertilack smiled. "Hurry now. I want your dragon ready to go battle as soon as possible."

"Of course!" Thorn said before dashing off to equip his dragon.

"That was a nice thing to say," Caldor said. "I was beginning to think he'd never get over it."

"I only told him the truth. If we've forced Baudrous's hand prematurely as I suspect we have, then we may still have a fighting chance."

"My armour will definitely give us that," Keldon said, speaking for the first time in the conversation.

"Yes, tell us," Bertilack said. "What's the secret to this armour of yours? Is there enough for all of us?"

The dwarf eyed his brother slyly and motioned them to follow him to the workshop's back. It was extremely dark here, like no other place in the building. The only light came from the furnace's glow in the adjacent room.

Bertilack and the others stumbled forwards behind the dwarf, tripping over bits of machinery and metallic debris as they went.

Keldon summoned Argast, who promptly gestured to several torches on the wall. They burst into flames and illuminated the room, making all assembled gasp in wonder.

Arrayed before them were enormous suits of dragon armour, physically identical to Argast's armour except for personal details fitted for each dragon. The baroque equipment hung on the wall in all its glory.

"Amazing . . . you were able to finish this many suits with the time you had . . . ," Bertilack said awestruck.

"I'm inclined to agree," Charlock said. "Your craftsmanship and speed rival that of the dragons of old."

"Such a compliment from you is praise indeed. However, I cannot take all the credit for Kazar had a hand also in this work," said the dwarf before turning, and admiring his work with a tear in his eye.

Caldor advanced to touch the metal. "What's this made out of?"

"It's mine and Kazar's own blend of magic and metal. We're calling it dragon steel," Keldon said. "Beautiful, isn't it?"

The group all agreed with his assessment.

"Unfortunately, I haven't had time to finish all the suits. Many still need more work, and few have been equipped to the dragons," Keldon said sadly.

"How much more time will you need?" Bertilack asked.

"A few more hours to finish the construction, and then time after that to equip the armour to the dragons."

"We'll just have to give you that time then, won't we?" Batras said as he entered the room with Gawain. "But it won't be easy. Bertilack, we have a problem. You should come and look."

Upon seeing the minotaur's face, Bertilack didn't argue. He and the assembled group followed Batras as he left the forge and headed to the spire's upper levels.

"What's going on, Batras? What happened after we left the fight?" Bertilack asked as they ascended the stairs.

"The ice dragons that were left were no match for our strength, but they weren't alone," the minotaur said grimly. "From the vortex that'd formed in the sky came more ice dragons and something else . . . large skeletal dinosaur-like flying creatures in huge numbers. We retreated here before we were overwhelmed."

They emerged on the spire's newly constructed battlements. What greeted them was a very different picture from the one they'd left scant moments before. The darkness that crept through the sky had surrounded the spire. Only the sky above the citadel itself was still clear. Ahead, where the vortex had been, all was darkness. The only thing the warriors could see was the area below them that'd been illuminated by the light coming from the spire's top.

"Upon seeing the vortex extend, we managed to get Kazar to erect what he called a light field to stop the darkness from reaching the spire's walls," Batras explained. "It should give us a brief respite."

Bertilack looked into the swirling maelstrom. The darkness beyond seemed almost alive. It continually battered against the shield like a living being and had effectively made them blind to their enemy's movements.

"Get one of the wizards up here. I want to know what our options are," instructed Bertilack. He could hear the fear in his own voice as Gawain departed to carry out his command.

"Something emerges from the darkness!"

Caldor yelled.

Bursting from the darkness like fish from the water, ice dragons descended on the spire, each one carrying a warrior on its back.

"Battle stations, all of you! Caldor, head down! Warn the others!"

One of the ice dragon's warrior counterparts leapt from its back to engage Bertilack, a further pair following to engage Batras.

"No, brother," Caldor said, dodging a vicious swing from one of the dark warriors. "I cannot leave you."

"Go! We need the others out here," Bertilack said, momentarily disengaging from his opponent in the hope of appealing to the elf's sense of duty.

Caldor hesitated but agreed to Bertilack's request.

"And hurry," Batras grunted as another warrior dropped in front of him.

Caldor paused again only briefly before descending the stairs.

"You ready?" Bertilack said to Charlock.

The black dragon nodded and took to the sky, growing to full-size to engage the ice dragons in the air. He was swiftly followed by Khrishaw, who'd been resting on Batras's shoulder.

Around them, the dark-garbed warriors

stopped their steeds as they viewed the great dragons rising into the air. Each of the evil dragons possessed a black armoured warrior and moved to intercept the dragons of the spire.

"A sight to behold, aren't they?" Bertilack said as he and Charlock grappled with the lead dragon and rider.

"That's nothing!" rasped the dark warrior deflecting Bertilack's attack. "Our master is the eldest of the dragons. All others are mere shadows before him!"

Bertilack just about managed to dodge a fierce jab as Charlock put some distance between himself and the ice dragon. Now closer to the light barrier, Bertilack could better see his attacker's features. He was young but not as young as Mark had been before the change. His opponent's face was nonetheless haggard by time. His eyes spoke of the harshness viewed in this world before his time. He closed once again with Bertilack, both clashing and wheeling each other, trying to get a hold of the other and deal a mortal blow.

Bertilack was struck by how skilled his opponent truly was. So far, he'd managed to match him move for move. Bertilack wondered how he could be so skilled. As the dark warrior came on, Bertilack deliberately blocked his attack with the flat of his blade and used all his might to push his opponent back.

"Why fight with Baudrous? You're human like me. You should be joining us, not battering us."

The dark warrior lowered his weapon and shook his head as their dragons once again parted.

"I'm nothing like you. You and those who follow you are weak and too afraid to accept the power our master brings."

Once again, the dark warrior came on lunging and slashing, with Bertilack struggling to parry the flurry of attacks as Charlock wrestled his own burden. Clearly, these warriors were a cut above the fodder they'd fought before.

"You're wrong, cur," Bertilack snarled as their swords clashed again. "Baudrous is evil incarnate. He cares nothing for you or our world!" Bertilack once again managed to force his opponent back.

"I'll cleave you in two," said the dark warrior, his eyes wide and mad.

Bertilack could barely fathom what could've happened to turn him this way. The dark warrior came rushing forwards again. In his haste, he misjudged the reach of Bertilack's emerald blade, and the sword's point smashed squarely into his ribcage. Blood poured from the wound, and the light faded from his eyes. Yet, he wouldn't be undone. Taking the blade in his hand, the dark warrior drew himself towards Bertilack but, at the last moment, couldn't find the strength to wield his sword. He spat from blood-flecked lips onto Bertilack's armour and smiled bitterly.

"You might've killed me, but my master waits for you, and he'll be your undoing."

Beneath him, the ice dragon roared. Momentarily distracted, it allowed Charlock to rent a great hole in its chest and fell from the sky.

"If your master has the courage to face me, then death awaits him. Go to your grave, evil one. Don't fret, your master will be with you soon."

Bertilack cared little if he'd been heard, for no sooner had his foe disappeared from sight than another was upon him, and the dance of death continued.

CHAPTER TWENTY

The battle atop the ramparts was short-lived once the two dragons flew into the air. The ice dragons erupting from the darkness were dumbfounded when they suddenly found themselves facing Charlock and Khrishaw on the other side.

Without the ice dragons to deploy them, the dark warriors soon ceased their attack. Still, this was by no means the end of the fight. Bertilack surmised that this was merely a preliminary engagement meant to test their defences. Posting Gawain and Batras as guards with their accompanying dragons, he once again retreated to the spire's bowels.

Their current problems were escalating out of control, Baudrous's forces seemed limitless, and they'd soon wear down the spire's warriors. He needed some way of reining them in.

Entering the forge, he found that both the aquatic dragons had been fitted with their armour, as had Sharos, who was even now preparing to relieve Khrishaw on the watch so that the red dragon could be equipped for battle. Charlock was also having his armour fitted, and Bertilack walked to his side.

"The armour suits you, my friend," Bertilack said.

"It feels wonderful," the great dragon said. "How can we lose now with such power?"

Even with the armour, Bertilack doubted it would be enough. Still, the scene before him was quite spectacular. Kazar's air elementals were moving armour and tools about as if they were straight out of a fantasy movie filled with child-like imagination and wonder.

"Where are Keldon and Caldor? I'd like to speak with them on a matter most urgent."

Charlock lowered his head so the elemental could install his helmet plate. "I believe they're both in the next chamber, although what they're doing is a mystery to me."

Caldor had returned briefly with Kazar and Gawain to assist in the battle on the ramparts, but had disappeared shortly after that, and Bertilack hadn't seen him since.

"Thank you, Charlock. Try and get these puffs of air to hurry along," the knight said, indicating the air elementals. "If I'm right, we'll be needing your help and the armours very soon."

An idea was forming in Bertilack's mind, and a smile sketched his face. If it worked, he wouldn't have to worry about being outnumbered. Walking into the dimly lit area, he didn't at first see his brothers. Both Keldon and Caldor were seated at a small table off to one corner of the structure, and it took some time to locate them.

"Brothers," he called as he approached. "We missed you on the ramparts, Caldor. Where'd you go?"

Caldor looked up from the diagram that he and Keldon were working on to regard his brother.

"Apologies, but I had a sudden inspiration," Caldor said, directing Bertilack's attention to the drawing in front of them. "I asked Keldon whether the armour he'd built could be changed so that it could emanate an aura of light. If possible, we could fly the dragons through that fog of darkness."

"Damn unsporting that," Keldon growled. "A warrior should at least be able to see his enemy."

"Agreed," said Bertilack. "I had the same idea. It could be our only hope of breaching the enemy's lines."

"I fear, though, we're approaching this the wrong way," Keldon said. "We're going to need Kazar's help."

"Of course, he created the light barrier to keep the darkness back," said Bertilack. "With luck, he can distort the spell to react with the armour."

"I'm unsure if we can lay the spell on all the armour. Would Kazar have that much strength?" asked Keldon.

"We'd have to ask Thorn to assist him," said Caldor.

Bertilack pondered this for a moment. "We'll need most, if not all, of our warriors battling. If this isn't possible, then it's a fool's errand."

"Not necessarily," Caldor said. "Perhaps

there's a way to shut this darkness off at the source."

"But the source will be Baudrous," Bertilack said. "Fighting him in his home territory is madness."

Baudrous was, after all, the author of all their troubles. It was doubtful he'd trust anyone but himself with the power for this spell.

"That may not be the case," the elf said. "When Thorn and I were in the other dimension, we heard tell of a massive fortress that Baudrous had constructed, a structure invisible to all but his most trusted lieutenants. We found out that he was storing his magic within it to use as a weapon against us. Try as we might, we could never find it, but Thorn said if he'd brought his magic tools from his lab, he could have."

"And you believe that Baudrous is somehow channelling his energies through this structure to create the darkness?" Bertilack asked.

"Considering how badly we must've bruised his ego, I'm sure he'll want to be at the forefront of our defeat."

Baudrous was so confident in his abilities and of his eventual victory that he'd undoubtedly be nearby. Still, would the evil dragon trust someone else with his power? Perhaps he would if he'd designed some form of restraint to keep his power in check.

"It might just work," Bertilack said after a long silence. "Quickly, fetch Kazar and Thorn and put them to work. I want three dragons at least outfitted with this magical shining armour, including Charlock."

Caldor stood up in protest. "I'll go in your place."

"No, brother. If we're wrong and Baudrous isn't where he's supposed to be, it'll be putting you and whoever goes with you at great risk. I'm the only one who stands a chance of defeating him."

Bertilack could see Caldor's displeasure.

"I'm going with you anyway. You're not leaving me behind, understood?"

Bertilack sighed. "Very well."

"That leaves just one other," Keldon said. "And it'll have to be one of the wizards if you hope to find a way into this invisible fortress."

"But which one?" Caldor said.

"Why don't we let them decide?" Bertilack said. "They know their abilities better than we do."

Bertilack's brothers nodded and filed out to look for the two enchanters. Once they'd gone, Bertilack was left alone to his thoughts to ponder his plan's effectiveness. It was daring, he had to admit, but could he ask the others to put their lives on the line for what was essentially a gamble? There were just too many variables and not enough time to consider them all.

Charlock entered the room, bowing under the lower ceiling, his armour was still unfinished, and the elementals struggled to fix it as the dragon moved.

"Did you hear our plan then?" Bertilack asked.

Charlock smiled before answering. "Of course! I have exceptional hearing, you know."

"Really?" Bertilack said comically. "I'd never have guessed! How'd you keep it from me for so long?"

"It wasn't easy," the dragon said, still carrying on the joke. "But I managed."

Bertilack smiled once more and then grew serious. "How do you like our chances?"

Charlock shifted his great frame uncomfortably in the doorway before he answered. "Difficult to say, but one thing of which I'm sure is you'll not do this alone. I'll be by your side, regardless of the outcome."

Bertilack grew more confident from the dragon's words and stood to walk over to him. "I'd never have doubted you, Charlock, but I must ask you something," Bertilack said, his face grim. "If we're to do this, cross into the unknown, we may have no way of returning. If Baudrous is on the other side, he'll undoubtedly be waiting for us, and if not, we'll still not know what we may face. I don't want my brothers coming through with us. Once the gateway to Baudrous's realm opens, we'll cross alone, and seal it, so that none will follow us."

Charlock looked at him, shocked. "But, Bertilack, that'd mean we'd have to lie to them both!"

"I know, but it's the only way. Hurry now. Before they return, you must be ready to leave."

Charlock did as he was bid. Still, the black dragon clearly wasn't happy. Never had he felt so bad at having to obey one of Bertilack's instructions, but he would comply. Though he didn't quite understand the knight's reasoning, he'd still follow him.

This was as Bertilack had suspected, which was why he'd told the dragon now. Charlock was more than capable of keeping a secret, and Bertilack needed to know that during the fighting, when it became heavy, Charlock wouldn't hesitate to follow Bertilack's instructions. He watched for a time as Charlock was outfitted with the last of his armour before leaving to find the mages himself. Time was of the essence, and Bertilack was eager to get this plan underway as soon as possible.

***

Almost an hour later, Bertilack stood with Charlock on the dragon ports. It hadn't been difficult to turn the spire defence spell to their own use, but the task had taken a lot out of Kazar. The wizard was now resting comfortably in his room.

During the time, there'd been sporadic attacks across the spire's defences, and so far, Gawain and Batras had kept them at bay with help from the other warriors when needed. However, it was these times that made Bertilack worried, for it seemed that each attack was becoming stronger, and then it all just stopped.

For a time, they had calm, but Bertilack knew this was only the beginning. Soon Baudrous would launch a massive attack.

Charlock had already been kitted out with his new armour, and Bertilack had to admit this made the already fearsome-looking dragon appear even more daunting. The armour was black and very baroque. It possessed a main chest and back guard extending outward to Charlock's wings. In addition, he'd also been fitted with leg and tail guards for extra protection.

The plan was now in motion. Caldor and Sharos had been fully equipped, with Thorn and Khrishaw just finishing up. It'd been decided that Batras's mount would serve as Thorn's conveyance for this affair. His orders were simple—get Thorn to where he was going, open the portal, and get back as soon as possible to defend the spire. Once the enemy saw them coming, Bertilack figured all hell would break loose.

The pair surveyed the darkness before them.

"A dangerous task, isn't it?" Charlock said.

"Indeed, my friend, indeed," Bertilack answered, his mind elsewhere. Bertilack fancied that he could see the darkness shifting differently as if it sensed the oncoming clash. Any moment Keldon would appear and give them the go-ahead to fly. They just had to be patient.

***

"What's taking so long?" Khrishaw rumbled as Keldon busied himself with the armour improvements.

"Not much longer. Your frame is slightly more irregular than the others," the dwarf gasped as he frantically hammered more armour plates into place. He did so hate to be hurried. He was an artist—didn't people understand the work he put in to accomplish his goals? Sometimes he received no respect.

The armour on Khrishaw had taken twice as long as usual, and Keldon was at a loss to explain it. It'd taken so long that they had to move the operation to the dragon ports to speed things up. Thorn had been here for a while but had departed once the spell was complete, claiming he had to gather more equipment from his lab for use in the coming endeavour.

Keldon glanced upwards briefly to observe the evil shroud that had encircled them. He smiled to himself. The enemy thought they were invincible, but that was all going to change once his work was complete. Oh yes, it would all change.

"There, finished!" the dwarf said smartly. "And not a moment too soon. Right, you big gecko?"

"I wish you wouldn't call me that," Khrishaw growled. "Besides, what're you doing standing around? You must get Thorn and tell the others we're ready!"

"Yes, your majesty," the dwarf bowed mockingly. "I've only just spent the last hour or so building that rig for you to protect your lofty britches from certain doom, and that's the thanks I get?"

"I'm sorry," Khrishaw said. "But we're in a hurry."

"I know, I know," Keldon sighed. "I'm going, but incidentally, if you're really that sorry, you can do me a favour and keep an eye on that brother of mine. Make damn sure he comes back alive."

"On my honour, no harm shall befall him whilst I fly close."

"Thank you, and good luck."

Khrishaw nodded grimly as Keldon left and rushed down the tunnel. He'd gone a scant few metres when he bumped into Thorn.

"I trust everything is in order," said Thorn.

"Aye, that it is, my friend. Look after yourself out there, and make sure you bring your pointy-eared self back here in one piece, you got me?"

"But of course. I've complete faith in your abilities as a craftsman and even more faith in my abilities as a sorcerer."

The two bid each other goodbye and went their separate ways. Keldon couldn't wait to break the news to Bertilack that they were finally ready. He picked up his pace when he entered the vicinity of Charlock's dragon port but was instantly thrown off his feet as something impacted the spire.

"Damn," the dwarf said as he struggled to his feet. "What was that?"

Another blast struck the spire and then another with alarming frequency.

"Oh no, we must be under attack! I've got to get to Bertilack!"

As more tremors rippled through the castle, Keldon braced himself before he toppled over. He hugged the wall and inched further along the tunnel as more impacts hit and masonry fell from the ceiling. He could see the tunnel opening ahead, which was now and again illuminated by gouts of flame as Charlock tried to repel an as yet unseen attacker. Keldon saw Bertilack in the doorway as the knight struggled with an ebony armoured assailant.

"Hold on, brother!" Keldon yelled, cradling his hammer. Charging in and coming from the dark warrior's blind side, the dwarf struck out with all his force and caved the side of the man's face in.

His opponent went limp and fell to the ground as Bertilack watched, stunned.

"Your timing is impeccable. Tell me, are the preparations for Khrishaw complete?"

"That's why I'm here, but it seems instead

bailing you out of tight spots is a full-time job for me."

Bertilack suppressed a witty retort as he scanned the sky for more opponents though none for the time were forthcoming. Bertilack couldn't believe the timing. Just a few more moments, and he'd have been on his way.

"What're you standing around for?" Keldon said. "Get on that dragon of yours and get out of here."

"I can't. If this is Baudrous's main attack, I must be here to help."

"I can see what you're thinking," Keldon said. "And don't. If you'd gone up there earlier, you'd have been caught in the first attack wave."

Bertilack couldn't decide the best course of action. The decision, however, was taken out of his hands as Charlock's jaws came down and clamped on the knight's armour, dragging him off his feet and depositing him unceremoniously in the saddle.

"Charlock," Bertilack sputtered. "What're you doing?"

The dragon's head came back round so he could more easily engage with the knight. "Beginning our mission. Both Khrishaw and Sharos will be ready to fly in moments. If we aren't there to do our part, the entire plan will collapse, and their lives will be in danger."

Bertilack still couldn't bring himself to abandon the spire and his friends.

"That dragon of yours has at least a sense of priority," Keldon said. "We'll be fine until your return, but if you don't beat Baudrous and end this spell, none of us are getting out of here alive."

It went against the grain to flee a battle such as this, but Charlock was right. They were needed elsewhere.

"Okay, I guess you're right, Keldon. I trust you can raise this port's defence and lower the portcullis?"

"If I can't, I'll hang up my hammer. Now get going."

Beneath Bertilack, Charlock needed no further encouragement. The mighty black dragon beat his wings as hard as he could and lifted himself and Bertilack clear into the skies. Behind them, Keldon rushed to close the gate that would seal the invaders from the spire.

Bertilack risked a hesitant glance behind him. "Good luck, my friends," he said as the gate slid firmly into place. "I pray you remain safe."

Within moments the spire fell away, and Charlock plunged into the darkness. Bertilack whipped his head forwards as the clawing mist enveloped them, threatening to drag them into a world of darkness and despair. The darkness was like some huge living entity threatening to rob them of their minds and courage. Bertilack found that for all his strength, he couldn't fight the madness. He lost control and felt his grip slacken on Charlock's reigns.

It was then that the armour burst into life. Charlock's body was covered in a bright veil of energy that brought Bertilack back from the dark abyss's edge. He floundered for a moment, unsure what to do, his mind reeling. Still, little by little, he made it back to reality. He gripped Charlock's reigns more firmly, and the dragon turned his head to regard him.

"Almost thought I'd lost you for a moment."

"Almost," said Bertilack, his voice weak. "Tell me, are we still on course?"

"Yes, the others are up ahead. See for yourself."

In the distance, Bertilack saw them first as two bright halos against the dark mist. As they approached, he could discern other shapes in the gloom—ice dragons and undead beasts assailed them from all sides. Still, the two riders fought without wavering.

Charlock and Bertilack approached. The dragon released a thunderous roaring challenge to the assembled winged nightmares.

At heart, it seemed that the ice dragons were cowards, for they fled almost immediately, leaving only the undead that were easily dispatched once Bertilack had fully joined the fray.

"Brother!" Caldor yelled. "Glad to see you could join us," the elf said, a smile playing on his lips.

"You have my apologies. My hesitation nearly cost us dearly, but I'm here now. That's what matters. Tell me, do you know where the portal is to be found?"

"We don't," Thorn said. "But the dragons do. Sharos said he's been able to sense its presence since we entered the cloud."

"Is this true, Sharos?" Bertilack said.

"Indeed it is, but don't take my word for it. I'm sure that Charlock can detect it as well."

Bertilack looked to his mount, who turned and nodded in response.

"Can you take us to it, Charlock? Even if you can't see where you're going?"

"It won't be easy, but together we can manage."

"Then let us waste no more time!" Bertilack yelled. "Onwards to the portal and the world of Baudrous."

Charlock turned in response to his words and set off in the direction where he felt the portal's pull more tangible. Behind him, the other dragons formed in a rough v-shape, and together, the warriors probed the depths of the inky black darkness.

Resistance to their incursion was fierce, with countless unnamed horrors erupting from the mist to battle them. Creatures with too many heads or limbs flew towards them on black wings but found only death waiting for them when they closed with the knights of the spire.

Some of the creatures were so full of the darkness that they couldn't even stand the light from the enchanted armour and disintegrated on contact.

Bertilack found himself wondering what vile sorceries had Baudrous wrought to conjure these abominations. Even the ice dragons seemed hesitant at battling beside these chaos-spawned monstrosities, for they kept their distance in almost every engagement where the beasts fought.

In time though, the great portal was before them, pulsing with darkness and radiating waves of pure malice and hatred. It stood like a gaping sore in the sky.

For a while, no creatures erupted. Bertilack fancied that they'd never have a better chance.

"My friends, it's time! Thorn, come forwards and use your spells on this ring of darkness. We must be assured that when I pass its boundaries, I'll end up in Baudrous's stronghold."

Thorn motioned his dragon forwards and began work, weaving his spell. He had to be quick. If Baudrous sensed something was wrong with the portal, he'd undoubtedly send agents to stop them.

Caldor urged Sharos forwards at this point so he'd be aligned with Charlock and Bertilack.

"Are you sure you're set on this course of action?" asked Caldor. The two stared together fixedly at the portal, and the elf felt a shiver run down his spine. "You know I'm more than willing to take your place at a moment's notice."

"Caldor, I've no doubt in my mind that my destiny, and our eventual victory, lie beyond this door," said Bertilack. He turned to face his brother. "We've changed considerably since meeting the dragons, haven't we, brother? Though you take your role as eldest very seriously, in these times, such thoughts for my safety are unnecessary. We both know I give this mission the best chance of success."

Caldor returned his brother's gaze. Even through the armour, he could still only see the young boy he'd had to save from being picked on at school. And yet he knew nothing he could say would shake Bertilack from his chosen course. This time he'd have to let his brother fight this foe alone and allow him to stand on his own two feet. With a tear in his eye, Caldor bowed respectfully and retook his place in the formation.

"Thorn, how are we doing?" Bertilack asked the wizard as sparks of magical energy flew from the elve's hand.

"Nearly there," the elf said through gritted teeth. "I've locked onto your destination, but it's taking all my will to bring this side of the portal into alignment with the other side." Thorn's hand came up to his chest, allowing his hand to grasp his power amulet. "Once I make contact, you'll only have seconds to enter the portal. I can't hold it longer than that."

"Understood," Bertilack said, his face a mask of grim determination. "Ready, Charlock?"

The dragon swung his head around and merely nodded, for it seemed he too was having trouble. The storm around them was rising in intensity, and he, like the others, was having trouble remaining aloft.

"Bertilack!" Caldor yelled from behind. "We have company and lots of it!"

Bertilack turned in his saddle as much as he could and witnessed the arrival of no fewer than five ice dragons as well as an attendant menagerie of the flying undead. "Engage them as far away from the portal and Thorn as possible!" the green knight commanded.

"Right!" Caldor slapped the reigns hard against Sharos's silvery flanks, and the two spurred off to meet their enemy. However, it was an impossible battle. Even with the armour, those undead creatures had such numbers so as to be more than just a problem for the dragon and the elf—their only hope was that Thorn would be ready in time to help.

"I've done it!" Thorn finally yelled into the storm. "The gate is ready, but act quickly. I'm losing it already!"

Bertilack looked once more at his brother before indicating to Thorn his last command.

The elf mage tore his gaze away from the portal in Bertilack's direction and saw what the knight was trying to indicate.

"I'll aid him as soon as you're through. Now

hurry, or all we've done will be for naught!"

"Thank you, my friend," said Bertilack.

Sensing the swiftly receding energy stored in the portal gate, Charlock spurred the pair of them forwards and took them both into the magic circle.

Bertilack had scant moments to take in what was occurring before the vast gate's energy hit him, and he lost consciousness.

CHAPTER TWENTY-ONE

Darkness. By God, why was it so dark? Ah, but this darkness was a safe haven, a paradise. No one could hurt him here. It was a good place. A place to rest.

At the corner of his awareness, a voice called out a name. That name rang a bell ... *Bertilack* ... but where had he heard that name before?

Whatever. It didn't matter to him. He just wanted to sleep. He tried to shift his bulk and make himself more comfortable, but the floor was hard. And coupled with the irritating voice that kept repeatedly shouting that familiar name, he was finding it arduous to relax.

"Bertilack! Bertilack, are you okay?"

Of course, he was okay. He was more than okay . . . wait a minute . . . was he Bertilack? Was that his name? He struggled to remember anything before the great darkness. He remembered the silence, the calm, the peace, and the unyielding need just to sleep. Still, why couldn't he remember his own name?

"Bertilack, wake up. We'll be in danger if we stay here for much longer."

Danger? If only they hadn't gone through the portal, they wouldn't be in danger. Wait . . . portal? What portal?

Slowly, his memory returned. He remembered falling through the dimensional barrier, remembered the light, and recalled feeling the power of the place that'd surrounded them.

"Bertilack?"

He opened his eyes. "Charlock?"

"My fricnd, you're awake."

"Where are we?" the knight said.

They were lying on the floor of an immensely high-walled room. Try as he might, Bertilack couldn't see the room's ceiling, which was lost in the inky blackness, some fathomless distance above.

With Charlock's aide, he managed to stand and perceive what'd happened. The dragon prince had managed to stay conscious through most of the journey and said that as they travelled through the portal, he'd felt some other will set against them. Something that dwelt in this place had felt their approach and had sabotaged their efforts to make it here.

"Are we still where we need to be, though?" Bertilack asked. "If someone was trying to kill us, couldn't they have also changed the direction we were headed?"

Charlock pulled back away from the knight and looked around. "I believe we've made it to Baudrous's black fortress. Whoever was abusing the portal probably wouldn't have had the power to change its course against Thorn's will."

"With luck, our unseen adversary will think we perished in the portal. If not, we may find our way difficult to traverse."

Charlock nodded in agreement. Together, the

warrior and dragon made their way away from the portal.

The cavernous chamber in which they walked was immense beyond compare. The companions could only hope they were heading in the right direction.

After what seemed like an age trapped within the clawing darkness, Bertilack and Charlock found themselves confronted by a huge doorway consisting of two ornately carved panels that ascended into an arch.

"Who or what would need such a door? The size dwarfs even me," said Charlock.

Bertilack was inclined to agree and hoped that whatever it was, it wasn't still in residence.

"Nothing for it, I suppose, no other way to go."

Bertilack moved aside, allowing Charlock to focus his considerable strength against the door. The black dragon reared up on his hind legs and applied all of his weight to the task. Gradually, the great carved doors gave way, opening into another equally dim-looking corridor.

Bertilack stepped through first, sword at the ready but was surprised to find no guards or signs of life. "I don't understand, Charlock. Where's the welcome committee?" the knight said, still looking around as if expecting demons to begin flooding out the walls.

"Perhaps our hosts are too busy elsewhere. The simple fact that we're not accosted straight away by our enemy would attest to that."

"Baudrous's overconfidence in his own abilities will be his downfall. Well, we can't stay here forever. Which way would you like to go?"

Charlock glanced around them, sniffing the air, trying to make up his mind. "I'm detecting a low sub-surface pulse of magic. It emanates from that direction."

He pointed his scaled snout to the right, and the pair moved together but this time more guardedly. In the last chamber, there'd been plenty of room to manoeuvre. With Charlock's superior eyesight, they would've seen their attackers long before they were seen. Unfortunately, they didn't have those luxuries in these confined tunnels, so stealth would have to do.

Following the tunnel led them to a dark flight of stairs that seemed large enough to facilitate an immense creature of some sort. The stairs were easily traversable. Bertilack and Charlock reached the bottom without incident before continuing down another winding passageway.

"I hate how quiet it is," Bertilack whispered.

"It won't be for long," Charlock said as they neared a turning. "I sense we're not alone."

Bertilack nodded, turning the corner and standing once again before an immense set of metal doors. However, unlike the first, these particular doors were guarded—a group of skeletal warriors, each mounted on some form of fast-moving dinosaur. In the dim light, Bertilack could not make out the species. In a few moments, the point would be moot.

The undead riders turned as one towards their new visitor and charged headlong towards Bertilack, shouting silent screams from long dead throats. The effect was daunting, but Bertilack held his ground. Each skeletal rider wielded a wickedly barbed lance in mockery of the ancient knighthoods of medieval day, and each had it pointed at Bertilack.

Charlock brought his wing down in front of Bertilack to stave off the horde's advance. Bertilack, however, wouldn't allow Charlock to be hurt for his protection and leapt out from behind his partner's wing. He would apologise and thank the dragon for the thought later, but the young warrior wouldn't back down from a fight.

Bertilack prepared well for the charge and

tried to calculate how best to strike his enemies. Their lances were longer than his blade, so he'd have to get underneath their guard whilst avoiding the undead mounts' teeth. They were almost on him. Bertilack prepared to fight but heard a great intake of breath from behind him.

Quickly realising what Charlock had planned and berating himself for not seeing the dragon's plan sooner, he rushed behind the dragon's outstretched wing again as Charlock released a torrent of blistering flame that consumed all but two of the skeletal creatures.

The remaining pair approached. Now it was truly time for Bertilack to be involved. Leaping once more from the dragon's protection, he engaged the last two. Taken out of their charge by Charlock's assault, the skeletal warriors were less difficult to battle, but this didn't make them easy by any means.

Bertilack parried a blow from the nearest skeleton's lance and then kicked its mount hard in the ribcage, crushing the bones. Injured and taken out of stride, the beast fell to its knees only to be beheaded by the knight as its rider was flung free towards the waiting dragon's jaws. Charlock made quick work of his opponent, but Bertilack was still in danger.

The second rider was faster than Bertilack had thought and managed to pin Bertilack down with its claws. The knight struggled to free himself but found that he couldn't move his sword arm. His strength couldn't break the skeleton's grip and lift the blade.

Bertilack swore, but he wasn't finished. After all, he still had another arm. The skeletal creature snapped at him as he tried to wrest his other hand free, its fetid breath choking him. Bertilack dodged several attempts before finally managing to free his other arm. Bringing it up, he clouted the beast with his heavily mailed fist repeatedly, eventually shattering the creature's head.

The skeletal rider had learnt much from its friend's mistake and leapt free before the mount fell, landing on the floor a few feet away from Bertilack, who was still struggling under the fallen creature's weight.

Seeing what it thought to be a golden opportunity, the skeletal warrior charged again, seeking to throttle the knight with his bare hands. Charlock, on the other hand, had a different idea. He'd positioned himself better in the narrow confines and now stood ready to assist. He effortlessly extended a claw and destroyed the skeletal warrior before disentangling Bertilack.

"I'm willing to bet that whatever we seek lies beyond that door," the knight said as he regarded the immense doors before them.

"Shall I open them?" Charlock asked.

"Yes," Bertilack said. "But carefully. I don't like the way this feels."

The fact they'd so far met little opposition unnerved Bertilack. If their information was accurate, they were in the heart of an enemy stronghold. So, why wasn't it more heavily guarded?

The dragon pulled his wings tight into his body to better fit down the confined passage before moving to place his hands on the door. Strangely, however, this was unnecessary for the doors opened by themselves as they approached.

Bertilack leapt back, sword drawn, and braced himself for the worst. He thought this was the reason there'd been no guards. They'd been lured here into this corridor so that Charlock would be restrained in movement and easily overcome. Bertilack cursed himself inwardly for his mistake but was surprised to find no hordes of creatures leaping forth. The door had just opened by itself into another dimly lit chamber, and in the centre of the room glowed an immense ruby light that pulsed with an almost heartbeat-like rhythm.

"Well, that was anticlimactic," said Bertilack. He stepped through the door and was instantly aware that he and Charlock weren't alone.

The red light emanated from an orb in the room's centre but standing beside the orb was one of Baudrous's cloaked sorcerers.

"I knew I didn't like the feel of this," Bertilack said as they neared the motionless form.

Charlock growled in agreement. The red orb emanated a malevolence most foul that Charlock found at once both familiar and strangely different. He couldn't place where he'd felt that energy before.

Bertilack continued his approach towards the motionless figure when it suddenly turned around, revealing an elderly man's features. He stared through the pair as if they didn't exist before speaking in an earthy yet tired voice.

"My master said you'd come. It was inevitable."

The elderly figure appeared unperturbed by the pair's sudden arrival. In fact, he acted as if Bertilack and Charlock were beneath his notice and returned his gaze to the ruby orb.

Bertilack looked at Charlock and shrugged. He'd expected many things to be beyond the great doors, but this wasn't exactly what he'd had in mind. However, never one to be so easily dismissed, Bertilack once again advanced upon the man.

"Excuse me, but who the hell are you, and what in the world are you doing here?" the knight asked. He waited for a few moments but received no answer.

"Listen, friend. I suppose you know by now that this is a terrible place to be just standing around in. I'd like to affirm whose side you're on."

At this, the old man turned. His eyes crackled briefly with magic energy, and all of a sudden, Bertilack found himself being hurled across the chamber. He crashed into the room's far side and winced in surprise and pain. Charlock roared his mightiest bellow, fully preparing to leap upon the old human. Bertilack, however, was back on his feet and bade the dragon to stop.

"That was a cheap shot, but at least we know your allegiance lies with that twin-headed snake."

"You dare insult the master, you foul-mouthed little bug?" the man roared, showing for the first time some hint of emotion. "I'll tear out your heart! I'll boil the blood in your veins. Don't think my powers will be turned aside by your armour as other weaker spells have. Mine are too powerful, even for you!"

"That still doesn't answer my question," Bertilack said, his head ringing from the fall.

"Not that it matters," the man said. "But my name is Scott Thomas. I freed Master from the ice and have been with him from the beginning . . ."

Bertilack surmised that this man was clearly deranged. He seemed to talk to himself more than the knight and enjoyed reciting his tale. Still, at least it would allow Bertilack to approach. If he could get near enough, he could take this lunatic down without killing him.

"I bet you're wondering what I'm doing here now. Of course, it's not like your feeble brain could understand, but I'll speak slowly . . ."

Bertilack continued to approach and said nothing, hoping the sorcerer would stay in his dreamland.

Charlock watched his friend's movements and stood still, realising his intentions.

"My time with Master has been well spent. I've gained power above and beyond that of mortal men, and soon, when the last of my master's armies cross over into your dimension, he'll rein supreme with me at his side."

The insane robed figure stared off into space for a moment as if picturing his dream unfolding. Then he abruptly turned to face Bertilack.

"I know what you plan, fool," the maniac growled. "You think me unaware of you edging closer. Perhaps you wish me a quick death, but your efforts are wasted and your logic flawed."

Again, the man's eyes crackled with energy.

"Wait!" Bertilack said, hoping to buy more time. "Tell me more of your tale."

The old man stopped, and the energy faded from his eyes. "Why should I?" the man asked inquisitively.

"If I'm to die by the hands of Baudrous's strongest mage, I'd at least like to know his full story."

It was a terrible excuse, thought Bertilack. Still, perhaps he was just crazy enough to go for it.

"Yes, I suppose you're right. It's the least I can do, for soon you shall die," said the man, wiping a tear from his eye. "Very well. So, as I was saying before, I freed Baudrous from the ice. It was I that first awoke him in this world. In return, he gave me a position of power and charged me later with ensuring that this ruby orb stays intact, allowing the black mist to stray over your dimension. A most impressive plan, if I do say so myself."

The maniacal laughter that followed Scott's rant was all the indication Bertilack needed. He rushed forwards and brought his sword around in an arc, focusing his efforts on his blade's flat so that he'd only knock his opponent unconscious.

However, his strike never connected.

Scott never let his guard down and used his powers once again to repel Bertilack and send him flying.

Charlock reared up and belched forth a sheet of white-hot flame towards the wizard. The flames came as a great wave but dissolved and fell short of their mark. The dragon looked at the melting flame, stupidly wondering what'd just happened.

"So, you're supposed to be the greatest of the light dragons? And yet, you couldn't sense the shield I'd erected. Pity, such pity," said Scott. He raised his arms, allowing bolts of energy to shoot out and impact Charlock's wings and chest.

The magic projectiles cleaved easily through the great dragon's armour and deep into his flesh, forcing him to roar in pain and outrage. Stumbling, Charlock fell backwards into the wall. Knocking his head, he hit the ground and lay still.

Scott naturally believed his work was done. Baudrous had said that he wasn't to harm either of these particular enemies. His task was to subdue them for torture later. He turned back to the ruby-coloured globe, a faint smile playing on his lips as he considered how easy their defeat had been.

However, had he been watching more closely, he'd have noticed movement from the pair.

Bertilack had just about been awake in time to see Charlock injured. Slowly, all the time watching Scott for movement, the green knight rose to his feet. He looked briefly to Charlock and saw the great dragon's eyes flutter open. Nodding to the dragon, Bertilack brought his sword up and crept around to Scott's blind side. In his last failed attempt, he was hoping not to kill the sorcerer. However, this time, he was afraid there'd be no alternative. If he didn't overcome his enemy soon, there might not be a spire to return to.

Using slow, deliberate movements, Bertilack approached the robed maniac, but as he did, a shimmering force appeared, and denied the knight access.

"Admiring my force field?" Scott smiled. "After your earlier attempt at attacking me, I thought it prudent to take more precautions."

"Do you fear us, sorcerer?" Bertilack said, testing the field with his sword's tip.

"On the contrary," Scott replied. "I merely have no more time to deal with the likes of you. I've already expended enough energy on your account."

Ending the conversation, Scott once again

turned his back on the knight. Bertilack fancied he could hear light chanting from the mage.

Considering the need for secrecy well and truly over, Charlock rose to his feet and came to stand at Bertilack's side. He brought his claws up and tested the field's strength for himself. Pushing down on it with all his might, he was surprised to find that even his strength wasn't enough.

"Blast that mage," the dragon growled. "We don't have time for this."

"Charlock, you know much about magic," said Bertilack. "Wouldn't the mage concentrating on his current spell added to the energy it takes to keep up this personal force field be rather taxing?"

"Indeed," the dragon said. "Especially if the other spell he's casting is a strong one."

"Like, say, keeping a huge dimensional portal open and flooding a dimension with magical mist?"

"Yes, just like that," the dragon answered. "Why?"

"I wonder what would happen if we were to apply more pressure to the shield. Both of us attacking and hammering at it simultaneously, wouldn't it take more energy and concentration to keep intact?"

Charlock at once saw what the knight was

hinting at. If they could apply more pressure and drain the wizard's magic, he'd have to stop one of the spells to compensate. He only hoped they could do enough. Scott had already demonstrated that he was a formidable foe.

Bertilack struck the barrier with his sword as hard as he could whilst Charlock swung at it with his claws. They rained blow after blow upon the shield, and after a while, it appeared to be working.

Scott faltered in his chanting, and his face wrinkled even more in concentration. "Fools! You only serve to tire yourselves!" he rasped. "None can break that spell!"

Under normal circumstances, that might've been true, but this was far from normal circumstances. Scott couldn't even force the tiredness from his voice. He'd obviously been working the spell for Baudrous since the attack began, and now he was almost spent.

"No!" the wizard cried in anger. "I won't be beaten!"

Yet the exertion was taking its toll, and still, the two warriors continued to strike at the shield.

"No, no, no!" Scott shrieked as the barrier flashed and died. Raising his hand, the wizard pointed them at Bertilack and struck the knight with an intense bolt of energy which coursed through Bertilack and forced the knight to his knees. Unfortunately for Scott, he only had time for one spell. From the other direction came Charlock in a rush, barrelling into the wizard and pinning him to the ground. Sitting atop his enemy, Charlock roared a roar that shook the very castle.

"Ha!" Scott laughed. "You might've defeated me, but this too was expected. Before my shield fell, I finished the spell. As long as the ruby globe is intact, the spell cannot be stopped. You lose!"

"Then we'll have to do something about that, won't we?" Bertilack said, his voice sounding weak as he limped towards the dragon and his prisoner.

"Impossible," Scott said. "There should've been enough magic in that last spell to finish you. How can you be alive?"

Bertilack continued to advance on the globe, his face determined. He could feel his strength return with every step. "Perhaps my armour is more resilient than you were led to believe," the knight said. "Now watch as I smash this little bauble to pieces."

Bertilack had almost reached his goal and brought his sword around in a wide arc.

"F-fool . . . do you really believe your weak

magic and strength can overcome the power of the orb?"

"The hesitation in your voice betrays you, mage."

As Bertilack brought down his blade, he heard Scott scream in despair. The dark mage struggled impotently against the dragon's grip as he watched his nemesis shatter the ruby globe.

"Fool! Do you realise what you've done? You've doomed us all."

Ruby crystal debris showered upon Bertilack, striking him with an immense concussive force. And though he was still standing, the castle around them began to crumble.

CHAPTER TWENTY-TWO

In the realm of the spire, the situation was looking grim. Even though the cloud that'd enveloped them had suddenly disappeared—dispelling many of Baudrous's creatures that needed it to survive—they were still hopelessly outnumbered.

After Bertilack's departure, Caldor had taken over leading the spire's defence. He'd returned to the front lines where he now flew, flanked by Batras and Gawain mounted on their respective dragons. The banishing of the darkness had given them a monetary lapse in fighting, but it wouldn't be long before conflict renewed.

"Bertilack must've succeeded," Gawain said from his position behind Caldor.

"Indeed. It now serves to highlight the fullness of our predicament," Caldor said as he surveyed the dark tide that struggled to assemble not minutes away from them.

"We should take them now," Batras said, growling. "If we hit them whilst they're confused, we can win this."

Caldor continued to stare off, making Batras think that he hadn't heard.

"Caldor, are you listening? I said—"

"It won't work," the grim-faced elf explained. "Even so disorganised, the enemy far outnumbers us. We cannot hope to win against them. Our only hope is battling under the protection of the spire. Only with all our powers together can we best that horde."

Feeling suitably chastised and more than a little irritated, Batras leaned back in his saddle.

"I think it'll work, Batras," Khrishaw said beneath the minotaur.

"Thank you, my friend, but Caldor is in charge, and his word is absolute."

Although Batras didn't like it, he preferred to lead from the front with less of this flying around and doing nothing all the time.

It was then that Gawain suddenly spoke up. "Hey, lads? What the heck is that?" the big knight said in a tone that could only be described as a deep shock. The others turned to see what'd so wrapped Gawain's attention. Before their eyes, something materialised on a distant mountain peeking east of the battlefield. At first, it was just an outline. Then it began to fill in. The shape was enormous and almost bigger than the spire. As it solidified, fear gripped the pit of Caldor's stomach.

Before them, grinning evilly was none other than Baudrous himself but grown to gargantuan size.

"Puny scum of light, prepare to die," the two mouths spoke, and though he was far away, Caldor was sure that all the spire's warriors heard the proclamation.

***

Bertilack and Charlock tore through what remained of the dark citadel. Scott had completely lost his mind during the last moments after the red orb shattered, and his body now lay a lifeless husk on Charlock's back. Bertilack couldn't bring himself to leave the crazed sorcerer there and had instructed Charlock to carry him.

"We have to get back to the portal," Bertilack said amidst the explosions and falling masonry brought on by the citadel's death throws.

"How can we be sure it's still open?"

"We can't, but at the moment, we've little choice."

Through the gaps, Bertilack could see what lay outside the citadel. It wasn't much, just an endless crimson void that boiled around them like an immense, unfathomable sea. Bertilack imagined that if they were trapped here, they wouldn't survive for long.

They approached the portal chamber. The great doors they'd passed through earlier still stood before them, looking ready to fall apart at any moment.

As Charlock drew closer, the right-side door tumbled forwards, forcing the dragon of light to leap out the way. Dust and debris erupted forth from the doors and impact crater.

"Another close one," said Bertilack.

There was hardly any building left, and what

remained was rapidly diminishing. Charlock continued to run full tilt with Bertilack holding on for dear life as they raced across the open floor. The support columns holding the ceiling failed and rolled towards the dragon and the knight. The dragon jumped and glided past as best he could. It was then that Bertilack finally saw the portal.

Suspended where it had been when they'd left, it still stood resolute with its swirling mass.

"Look, Charlock! The portal's still open!"

"Yes," the dragon grunted, concentrating. "It must be powered by some other means."

"Well, all that matters is that it's working."

"We may still have a problem," the dragon said, avoiding a large piece of side walling. "We've no idea if the portal is still set for our realm."

Bertilack looked behind them and stared into the increasingly growing red maelstrom.

"Anywhere's better than here."

Charlock was inclined to agree. In one fluid movement, the dragon folded his wings and leapt through the gateway. The journey this time seemed much faster. Erupting forth from the other side of the portal, Charlock struggled to remain aloft as he was thrown out and into the air.

Beyond them, the spire loomed large as life, its walls shining in the sunlight. As Charlock righted himself, Bertilack could better view his surroundings. What he saw shocked him and Charlock to the core of their beings.

Both armies had stopped fighting and stared at each other across the sky, but this wasn't the main problem. Neither was it the sight that'd so terrified Bertilack and Charlock. A small distance away, swelled to unbelievable proportions, Baudrous laughed as his leviathan-sized form stomped towards the spire.

Bertilack's warriors seemed transfixed by the horror of it all, and none moved to stop their nemesis from carrying out his evil plan. Baudrous's soldiers seemed content to allow their master to enjoy his fun and flew idly in the air, watching the spire's knights.

Charlock landed on a hill not too far off, so they could put Scott down and better assess the situation.

"What do we do now?" Charlock asked, watching the scene unfold.

It seemed that the evil red orb they'd shattered had done more than just keep the darkness going. Baudrous must've fed on its energy, for he now pulsed with a sickly red glow that radiated the same malicious aura as the orb. The only upside of this was that Baudrous's great bulk was taking its time to reach the spire.

"We do what we came here to do," Bertilack said, sliding off Charlock's back. "We take him down."

Charlock looked once again at Baudrous's great form and shook his head. "I see no victory for us here," the dragon said grimly.

Bertilack refused to listen. So far, for as long as they'd fought, there'd been a way. Some force, some guiding light, watched over them and had led them here. He was sure of it. They just had to continue having faith.

"Fortune favours the bold, my friend," Bertilack said, staring defiantly at the approaching monstrosity. "We'll find a way. I'm sure of it."

"Perhaps, but—"

At that moment, Bertilack's sword glowed a deep emerald green. Both he and Charlock stood perplexed as the blade not only glowed but grew larger and more radiant than it had ever been. Turning and twisting, it formed into an immense lance. Bertilack stumbled briefly under the weight and brought his other hand up to balance himself. Surely no footman nor horse rider could adequately wield such a weapon. No, this lance was meant to be mounted on a dragon. As Bertilack held it in his hands, he and Charlock heard a voice in their heads. It was the voice of the guardian, the one whom they'd addressed back at the hatchery caves where this had all begun.

"You hold in your hands now the instrument of dragonkind's salvation, the ever-lance. Forged millennia ago to ensure Baudrous's destruction, it was hidden within the ever-stone when it appeared that all would be lost to dragonkind. You are the chosen one. Only your courage and spirit combined could conjure the lance when it was truly needed, and now it'll always be yours when the time is right."

With that, the voice faded and left Bertilack and Charlock alone to ponder its words. Bertilack marvelled at the weapon in his hands. The instrument made to kill Baudrous was the awesome power that Bertilack had carried with him all this time. And now, with Baudrous at his zenith of power and inhabiting a body that couldn't readily avoid the great weapon, they finally had a chance.

"Charlock, did you hear the guardian?"

"I did. We've been given a most wondrous gift!"

Bertilack climbed into Charlock's saddle.

"Shall we get their attention then?"

Positioning himself at the hill's very edge,

where he was more visible to the two armies, the great dragon reared up and released a great and immense roar across the battlefield.

Ahead the two warring forces turned to observe this new disturbance, and even Baudrous himself stopped his advance to see what'd distracted him.

Bertilack brought the lance up and positioned it in the saddle so he could wield it effectively in flight.

"Head for Baudrous," Bertilack instructed. "With luck, our friends will see what we're doing and keep that army of his from interfering."

Charlock took to the air, swooping low off the hill and rising to meet the others' level.

"You've come to me at last," said a dark malicious voice in Bertilack's mind. It was unmistakably Baudrous. Bertilack had never been able to forget that voice since their first encounter at the museum.

"Turn around, little knight. You can't stop me."

Something about Baudrous's evil voice seeped doubt into Bertilack's mind. How could he win? Even with the ever-lance at his side, even with the power of Charlock beneath him, how could he win? Baudrous was virtually invincible with powers beyond Bertilack's reckoning. What good were mortal hands against such unbridled power?

Bertilack faltered, the spell of despair washing over him, robbing him of his strength and courage. His grip on his weapon loosened, and it was then that Baudrous gave the go-ahead to attack.

The flights of dragons under his thrall, as well as the undead horde, turned as one towards the weakened knight. Beneath him and unaffected by the magic, Charlock tried to bring Bertilack out of his trance as the enemy approached, but it was to no avail. Baudrous's hold was too strong.

Charlock, however, swore to himself that none among them would lay a clawed hand upon his friend. He paused, hovering in the air, awaiting the enemy.

"Charlock," Baudrous said for the first time, addressing the black dragon. "Why throw your life away for the protection of this one? He's not worth it."

"Out of my head, foul one. Peddle your poisons elsewhere. You've no power over me," Charlock said, suddenly charging towards the evil army of darkness.

"May you die in agony, you foolish dragon."

Baudrous went silent and continued his

march towards the spire as his minions moved to remove Bertilack and Charlock from their master's misery.

"Bertilack, please, snap out of it," Charlock pleaded as they neared the battleline. "I can't do this alone."

It was then that Charlock heard a familiar voice.

"Worry not, for you won't have to," said Caldor.

Charlock's spirit lifted as the spire's warriors spurred into action. Bertilack's brother led the entire combined might in a rear attack against Baudrous's forces, and the black dragon roared in approval as he watched the army of darkness shatter.

On the ground, Baudrous's forces were faring no better. The evil dragon had crafted an immense skeletal legion for himself, but this was slowly being whittled down by Kazar and Thorn upon their water dragons. The mages had crafted an immense enchanted moat that, whilst protecting them, was also allowing the water dragons to reach their full aggressive potential.

"Bertilack," said Charlock now that they were once again clear of battle. "Your friends are battling for you. They're fighting to protect you.

The very presence you inspire is driving them on. You must lead them."

"My friends," Bertilack said as he looked around with glazed-over eyes. "My friends are with me."

"Yes, Bertilack," said Charlock. "They're all with you, and I'm with you too. Please, come back to us."

Bertilack's mind struggled to fight off Baudrous's hold. He looked to his hand and saw the ever-lance resting there. Its presence lent its aid to awakening him and returning him to the real world.

"Hold the weapon aloft and cry its name. Show the tyrant that he has no power over you," said Charlock.

Bertilack tried to raze his arm, but it felt like lead. He concentrated hard, straining with the exertion. "I can win," he said under his breath before shouting his next words. "Baudrous! You've no hold over me! The ever-lance will be your end!"

And with a final push, Bertilack broke through the enchanted mist and pointed the lance at his enemy.

"Come to me, little knight. Come and see how futile and impotent you are against the majesty of

Baudrous," the dark dragon said, stopping in his advance once again.

They needed no further encouragement. Charlock allowed the wind to fill his wings once again and dived headlong through the vicious melee that raged around them, heading straight for the evil dragon.

A few times, ice dragons tried to impede their progress but found their flesh easily rendered by the ever-lance's power. The emerald weapon cleaved scale and flesh in equal measure, then allowed itself to be withdrawn quickly as the latest of Bertilack and Charlock's opponents spiralled to the ground. Soon none would challenge them, and the pair sped easily to Baudrous.

The dark dragon loomed large before them and showed no further signs of stopping. He carried on through the land, crushing trees and boulders as if they were nothing, making his way towards the spire.

Bertilack and Charlock stopped just short of the dragon and yelled a challenge. "Hold, cur, and fight us!"

"Cur? You insect! You dare to insult me?" Baudrous stopped his approach and faced the pair. He laughed in a deep booming way. "So easily you come to your doom, young one! Know, however, that I've no mercy to give. You'll experience torments untold, but you won't die. My sorcery will keep you alive to be tortured continuously for eternity."

The ramifications of Baudrous's words hit home once more. Bertilack almost felt himself succumb to the terror again. Still, before his emotions took hold, Baudrous acted and released a twin torrent of flame directly at Charlock and Bertilack.

Luckily, the younger dragon was prepared, and he banked easily away from danger. Falling into a roll, he came towards Baudrous and released some flame of his own, which failed to do more than irritate the larger dragon. Charlock pulled away in surprise and watched in horror as Baudrous brushed his scorched scales, as if he had an annoying itch.

"Was that it, little prince? Was that the power of your house? Your father wasn't much of a warrior, but he at least fought better than that," snarled Baudrous. He then released more flame at Charlock. This time, the black dragon only just avoided being barbequed.

"We have to get close enough to use the lance. It's our only chance," said Bertilack.

Nodding, Charlock once again took them into

the fray, dodging yet more fire and swinging around Baudrous's back, where he managed to rake his claws across the ancient dragon and draw blood.

"You're not as invincible as you thought, dragon!" Bertilack crowed. "Perhaps we've hope yet."

"A scratch, fool. It'll take much more to destroy me," Baudrous said, enraged. He charged at the pair and attempted to bat the smaller dragon out of the sky.

"Now, Charlock! Whilst he's distracted, attack!"

Swooping in again and slithering once more under Baudrous's guard, Bertilack was ideally placed to put the point of the ever-lance deep into Baudrous's shoulder, forcing the evil dragon to roar in pain.

The lance bit deeper and deeper. Though it looked like little more than a toothpick compared with the great dragon, it still seemed to be making him very uncomfortable.

Baudrous cried in pain and attempted to grab Charlock and remove the source of his irritation. Fortunately for the knight and dragon, the lance came out of Baudrous just as easily as it had come out of the ice dragon, and the pair could avoid the strike.

"Does it hurt, dragon?" Bertilack cried. "That's for trying to conquer our world. We'll make you pay for every evil you've committed!"

"You dare to judge?" Baudrous said, holding a claw over his wounded shoulder. "I'm older and wiser beyond the years of men. What I tried to do was for the good of all dragonkind. Those ancient dragons would've kept the entire population of this planet at peace and completely oblivious to their true calling."

"True calling? You monster!" Charlock spat. "You killed an entire race for your vision. You killed my family! There are no dragons left to realise your dark dream."

"They're better off dead than living a lie," Baudrous laughed. "We dragons were born to rule the stars themselves, not just this pathetic little mudball world. You both should thank me."

Baudrous shot another dual stream of fire at the pair.

"Nice try," Bertilack said as Charlock deftly avoided the blast. "But you're too old and slow to best us."

These words triggered Baudrous. He flew into a rage, breathing fire in all directions and vainly hoping to strike Bertilack and Charlock with a lucky blow.

"You're dead! Do you hear me? All of you, dead!"

As Charlock flew, he briefly turned to regard their unruly enemy. Yet, this proved a mistake, for he was hit full in the face by one of Baudrous's fire shots. The searing heat washed over him, and luckily Bertilack managed to get his shield up to defend him, but it was too late for Charlock. The black dragon lost consciousness and plummeted to the ground.

"Ha!" Baudrous said with malicious glee before advancing on the prone warriors. "Too old for you, am I? Well, look at you now! I've bested you!"

The ground rumbled with his heavy footfalls, and Baudrous was now directly over Charlock when he noticed that Bertilack was no longer in residence. The saddle still clung to Charlock's back, but the knight and the lance had gone. The ancient dragon glanced around the ground, desperate to find Bertilack and the deadly weapon he carried.

"Where are you, knight?" the dragon growled, turning his great bulk around as he searched in vain. He continued to pace around before finally returning to the unconscious Charlock.

"Well, young dragon, it'd seem that your friend has abandoned you. Don't worry. I'll keep you company."

Baudrous reached down with one of his house-sized claws and attempted to roll the prone dragon over.

"Hold, dragon!"

Baudrous spun round and spied Bertilack standing upon one of the fallen trees in the great dragon's path.

"Wait your turn, human filth. I'm going to destroy this traitor to my race first, and then I'll deal with you."

Baudrous turned his massive bulk so that he was once again facing Charlock.

"I said hold, dragon!" Bertilack repeated. "Before you destroy him, you're forgetting one crucial thing."

"And what would that be?" Baudrous hissed, turning once more to face the knight.

"If you hadn't noticed, I no longer carry the ever-lance."

Baudrous assimilated this information and again scanned the immediate area with his eyes.

"So," Baudrous said, smiling. "You've lost the one weapon that could've harmed me. Thank you for that small fragment of information. I may make your end quicker because of it."

"Oh, I never said I had lost it," Bertilack said. "I merely said I no longer carried it."

"What?" said Baudrous. It was then that a fountain of blood erupted from his chest, followed by the ever-lance's point. Realisation slowly dawned on the dark dragon as he turned to face his attacker.

Charlock had been playing possum the entire time. The dragon had merely been waiting for this moment. "It's over," Charlock said as he watched Baudrous's lifeblood ebb away. "You've lost. Even now, your forces are in retreat, and with your end, the new age of the dragons begins, unencumbered by your evil."

"No, you haven't bested me yet," Baudrous moaned as his claw came up and tore the ever-lance from his chest. "You might've wounded me in this form, but I don't need it to destroy you!"

As the companions watched, Baudrous returned to his original size and hovered in the air above Charlock. The ever-lance clutched in a bloodied claw.

"Without this, you're nothing!" Baudrous shook the ever-lance furiously. "You still cannot fathom my power, can you? I am immortal. No weapon can kill me!"

Baudrous flung the ever-lance away. "Now, dragon prince, it's just you and me. I shan't allow that infection over there to interfere."

Baudrous turned and breathed a twin stream of fire at the hill on which Bertilack stood, incinerating everything in its path.

Charlock watched as the spot on which Bertilack stood was set aflame.

"No!" Charlock screamed. The rage was building in him once again. The same fiery rage that had consumed the dragon the last time he'd anguished over Bertilack's fate. That time the mage had felt his pure rage. This time it would be Baudrous. Breaking into the sky, wreathed in vengeful flame like some newly risen phoenix, Charlock sped towards Baudrous like a comet.

"Murderer!" the black dragon snarled. All rational thought left the black dragon. He merely strove to kill Baudrous. He'd become a weapon—a weapon of single-minded purpose, devoid of emotion, his only wish to see Baudrous dead by his claws. He charged forth and raked the evil dragon across the chest, blowing fire into the wound. For a moment, Baudrous seemed to be taken back by the younger dragon's furious charge but soon regained his footing and dealt Charlock a vicious blow to the face. Charlock fell back, stunned.

"That's what I wanted to see! Your parents had dismissed that part of their nature, but I see it's still alive within you!"

"I won't listen to your taunts, demon!" Charlock spat, still in the grips of the red mist. "I'll show you how wrong you are!"

Charlock once again attacked Baudrous. Grasping him by surprise, he flung the older dragon to the ground. "You see?" Charlock crowed over his fallen enemy. "My parents fought you with all their strength as I do."

Baudrous rose from the crater he'd made by his fall and dusted himself off. Charlock's attack had done him no damage. In fact, it'd done little more than annoy.

"I applaud your efforts. Had your parents made a similar choice, they might not have lost to me."

Baudrous remained on the ground, content to look up and sneer at his adversary. "You have what they lacked. You have the will to fight, the will to kill."

"No, serpent. I merely do what I must," Charlock glowered down.

"Yes, and every step you take on this road leads you closer to me."

"Monster!" Charlock screamed, dive bombing his evil opponent.

Baudrous, however, was prepared for this angered response and had counted on it. As Charlock came on, the evil dragon raised his arms and caught Charlock around the wings.

"See how easily I manipulate you?" Baudrous hissed, blowing smoke into Charlock's face. "A few choice words, and you crumble before me."

Baudrous increased the pressure he was applying to his gigantic bear hug.

Charlock attempted to free himself but found the dark dragon's grip too strong and felt his strength fade. "Bertilack . . . I'm sorry, I couldn't avenge you."

"Not yet, my friend!"

Charlock heard the voice within his own head. It was unmistakably Bertilack speaking to him telepathically. His presence, and the fact that his friend was alive, gave Charlock new strength and energy to fight, and he once again struggled to free himself.

"So, you have some spirit left, after all!" Baudrous said, grunting with the exertion needed to hold Charlock. "Why do you fight? Your friend is gone. The human germ you clung so diligently to and defended is dead. And once I finish with you, the rest of your friends are next."

"Not quite," said a voice from behind Baudrous. It sounded weak and tired but familiar.

"No!" Baudrous said in surprise. Still, it was too late, for Bertilack had changed the lance back into his sword and, at that moment, hacked at the evil dragon's flanks. Purple blood erupted from the wounds on Baudrous's back. They were nowhere near enough to stop him, but they provided Charlock with an adequate distraction.

Whilst the great dragon flinched and shook from the impacts, he slowly released his grip, enabling Charlock to free a clawed arm and seize Baudrous around the neck. Scale and bone shattered as the black dragon dug deeper into the neck of his nemesis, slowly squeezing the life from his opponent.

"No!" Baudrous gurgled. "I won't be defeated!"

"Go to Hell, demon!"

Charlock tore out Baudrous's neck and watched as the older dragon's life was extinguished. He laid on the ground, one head crushed at the windpipe and the other flailing around, unaware that his other head had died. Slowly it too laid still, and Charlock was left standing triumphant over his greatest enemy's body.

"Finally," Bertilack said, approaching from Charlock's side. "It's over."

"Yes, my friend, but for some reason, I'm left feeling empty," said the black dragon. His eyes stared at his friend, full of sorrow. "I thought that with Baudrous gone, the pain of my family's death would leave too, but it hasn't. With him gone, I'm left without a purpose."

Bertilack pondered Charlock's words for a moment before turning to look at how the others were faring. He was surprised to see the entire team of spire warriors heading towards him.

"He hasn't left you without a purpose."

Charlock turned to see what his friend had indicated and noted with joy his fellow dragons and friends returning from battle.

"They're your responsibility now, Charlock. With Baudrous gone, they've fulfilled their destiny and yours. Since you hatched, you've been under that yoke, but now you're free to decide your own fate, your own future. It'll be daunting, but we'll be here as often as we can."

"You're not staying?" Charlock asked.

"I'm afraid not. Some of the others may wish to, but I can't. I have a life back home, people who care about me. Without the threat of Baudrous looming over us, we've no need to be here all the time. This land belongs to you and your kind now."

"Hey, brother!" Caldor yelled as Sharos let out an ear-splitting cry. "Good to see you made it."

"And the same to you!"

Sharos landed with the others trailing behind.

"No real concerns," the elf smiled, leaping from his dragon's back. "Nor should there be. Although I must admit, they did have me concerned for a while, then suddenly the skeletal hordes crumbled to dust, and the ice dragon fled with their human allies."

"We may see them again," Sharos said.

"I doubt it'll be any time soon," Bertilack said, smiling. "Without Baudrous to lead them, we have nothing to fear unless one emerges that can lay claim to his power."

"Which won't happen," Keldon said as the others finally came to land. "As soon as we're ready, Argast and I are going looking for them."

"And you can count on us," Batras yelled, speaking for himself and Khrishaw.

"And us!" Gawain concurred on behalf of himself and Bloodstone.

"You guys are crazy," Kazar said. "All I'm looking forwards to is a bit of rest and relaxation."

"Hear, hear," his dragon agreed. "A good bit of

swimming and fishing is just what the doctor ordered."

Bertilack smiled and looked at Charlock as the others joined the conversation to decide what path each of them would take. "Well, Charlock," he said. "Looks like I'll be around for a little longer."

"Glad to hear it," Charlock said, heading towards the spire on foot. "We've so many more places to fly and dimensions to explore. And who knows, perhaps we'll find some more adventure along the way."

Thanks for reading!
If you enjoyed this book, please add a short review on Amazon. It helps more than you know!

Acknowledgments

This book has been a long time coming, and there is no way I can thank all the people that have helped me with this over the twenty plus years I've been toying around with it, but I shall endeavour to try. First, I would like to thank Sikandar Vayani, without whom, publishing this wouldn't have been possible. I would also like to thank all my friends and family for their roles, making it almost in part, a biography, as much as a fantasy. Thank you to Emma Chapman, for holding onto the original drafts when I thought them lost. To my daughter, Elle, and my partner, Shauni, for always believing in me. And my friends, Aaron Pearson, Connor Sims, and Owen Jones, for having faith in me, when I had precious little in myself.

If you loved Dragon Knights of the Emerald Spire, then check out Terry Silverman and the Demon Wolf! [Available now!](#)

Enjoy a free sample on the next page!

PREVIEW

"You're in my seat," said Terry, squeezing between the two of them.

The boy didn't take too kindly to the interruption. "What's your problem?" he said in a plummy voice. He stood up, bringing himself face-to-face with Terry, and bared his fangs at him.

Maybe this wasn't such a bright idea. Only now did it dawn on Terry that he was picking a fight with a fully-fledged bloodsucking vampire. He was also acutely aware of the possibility that he may be starting a scene and creating unnecessary attention for himself. But wait, why should he be scared? Terry was a vampire too, and not just any vampire, he was a vampire who could walk in broad daylight and not get burnt to a crisp by doing so. In this battle between fang-bearers, he had the high ground. Terry tried his best not to move, maintaining a steady gaze.

"Well?" said the smug boy.

"I said you're in my seat," he repeated. "That's the problem."

"I don't see your name on it."

"No, but it has my ticket number on it." Terry's confidence was rising. He was on a roll. "Or can't you count, you blockhead?"

Okay, so maybe the last part wasn't really necessary, and *blockhead?* Really? Great choice of words, Terry. But someone had to tell the kid or else he'd never learn.

Some of the surrounding students started to take an interest. The smug boy clenched his fist, looking like he was ready to hit Terry, but before he could say or do anything more, a minotaur in a fitted blue suit and red bow tie raised his head from a seat in the front row.

"Ahem! And what, may I ask, is going on here?" said the minotaur with a loud, authoritative voice that drew everybody's attention.

"It's Tompkins, the deputy headmaster," whispered one of the male students covered in silvery fish-like scales.

"I heard he tamed a basilisk with just a glare," said a tall female elf with light blue skin and dark blonde hair.

"I heard he killed an ogre with his bare hands," said the twin elf sitting next to her.

Tompkins got out of his seat and strode towards Terry and the smug boy, steam exhaling from his long snout. He had a human body, but his eyes inside his bullish head were small white slits with no pupils, nor irises, giving the impression of a soulless being. "Ah Kurt, I should have known," he said, addressing the smug boy first. "I would think that you'd know better now that you're joining intermediary school."

"Sorry, sir, we just had a small misunderstanding," said Kurt, bowing his head slightly.

"And you are?" asked Tompkins as he turned to Terry.

Terry gave a small, courteous bow by placing his right hand across his chest and nodding his head briefly before introducing himself. "Terry Silverman."

Tompkins studied him for a moment, rubbing his chin thoughtfully. "Hmm," said the minotaur, "I don't recall seeing you at Grimerth Foundation School."

Terry lowered his right hand. "I'm a new student, sir," he explained. "I've only attended human schools prior to today."

"That must be why I don't recognise you. So, Terry, can you tell me what happened?"

"He's in my seat," said Terry. "I asked him to move and he refused."

"Like I said, there was a misunderstanding, sir. I was just making my way to my seat. I apologise," said Kurt. "I'll be going now." He turned, and as he did, he shoved Terry, pushing him backwards against the vampire girl's seat. "Oops, sorry about that," said Kurt.

Terry picked himself up off the floor. "You did that on purpose!"

"Ahem," said Tompkins, ensuring that both of them didn't forget his presence.

Kurt eyed Terry, but he said nothing more as he headed to his own seat, much further back.

"Well then, Terry, please, make yourself comfortable," said Tompkins.

"Thank you, sir." Terry nodded his head and sat down in his seat. He watched Tompkins head towards the front, past the drawn curtains and into the teacher's section.

"Well, that was interesting," said a meek voice sitting next to Terry. Terry turned and was taken aback by what he saw next, so much so that he almost fell off his seat with his jaw dropped in shock. The hooded cloak and downturned head had kept this person hidden earlier, but now Terry could see clearly. It was a skeleton! A real live talking skeleton! They really existed!

Of course, none of the other students around him paid the least bit of attention. The werewolf at the window seat was completely ignoring the fact that there was a talking pile of bones next to him. And why should he care anyway? For this werewolf, seeing a skeleton was probably just a normal everyday occurrence, nothing at all of interest. He was entirely immersed in his own little world, holding a mirror up to his face in one hand and busy plucking hairs off his bushy face with a tweezer in the other hand.

"They call me Fergus Gravestone," said the skeleton, removing his hood and revealing his bony skull. He held out a bony hand. "How do you do? Me? Well, can't complain. Least I'm still alive. No, wait. That's not quite right, is it?"

Terry chuckled in disbelief. "You're weird ... I like it." There was a certain splendour for him in seeing the unnatural after living life amongst mundane normality. He held out his hand with long pointed nails, clasped Fergus's bony fingers, and introduced himself.

The skeleton rattled, leaning in close, a little too close. His empty eye sockets peered deep into Terry's soul. "So, you're not from around here."

"Well, yes, I did just say that to the scary looking teacher."

He pulled back. "Fascinating. So, you're new. Well, I'll be damned. No wait, I already am. Long story though, you probably don't want to hear it. Say, you look like the kind of person that likes to play games. Do you want to play a game?" he asked as he pulled out a deck of trading cards from inside his cloak and began shuffling them like an expert. "These cards are based on famous monsters," he explained. "Before, it was only possible to get them in packs of gum, but then they realised they could sell the cards for more without the gum. Personally, I wasn't happy about that. It completely killed my allowance. I hardly have enough money left for food now. Lucky for me, school meals are free."

Once the plane had taken off, Fergus began setting up the cards on the table tray in front of the seat and explained the rules and strategy behind the game to Terry, going into a lot of detail. Lots and lots of detail. So much so that Terry's head was starting to hurt. Once the second game was over, Terry tried changing the subject.

"So, you're a skeleton?"

"I am? Hell's bells and buckets of blood! Does this mean I died, or was I born like this?"

"Which is it?"

"Good question. I'll let you know when I know."

A tall zombie with high heels, unsightly frizzy red hair, and a crimson stewardess outfit tapped Terry on the shoulder. She offered him a newspaper to read. He glanced at the paper and dismissed it with a wave. She then offered it to Fergus who also rejected it. The werewolf at the end ignored her entirely, still too busy plucking his never-ending facial hairs.

"It's always the same stuff," said the skeleton. "The Demon Wolf strikes again. Another missing monster found washed ashore, mutilated body of course. The usual speeches from UGOM about the safety of Grimerth and their promise to protect us and all that rubbish."

"Demon Wolf?" asked Terry.

"Ah, they call him that 'cause all the victims look like they transformed into some sort of demonic wolf before being completely ripped apart and destroyed."

Enjoy this sample?

You can buy the full story of Terry Silverman and the Demon Wolf at bookstores and online! Visit:

www.spellcraftpress.com

Lightning Source UK Ltd.
Milton Keynes UK
UKHW010614090223
416744UK00004B/305